# Taken by the Passion

by

## Maxine Mansfield

Taken By The Passion

Contact Information: info@thewildrosepress.com

Cover Art by *Diana Carlile*

The Wild Rose Press, Inc.
PO Box 708
Adams Basin, NY 14410-0708

Visit us at www.thewilderroses.com

Publishing History
First Scarlet Rose Edition, December 2012
Print ISBN 978-1-61217-795-3
Digital ISBN 978-1-61217-796-0

Published in the United States of America

**She'd been betrothed to the, stubborn, arrogant, egotistical, barbarian prince since the day she'd been born...**

He held out a hand toward her. "Spend this one night with me, Lizbeth, and if you still feel the same in the morning, we'll talk about you possibly going to the Academy and taking a few classes now and then. After all, how would it look to my family and friends if my brand new wife took off before the sun rises on her wedding night? I have appearances to uphold, we both do."

Lizbeth sizzled with anger. "I don't like you, remember? I couldn't care less how this looks, and...and I won't spend this night or any other with you until I have to, even on a bet."

Adan grinned. "Really? Not even on a bet? What if a bet was to get you exactly what you want most? A life of your own without a moment's interference from me until the day I do become king?"

Lizbeth shook her head.

"I never took you for a coward, Lizbeth, guess I was wrong. You say you know me better than I know myself. I say prove it, Lizard. If you can manage to answer ten...no make that five questions about me correctly, you win."

His grin grew even bigger. "And if you win, not only will I escort you to the front gate and wave you through the portal on your way to the Academy, I'll be happy to inform my family and friends you're leaving me. That you find a dusty, old institution more sexually appealing than you do your own husband."

The grin disappeared from his face. "But, if you don't answer all of the questions correctly, you'll spend this one night, this entire night, willingly in my bed, in my arms, as my wife, in every sense of the word. Deal?"

He held out his hand again, and Lizbeth stared at it. Her fingers itched to take him up on his offer. A life without interference or being under Adan's thumb, even for a short while, was more than a little tempting. Could she trust him, though?

Lizbeth hesitated, weighing her options. Other than being a bunny killer, Adan Hammerstrike was known far and wide for his word. Once he gave it, he never took it back.

She'd spent the majority of every day, for as long as she could remember, learning everything there was to know about the arrogant barbarian prince. She couldn't lose, and this was an opportunity she couldn't afford to pass up.

Lizbeth smiled as she shook his hand. "Deal."

## Dedication

To Rich, my real life hero. Thank you
for all you do, and all you put up with.
Love you honey.

To David Karopkat, as always,
thank you for your wonderful imagination,
and the use of one very special Mr. Leeky Shortz.

To my critique partners, Lizbeth Selvig,
Morgan Q Oriely, Tam Linsey, DeNise Woods, and
Jenifer Bernard. You guys are beyond priceless.

And of course, to my wonderful
editor and cover artist, Diana.
You make me look really good!

Touched by the Magic,
Tempted by the Storm,
Taken by the Passion…
A New Love is Born.

*"Though from scales of time or creature scales, bring forth life and let it not fail. Essence and oils, herbs and sand, sprinkle of scale dust held in your hand. Life for a moment or life everlasting, it's the choice you make while you're casting."*

## Chapter One

Lizbeth glanced at the gorgeous barbarian standing nonchalantly with his well-defined arms folded across the expanse of his wide, bare chest, and cringed. Who would have guessed such a cold-blooded, vicious murderer could end up with the face and body of a god? Yet, somehow, he had. She balled her hands into fists, clinging desperately to the one emotion she'd fostered concerning this man for as long as she could remember…anger.

One of the barbarian's friends laughed at something he said and, with the shake of his head, a lock of hair the color of summer wheat dislodged from behind his perfectly rounded ear, and fell across his forehead. Lizbeth had the strangest urge to tuck it securely back in place. Her fingers tingled with the desire to go to him, reach up, and do just that. It wasn't fair.

Prince Adan Zeth Conner Hammerstrike wasn't supposed to be devastatingly handsome or brilliantly witty or muscled beyond belief from head to toe like the barbarian warrior he was. He was still supposed to be the horrid troll of a boy he'd been when last she had the misfortune to be in his presence.

At least one thing about the man remained consistent. If the tilt of his chin and the arrogant smirk on his face were any indications, he still possessed the same annoying, egotistical, pompous-ass attitude he'd always had.

Lizbeth sighed. Perhaps his body had changed for the better, but the important details remained the same. He was still the crown prince of Alaria and the man destined to be the next king of the Barbarians, and she was as she'd always been, nothing more than property.

Turning from him and the sounds of celebration, she walked to the floor-to-ceiling windows of his family's castle and glanced out and upward at the night sky. The three moons of Albrath, each in a different phase, shone down, illuminating the icy-cold, barren landscape and high mountains of the far northern kingdom of Alaria. So this was home?

Tears threatened, and Lizbeth scrunched her eyes tight to prevent their escape. She would not cry today of all days. It was a promise she'd made. Her entire life had been in preparation for this day, and she had willingly done what duty dictated. Now, all she wanted was to get through the rest of this evening, say goodnight, gather her valise, and be on her way.

A single tear escaped past her defenses, and Lizbeth quickly swiped it away before anyone had a chance to notice. She wasn't a little girl anymore. As of twelve turns of the hourglass ago, she was twenty-one and a woman fully grown. And not just any woman, either. As of two turns ago of that same hourglass, she was the signed, sealed, and delivered wife of Prince Adan Hammerstrike. On parchment anyway. And that was more than she'd ever wanted from the man.

Happily-ever-afters with someone you loved and who loved you back were fairytales for children, not the reality of a royal's life on Albrath.

Lady Lizbeth Claire Soulenticer, now Princess Lizbeth Hammerstrike, future queen of the Barbarians certainly didn't believe in anything as silly as fairytales. She never had.

\*\*\*\*

Oh, God Draka, she wasn't crying was she? After being raised with four sisters, let alone his queen of a mother, he couldn't abide another moment of female drama. Adan sighed as he watched the slip of a girl wipe what looked suspiciously like a tear from her cheek. He shook his head and wondered, for not the first time this day, what he'd ever done to be saddled with such a wife. One who didn't have the capacity to be anything but what she'd always been—a whining, sniveling, pain in his arse, unwanted responsibility.

Not that he wouldn't still do her the honor of bedding her for, after all, it was his duty. And even if she wasn't the type of woman he would have chosen for a wife, had he been given the opportunity to choose, she wasn't horrid to look upon. As a matter of fact, she was stunning.

Hair the color of liquid toffee, rich and thick, hung well past her waist. Strands of copper with gold highlights danced in the glow of a hundred candles scattered throughout the room. Adan's fingers itched to gauge its weight. His chest ached to have it brush across his ribs and come to rest upon his shoulders as she gracefully rode him long into the coming night.

Skin the shade of warm cream, and lips, full and pouty with just a tint of peach, caused a stirring beneath his ceremonial kilt. The promise of breasts full and heavy below her lacey, white gown teased at his senses while her hips, just the right size to grasp with both hands, tormented his mind.

Surprisingly enough, however, it was her ears that totally enthralled him. They always had. All afternoon his tongue had been tempted to flick out and finally taste the crisp little points of her ears. Who would have thought dainty, pointed, half-wood-elf ears could be so damn sexy? Perhaps he wasn't quite as immune to his pretty little wife's charms as he thought.

Adan chuckled to himself. He didn't have to be immune. All he need do was crook a finger and beckon, and she would immediately come running to his side. It was her nature and in her training. All she'd ever known in life, from the moment she'd been born, was whatever Prince Adan wanted would one day be her duty to give. Every lesson she'd taken, every book she'd read, every single thing she ate, learned, and probably even dreamed of, had been for one purpose— to become the wife of and to please Prince Adan Hammerstrike.

For a fleeting moment, Adan wondered if she'd ever had more than a handful of thoughts in her pretty little head she could rightfully call her own. Thoughts that didn't revolve directly around him. Probably not. How boring.

Glancing about the room at his friends, Adan blew out a breath. To his right stood Uthiel Dragonheart, human paladin, protector of dragons, master of Castle

Kuropkat, and husband to the beautiful Briar, an amazing elf-human healer. Not a happier man in all of Albrath could be found.

That is unless you took into account the equally jovial Sarco Sunwalker, across the way to Adan's left. Sarco, heir to the Lordship of the Elves, wizard instructor at the Academy of Magical Arts, and husband to Adan's youngest sister, Lark.

Both were strong-minded men with wives who complemented and challenged them. Opinionated, smart, sometimes sassy, never boring, always in the thick of things, passionate wives.

And what kind of wife did Adan now have? He glanced toward Lizbeth, and the touch of sadness that flickered in her soft hazel eyes made him almost feel guilty about what he had planned. After all, it wasn't her fault if she was ordinary, predictable, and boring. She was what she was, and nothing more or less than a product of her upbringing.

Like it or not, enjoyable or not, it was still his duty to consummate this travesty of a marriage before he took his leave of her. And leave her was exactly what he planed to do.

When the sun rose in the morning, he would bid farewell to his uninteresting little responsibility. His parents could contend with her. Allowing him the freedom to return to the Academy with his comrades and continue his carefree life, unfettered by the likes of an unwanted wife, at least until such a time duty forced his return.

No doubt she would cry and beg him to stay, but in the end, it would do her no good. His mind was made up.

With a gesture and bow goodnight to his friends and family, Adan headed toward his bride.

****

Down a long corridor, they walked in silence. Up a staircase, past two hallways, one to the right then another to the left, through a drafty archway, and across the width of an expansive open-ended room until they stopped before a door.

Lizbeth could smell a hint of wood smoke, alder she guessed, as Adan turned and cupped her chin in his big, barbarian hand. Try as she might, she couldn't stop herself from trembling.

"Don't worry your little head about my pleasure or anything else this night. I'm sure you're quite eager to use some of those techniques you've been studying over the past few years to please me, but for this evening, allow me to simply do what needs to be done quickly and efficiently. My pleasure will come in good time, Lizard."

If his smile hadn't been so genuine and if Lizbeth hadn't been certain the only thing between the big buffoon's ears was more of the same hot air he'd been spouting all evening, she would have smacked the condescending look right off his face. Don't worry about his pleasure? Eager to use techniques to please him? And...and...Lizard? Who did he think he was?

Instead, she smiled at him innocently. "Lizard, seriously, Adan? Do I really remind you of a reptile? And your pleasure? You mistake my distress, my lord. I'm simply not accustomed to the extreme cold here in your kingdom. Hmm, I hadn't given your pleasure a single thought. Was I supposed to?"

Adan's look of genuine concern was almost

laughable. "I was under the impression husbands were supposed to come up with pet names for their wives. It's a rule, I think. I like Lizard. I mean, you don't look like one or anything, it's just…cute."

His eyes gleamed as he graced her with a smile she knew was meant to rattle her resolve and bring the fair maiden in her to her knees. "You have been adequately deflowered and schooled in all the arts of seduction, haven't you? You've taken the sex practices and theory classes all young people are required to take? I'm quite certain it was in the marriage contract your parents signed. You do understand what I'm talking about and what's about to happen, don't you? Please tell me you do, my lady."

It was all Lizbeth could do to respond with a straight face. "Yes, I've been properly deflowered and schooled in all forms of sexual functions. And as far as understanding, I know exactly what I'm about to do."

His smile gentled and became genuine. The sight of it almost made her feel guilty about the course of action she'd long ago decided upon…almost.

Adan opened the door to his room, and Lizbeth gaped and hesitated before stepping across the threshold. The parts of the castle she'd seen thus far had been bad enough with their stark walls of white stone and colorless decor, but this? This chamber was the most horrid of them all.

Her first impression of the room was one of ice. Cold, devoid of emotion or life, frosty, bitter aloneness. Lizbeth shivered and hugged her arms close to her body. From the white fur rugs scattered about the white stone floor to snow-white drapes hanging loosely open above the stark floor-to-ceiling windows, everything was devoid of color. Even the view was one of never-ending bleakness. And it was huge. No, huge wasn't the word. It was ridiculously huge for a sleeping chamber.

The only furnishings in the entire space consisted of a single, white, wooden chest against one wall and a white four-poster bed. The four posts were each carved in the image of fearsome dragon heads.

Lizbeth shuddered. The thought of dragons had chills racing along her spine. Let alone snow-white dragons with dead eyes and razor-sharp teeth. Words from a childhood poem came suddenly to mind and she shivered. *When the sun doth set and dusk draws near, If ye've misbehaved, ye have reason to fear. For by darkness of night, wings take flight, And seek out the naughty to devour by next light.*

Lizbeth shook her head to dispel the image. Knowing that even if she were standing here naked and freezing, the bed's coverlet of thick white fur wouldn't be enough to entice her to climb into that bed. Still, she couldn't force her gaze from the monstrosity. The thing was so big it took up most of the room. The horrendous sleeping space was situated in the very center and was large enough to accommodate an entire family of barbarians, and then some.

Lizbeth shivered once more. What kind of man could find peace enough to sleep surrounded by such...hopelessness?

There were very few things in the chamber that weren't white. Yellow flames licked at dark logs while red coals glowed like dragon's eyes in the fireplace on the far wall. The only other thing of any color was her one sad-looking, brown valise, sitting next to a white door across the room. The lone saving grace to the entire space was the familiar smell of wood smoke. It reminded her of home.

Lizbeth turned to Adan. "Is there somewhere I may change, my lord?"

Adan chuckled. "We're married, remember, Lizard. Feel free to change right here. I don't mind. As a matter of fact, why not simply slip off your gown and drop it to the floor. It will expedite things."

She hated herself for the rush of heat warming her cheeks. "I realize we're now wed, but I would prefer a touch of privacy. A bride looks forward to preparing for her wedding night. Surely even a barbarian can understand that?"

He raised an eyebrow but simply pointed to the door her valise set beside. "Suit yourself, and take all the time you need." He grinned wolfishly. "I'm a patient man, even for a barbarian, and I'll be right here waiting when you're ready to come out and play, Lizard."

Adan loosened the clasp holding his kilt together, and green and blue plaid wool slithered to the floor. For the space of forty-two heartbeats, Lizbeth stood frozen, staring at the glorious nakedness of her husband. Bronzed muscles rippled across his taut belly, while a halo of springy golden curls surrounded a broad, long cock.

The air in the room became agonizingly thin, and pinpricks of color floated before Lizbeth's eyes. It wasn't as if she'd never seen a naked man, but she'd certainly never seen one as marvelously made as this one.

His already more-than-adequate phallus began expanding until the veins running along its side pulsated. Lizbeth did the only thing she could think to do. She ran to her valise, snatched it up, opened the door, darted inside, and slammed the door closed behind her.

She wasn't sure how long she'd been in the small changing room, but she knew from her growing sense of claustrophobia it had been a while. God Draka, how she hated confined spaces, and it had already taken more than a few minutes just for her hands to stop shaking enough to manage the closures on her hideous white gown, let alone the ties of her corset or the multiple layers of snow-white petticoats. Manage them, though, she finally did. Then it took almost as long to rifle through her bag and find the garments she was searching for.

With a pounding heart, she slipped on her pale beige tunic and traveling pants, then stuffed her wedding gown with all its accessories haphazardly into the bag. Taking three deep calming breaths and blowing them slowly out, Lizbeth turned the doorknob, stepped out into the room, and faced her waiting husband.

If the look of surprise on Adan Hammerstrike's face hadn't been so priceless, Lizbeth knew she would've been tempted to lose her nerve as she nodded in his direction, walked right past the bed, and headed toward the door.

In his haste to rise, Adan became tangled in the white coverlet on the bed and, with a thud, ended up sprawled on the floor. "Where do you think you're going?"

Slowly, she turned and glanced at the angry barbarian. "To the portal, of course. Did I forget to mention I'm starting classes at The Academy of

Magical Arts in the morning? I really must be going. I don't wish to be late." She forced a smile. "It was a lovely wedding and reception. I truly am sorry my brothers were unavoidably detained and couldn't be here. They would've especially enjoyed the Alarian ale. Please give my regards to your family and friends."

The silk coverlet was forgotten as Adan leapt to his feet. "The Academy? What the VoT are you talking about, woman? You didn't say a word to me about any classes, and you well know it. This is unacceptable. You are my wife, and this is our wedding night. You can't just...just leave."

Lizbeth stiffened her spine and glared. "Prince or not, don't you dare curse at me, Adan Hammerstrike. If you wish to speak of the Valley of Torment then call it as such, and not that vulgar VoT word. And as for being your wife, that's only a technicality, and we both know it. We've been betrothed since the day I was born. My parents signed a contract pledging I would be your queen, not share your bed while you're still merely a prince."

She paced back and forth before the door. "You aren't king yet, and until you are, I will have the life I've been denied thus far. I'm now of age, and I wish to become an enchantress. As God Draka is my witness, I'm going to do just that. I'm through spending my days studying you and living your life instead of my own. I'm sick to death of you. I know more about you than you could possibly remember about yourself. And anyway, I wouldn't spend the night willingly in the same bed with a vicious murderer like you until duty dictates I must for all the platt in Albrath, husband or not."

She stopped and glared at him.

Adan ran his hand through his hair and took a deep breath. "So, that's what all this is about, huh? After all these years, you're still upset over the stupid rabbit? Lizbeth, I was fifteen and you were eleven, for God Draka's sake. I was trying to impress you with my elite hunting skills. How was I to know you'd made a pet of the thing? Rabbits are food. They're meant to be eaten, not played with. How many times must I say I'm sorry?"

He balled his fists at his side. "I am the prince and your husband. You'll immediately forgive me once and for all and stop this foolishness. I demand it."

Tears burned the back of her eyes, but Lizbeth forbade them to fall. "Demand it? Well, that certainly doesn't make you sound any sorrier now than you did then. For your information, I wasn't allowed to have pets. Did you know that? It took me weeks to get Horatio to come close enough so I could feed him from my hand and even longer to actually get him to trust me enough to touch him."

Lizbeth held up three fingers. "Do you have any idea how many times I got to pet his soft brown fur before you…you murdered him?"

Adan gulped, and Lizbeth knew he didn't want to answer the question. She waited, tapping her toe impatiently.

"Three?" he finally said.

Lizbeth nodded as her voice rose another octave. "Yes, only three times, and then I had to stand there and not shed a single tear while poor little Horatio was skinned and stuffed in a pot with vegetables."

She lifted her chin and stiffened her spine. "I didn't

dare tell mother why I was sick and couldn't possibly eat. I wasn't allowed to ever get dirty or play with creatures like other children were, let alone make a pet of one. I could never take the chance one of them might bite or scratch me and mar my perfect skin. Oh, no, the future queen of the barbarians, the future wife of Prince Adan Hammerstrike had to be without flaw. It was in the damnable marriage contract."

The tears did come to the surface then, and Lizbeth knew from the look on his face Adan had seen them. He started toward her as if he were going to offer comfort.

She held out a hand. "Don't! I neither need nor want your pity. All I want is my freedom until you become king. I give you my word, the day you accept your crown, even though I dread the thought of it, I'll do my duty. I'll come back here and be your wife."

He stood in all his naked splendor with his arms crossed looking as if he were contemplating the situation. He rubbed his jaw twice, nodded a couple of times then spoke. "I realize you can't stand the sight of me because I am, after all, the evil bunny slayer. But we have a duty to consummate this marriage."

He held out a hand out toward her. "Spend this one night with me, Lizbeth, and if you still feel the same in the morning, we'll talk about you possibly going to the Academy and taking a few classes now and then. After all, how would it look to my family and friends if my brand new wife took off before the sun rises on her wedding night? I have appearances to uphold, we both do."

Lizbeth sizzled with anger. "I don't like you, remember? I couldn't care less how this looks to anybody, and...and...and, I won't spend this night or any other with you, until I have to, even on a bet."

Adan grinned. "Really? Not even on a bet? What if a bet was to get you exactly what you say you want most? A life of your own without a moment's interference from me until the day I do become king?"

Lizbeth shook her head and turned to leave, yet Adan's next words not only stopped her forward motion but had her turning and facing him once more.

"I never took you for a coward, Lizbeth, guess I was wrong. You say you know me better than I know myself. I say prove it, Lizard. If you can manage to answer ten...no, make that five questions about me correctly, you win."

His grin grew even bigger. "And if you win, not only will I escort you to the front gate and wave you through the portal on your way to the Academy, I'll be happy to inform my family and friends that you're leaving me. That you find a dusty, old institution more sexually appealing than you do your own husband, and rightly so."

The grin disappeared from his face. "But if you don't answer all the questions correctly, you'll spend this one night, this entire night, willingly in my bed, in my arms, as my wife, in every sense of the word. Deal?"

He held out his hand again, and Lizbeth stared at it. Her fingers itched with the temptation to take him up on his offer. A life without interference or being under Adan's thumb, even for a short while, was more than a little tempting. Could she trust him, though?

Lizbeth hesitated, weighing her options. Other than being a bunny killer, Adan Hammerstrike was known far and wide for his word. Once he gave it, he never took it back.

She'd spent the majority of every day, for as long as she could remember, learning everything there was to know about the arrogant barbarian prince. She couldn't lose, and this was an opportunity she couldn't afford to pass up.

Lizbeth smiled as she shook his hand. "Deal."

## Chapter Two

Adan led Lizbeth to a white fur rug in front of the fireplace and gestured toward it. "Make yourself comfortable, Lizard, and we'll get started."

He watched as she bristled, then reluctantly kneeled, but he cared not that she was upset by his taunt. Instead, he was rather pleased with himself over her reaction.

So she wasn't the brainless little twit he'd thought after all. What a pleasant surprise. What she was, though, showed plainly on her face now that Adan knew what to look for. The slightest hint of a smile and the gleam in her eyes gave away her thoughts. She was angry and arrogant. Not simply arrogant, but arrogant to a fault. The little chit thought herself to be more intelligent, of quicker wit, and a better person than he.

Adan looked forward to the next few minutes and his bet with his pretty little wife more than he had anything in a very long time.

He paced back and forth before her, his hands clasped behind his back, and his cock lazily swinging back and forth like a pendulum. He couldn't help but smile as Lizbeth's eyes matched the movement. She gulped and pinkened.

Every moment he delayed asking the first question would increase her chances of making a mistake. Finally, when she was sufficiently nervous to give him the advantage, he began. "How many battles in the arena did I win last year and against whom?"

He had to give her credit. She didn't hesitate even a moment. "You won four battles in the arena last year, my lord. You win four battles every year. Oh, and you lost one, though it wasn't in the arena. It was at the Academy."

She held up four fingers, and Adan smiled at her antics.

She wiggled the first finger as she dropped it down. "You defeated Yarg, the troll champion in the spring Imbolc tournament." Another finger joined the first. "Then there was the dark-elf shadow-knight, Sergia, whom you felled during the Bealltuinn festival before the summer solstice games."

She tapped her lip with a fingertip for a moment before allowing the third finger to join the others. "During Lughnasadh, in the autumn, you defeated the ogre, Gar." Letting her last finger drop into place, Lizbeth sighed. "Right at the start of winter Samhain, even though I hear he put up a valiant fight, you bested the dwarf blademaster, Randa."

She grinned, and the impact of it had Adan's cock thickening.

"Then, you spoiled your perfect record by losing to your brother-in-law, Wizard Sarco Sunwalker, right after Yulemass. Such a pity, the great barbarian brought low by an elf."

She shrugged her shoulders. "I do hope you can do better than that, my lord, or I might as well be on my way right now and not waste any more of your time."

Adan sat on the fur rug directly before Lizbeth and crossed his legs in front of himself. "Don't worry your pretty little head about my time, Lizard. I'm having much too much fun to even think about stopping. Aren't you?"

She answered back sweetly, "Probably not quite as much as you. Question three please."

Adan laughed. He hadn't expected her to be as quick witted as she was. "That wasn't fair. It was an observation not one of the five questions, but I suppose in all fairness, I must give it to you."

Lizbeth had the grace to blush prettily, and the sight of it started a throbbing deep in his loins. How long had it been since a woman, any woman, had had this effect on him? Adan didn't verbalize what was running through his mind, however, he couldn't afford to give away another question so easily. Instead, he leaned over and nuzzled her neck.

The sound of her involuntary gasp and the feel of her shiver as his lips met soft skin disclosed more about his brand new wife than all the questions he could ever ask. She wasn't any more immune to him than he was to her. The thought made him smile as he formed his next inquiry. "What did I eat to break my fast yesterday and every other day this past week?"

Her giggle was like the tinkling of chimes to his ears, and Adan watched in wonder as her face gentled and again he saw the little girl she'd once been. "Yesterday was seventh day, so that means you had Alarian wild goose eggs, scrambled. On sixth day, you always have one of your favorites, cooked oats with tart winterberries. On fifth day, it was boar's kidneys, baked and wrapped in grape leaves."

She stopped, wrinkled her nose, grimaced, and stuck out her tongue.

Adan grinned.

"On fourth day, one of my favorites, buckwheat cakes with honey graces your plate. And on third day, you break your fast with mixed meat sausages and fresh fish. On second day, creamed raspberry sauce drizzled over crepes is placed before you."

She looked him straight in the eye. "And that, my princely husband, leaves us with today. First day, as is tradition, you were served Tambian pheasant, slow roasted and stuffed with wild rice as you always are to start your week."

She dropped her gaze to the floor. "And why do I know this? Because you eat the same thing week after week, and all of my life I've been forced to eat it, too."

Lizbeth glanced back up and rolled her eyes. "Seriously, Adan, what you've asked so far is common knowledge. Don't you read the section on the royal family in each season's *Barbarian Times*? Can't you think of anything harder? I must admit I wish to win, but I do want this to at least be somewhat of a challenge."

Adan continued to smile as he reached across the space between them and lightly stroked her leg at the hem of her tunic, making slow circles, growing higher with each pass. The pupils of her hazel-green eyes dilated, and her breathing became labored.

He leaned a hair's width from Lizbeth's lips and whispered, "How about something I doubt they cover in the *Barbarian Times*? At least, I hope they don't. What are my three favorite sexual positions, Lizbeth, and why?"

This time she did hesitate, and if Adan thought she had blushed before, there was certainly no question of it now. She glowed red from the top of her head all the way to her shoulders. Lizbeth Soulenticer-now-Hammerstrike was no quitter, however, and Adan was proud of his wife as she cleared her throat and answered.

"You like the traditional position of being on top best, because you enjoy looking your partner in the eye while, umm, while having intercourse with her. You're also partial to your partner taking the top, because you like watching her ride you. And...and...and you enjoy very much both the giving and receiving of oral copulation, because...well, because of how it feels, of course, and how very intimate it is."

Lizbeth stood, picked up her valise, and shuffled back and forth from one foot to the other. "Last question, Adan. Make it quick, please. I really do need to get going. Classes start bright and early in the morning."

Adan stood and faced her with his arms hanging loosely at his sides and his legs slightly parted. So, if being forced to discuss his sexual appetites bluntly hadn't made his wife stumble and make a mistake, perhaps touching him would. "Show me where on my body my scars are, Lizard, and tell me how many I have and how I received them?"

Lizbeth smiled and casually set her bag down once more. "I'm almost disappointed, my lord. This is the easiest question of them all."

Tentively, she reached out and ran a finger along a faint, raised white line slightly above his right collarbone. Heat from her touch radiated throughout Adan's chest.

"You have only three scars to mar your near

perfect body, husband. This one you received when you were but five years old. You thought you could fly like a dragon and jumped off the castle wall to prove it. Alas, like you are about most things, you were wrong."

She ran her hand down his right side until her fingers touched the puckered indentation he knew she would find, and Adan sucked in his breath as little shocks of pleasure exploded behind his eyes all the way to his loins.

"This one you received in your very first tournament. You were positive you were so quick that no man's blade could come close to piercing your flesh. A dwarf with lightning-fast reflexes and a sword longer than he was tall taught you how wrong you could be."

Next, she knelt before him and her hand hesitated for a fraction of a moment before she gently touched the inside of his left thigh and the slender white line running the length of it.

Adan knew himself to be of weak will as his cock twitched involuntarily toward her, seeking, begging for her touch.

She looked into his eyes and Adan forgot to breathe. "I was there the day you received this one. I bet you didn't know that. I didn't actually see you compete as we arrived too late for the tournament, but we were in the same village at the same time. My brothers always kept track of when and where your tournaments were being held, and they thought it would be a wonderful treat for my eighteenth birthday. They tried so hard to get us there on time and were sorely disappointed when they couldn't. To this day, I've never had the heart to tell them I abhor useless violence. This scar, however, didn't have anything to do with the tournament."

She lightly stroked the length of the thin white line while gazing at Adan. Time slowed as pleasure exploded into tiny sparks and fluttered unheeded through his groin and belly. The passion reflected in her eyes made his heart beat erratically, and his breathing became no more than short, ragged spurts. His mouth grew dry, and his palms began to sweat.

"This one you achieved after the tournament. The story was recounted all across the land for days. This one was from pulling a small child out of the way of a fast-moving cart. If it hadn't been for you, he would've been killed. It was the hoof of one of the horses that caused this gash. The town's people said you moved so fast you almost made it safely out of the horse's path yourself. Almost, but not quite."

Lizbeth suddenly patted his knee and stood, effectively breaking the spell. "Well, that's it, your only scars, husband. I've won, and I'll be on my way now."

She turned as if to go, but he grasped her and spun her around. Adan schooled his expression. "Before you attempt to make a hasty retreat, my lady, I have just one more question for you. Which do you prefer to spend the night upon, the fur rug here in front of the fire, the bed across the room, or perhaps simply on top of my near-perfect body? Your words, not mine." He chuckled.

Lizbeth sputtered. "What do you mean spend the night upon? I won fair and square, Adan Hammerstrike. I can't believe you would go back on your word."

"Oh, but you did not win, Lizard. I did." Adan raised his left arm and made a production of pointing to faint but distinctive marks high on the fleshy underside.

"You missed these."

Lizbeth shook her head. "Impossible. Don't you realize how important you are? Everything you do, everything you say, everything you eat, even how often you have bodily functions is cataloged, studied, and not only reported, but also set in missives to my instructors to be passed onto me. This can't be. Where and when did you get those?"

Adan looked her straight in the eye and told her the simple truth. "From you."

The sound of Lizbeth's gasp echoed off the walls. "I don't understand? I didn't, I never, I wouldn't have."

Adan grasped her shoulders and pulled her into him. She fit nicely beneath his chin and against his heart. She belonged there. "I know you think I'm nothing more than a sword-wielding barbarian, but remember when I brought the rabbit to you? I really was just trying to impress you." He slowly ran a hand up her back. "I had no idea he was a pet, Lizbeth, I swear I didn't. When I placed Horatio's limp body in your arms like a trophy, you screamed and dropped him. Then it appeared as if you were about to swoon, so I tried my best to catch you. You were beyond grief, though, and you latched so tightly onto my arm with your dainty hand and those razor sharp nails of yours you drew blood."

He slid his hand beneath the hem of her tunic until his fingers made contact with skin. Very warm skin. He tightened his embrace and rubbed his cheek against hers. "I never told anyone. I couldn't take the chance you might be punished for causing bodily harm to *the prince* when it was more my fault than yours, so I didn't get treatment for the wounds and they left scars."

Once more, he gazed into her confused hazel eyes. "I wasn't wrong to kill the rabbit, Lizbeth. For rabbits are meant to be eaten. But if it makes you feel any better, to this day I've never hunted another for my own table, and I can't bring myself to eat one. I really am sorry."

Adan tilted her chin until she had no choice but look him in the eye. "But being sorry doesn't change the fact. You lost, and it's time to pay up, wife."

She stiffened in his arms, but her eyes held his and her voice was clear and steady. "I'm ready, my lord. One request, though, if you don't mind. Let it be on the rug below us please. The thought of your bed makes me…ill. I don't…like dragons or the color white."

He nodded, and slowly, so as to not frighten her, Adan gently brushed his wife's lips with his own.

\*\*\*\*

Fur, soft and warm, against her backside was Lizbeth's first indication she was no longer standing. And the sight of her discarded tunic and traveling pants lying a scant few inches away on the floor, her second hint she was naked.

Glancing into the shadowy, deep blue eyes of her barbarian prince of a husband, Lizbeth asked, "How?"

It was the only word she got out before two very firm, warm, full lips met hers. The taste of need mingled with the scent of desire and wood smoke. His tongue flicked out and plundered the recesses of her mouth. Without thought or regret, she opened to him. Their lips took turns teasing and caressing as they stroked and delved. The very breath they took became one and the same.

Lizbeth tried unsuccessfully to hold onto the

memory that she detested this man. At the moment, however, all the reasons why eluded her.

Time slowed and finally stopped as Lizbeth's attention was drawn to goose bumps along the small of her back and down her spine. The pressure of each finger of Adan's big hands pressed her closer into him, forging them into one being. She quivered, and warmth flowed through her, around her, and inside her. A warmth that grew to a level of heat she'd never known before. Her pussy hummed with it.

He whispered against her skin and ripples of delight scampered to her toes. "What brings you pleasure, my lady?"

She stilled in his arms, not sure what to say.

He nuzzled her neck then nipped the very tip of her half-wood-elfin pointed ear. She shuddered as tingles of excitement scampered down her neck and across her shoulders before landing with a jolt in the pit of her belly.

"What brings you pleasure? Tell me," Adan whispered again.

She didn't know how to respond. She knew what brought him pleasure. After years of class after class on that particular subject alone, there was no way she couldn't know. But her own pleasure? It had never been a priority. As a matter of fact, even thinking about it had been discouraged. Sex in all its forms was to serve only one purpose, to please Prince Adan Hammerstrike. It was on the tip of her tongue to tell him whatever pleased him would please her when she realized she simply couldn't. "I don't know. It wasn't important."

Lizbeth heard his sudden intake of breath and worried for a moment she'd given him yet another wrong answer. "It's important to me." The tips of his fingers grazed a nipple, and Lizbeth arched upward, seeking to maintain the exquisite contact. Adan chuckled. "Mmm, I see you like that. It's a start."

He replaced his fingertips with his mouth and sucked, allowing his tongue to swirl around the pebbly hard nipple. Lizbeth had no control over the soft mewling sounds coming from her throat or the rhythmic throbbing that had begun deeper and much lower.

When he broke contact, she almost cried out, but he chuckled again. "It seems you like that, too."

His words brought a smile to her face.

Adan mumbled something against her skin as he made his way down her ribs and across her belly. She couldn't pay attention to anything he said, though, as his tongue delved into her navel and the stubble of tomorrow's beard lightly scratched and teased the skin right above the throbbing that had settled into a steady hum.

Her entire body pulsed, matching her heartbeat and growing stronger and more persistent with every stroke of Adan's chin against her skin. It was torment. It was wonderful.

And then he parted her folds and captured her swollen clit between his teeth. The word wonderful took on a whole new meaning.

Lights exploded behind her eyes and all sensation centered upon the small nodule. Lizbeth didn't realize she'd wound her fingers in Adan's hair and begun to rock. Her years of training disappeared, and all she knew was there was somewhere she needed to get and the only way to get there was with this man. Though she wasn't so sure if she'd survive the journey.

She heard herself beg him to stop because it was too much, then in the same breath, plead with him for more. She no longer recognized this stranger she'd become, and she didn't care. Just when she thought nothing in all of Albrath could possibly feel better than his tongue upon the tender membranes of her pussy, Adan slid up her body and, in a single powerful thrust, entered her.

Lizbeth couldn't breath. He was big, oh, God Draka, he was big, and so very hard and hot. The pulsing of his cock deep within her core matched perfectly the combined beat of their hearts.

Then he moved, and the world tilted upside down.

Slowly at first, then faster and faster, he rode. Lizbeth held on tightly as she chanced a glance into the eyes of her barbarian. The passion reflected in them gave her the courage to meet his thrusts with her own.

She ground her hips hard against his with every downstroke and was rewarded with his quick intake of breath. She did it again with the upstrokes, and his eyes crossed in pleasure.

Lizbeth smiled and was pleased when he offered a mischievous grin in response. Adan's pace quickened, slowed, and then quickened again. She matched his cadence thrust for thrust, as if they were two halves of a whole coming back together.

Then it happened. Not a slow building she could've prepared for, but an all-out implosion of such sweet, intense pleasure it brought tears to her eyes. Wave after wave of delightful spasms rolled through her.

A moment later, she gloried in the hot essence and strength of Adan's release as he plunged one last time deep within her, bellowed her name to the rafters, and then, with a shudder that racked his entire body, relaxed.

Before her breath could slow, Adan flipped them until he was flat on his back with Lizbeth straddled on top of him. His cock was still buried deep within her. She started to rise, but he shook his head and held her in place. "Not yet, my lady. Lie upon me and allow me the pleasure of your body for a while longer."

Lizbeth sighed with satisfaction as she lay her head upon Adan's chest and listened as the thump-thumping of his heart slowed to a normal cadence. She wrapped her arms about his sides and marveled at how strong-as-titanium muscles could feel so very soft to the touch. For the first time in a very long time, she belonged somewhere and to someone. The thought disturbed her more than it brought comfort.

She rose just far enough to look Adan in the eye. "This doesn't change anything, you know. I'm still leaving for the Academy in the morning."

He gently pressed her head close to his heart and wrapped his arms about her. "I know, my lady. I know."

## Chapter Three

She hadn't slept more than a few moments all night. Lizbeth lay in the same position she'd been in for many turns of the hourglass. Yawning, she snuggled deeper into Adan's embrace, the warmth of his arms about her and his breath against her hair a gentle reminder of what had transpired the evening before. Even his cock, now soft and snug against her belly, and the firmness of the rest of his body beneath her had become comforts she was not yet ready to give up.

She didn't want to move, although she knew she must. The very faintest streaks of light crossed the horizon and filtered through the window on the other side of the room. It was time to rise. Soon she must go.

Lizbeth closed her eyes tight to ward off the coming of the dawn a few more moments. It wasn't supposed to be like this. She hated him, didn't she? She'd been forced to live, breath, eat, sleep, and even pray for Adan Hammerstrike every day of her life for as long as she could remember. Getting up and walking away was supposed to be easy. This span of time before he became king was supposed to be her payoff for the hours, days, seasons, and years she'd spent living only for him.

Why, then, did it feel as if she were running away from her destiny instead of rushing toward it?

She didn't even want to be his wife, did she? She

wanted to be an enchantress, and she didn't want it just a little bit, she wanted it more than anything in the whole of Albrath. It was her dream.

Ever since she'd been a little girl and had found the old dusty tome full of wonderful spells while playing in the underbelly of her family's small castle, becoming an enchantress had been all she'd dreamed of. The hope of one day being able to instill magic into ordinary objects and thus make them extraordinary was the one thing that had gotten her through the long years of never-ending Adan Hammerstrike classes with her sanity mostly intact.

She shifted her weight and Adan stirred. Holding her breath so as not to awaken him, Lizbeth waited. A moment later, he grew still and relaxed. She didn't wish him to wake. It would be easier to slip away in the space of a few grains of sand if he remained asleep. The thought didn't bring her much comfort.

Why weren't things ever as simple as they should be? The marriage contract had been so straightforward. On the twenty-first anniversary of her birth, she was to become the bride of Prince Adan Hammerstrike, and when he became king, it was her responsibility to be his queen and give him an heir.

The time between her birthday and his coronation was never covered so, to Lizbeth's way of thinking, it was her own to do with as she pleased. It was her time to finally be on her own and not have to answer to anyone but herself. Not her brothers, not her Hammerstrike-class instructors, not Adan himself, and, most of all, not his mother Queen Allanna Zanlynn Calista Hammerstrike or those loyal to her.

Lizbeth shivered, though she wasn't cold.

Adan stirred once more, his cock thickening against her belly as his lips grazed the top of her head. "If I'm not keeping you warm enough, my lady, I'd be happy to retrieve the coverlet or a fur or warm you in other ways." He lifted her slightly and rotated his hips until his cock slipped inside her pussy as if seeking where it was meant to be.

She smiled against his skin as she squirmed. "Oh, no, you don't. Take that thing out and go back to sleep, Barbarian. It's too early, I'm much too tender, and I'm plenty warm just as I am."

But Lizbeth couldn't help herself as she giggled at his antics and tried to pull away.

In a single motion, Adan rotated them until she was once more beneath him. He slid his cock out then slowly buried himself within her pussy once more, growing larger and harder with every passing second. "I'll be as gentle as a barbarian can be, my lady. I promise.

"If you truly don't wish this," he whispered against her ear, "or really are too tender for my attention, just say the word and I swear, I'll stop. Though as I've no doubt you know, I am used to getting my way." He slid out again until just the very tip of his cock remained inside, and then quickly plunged back in, all the way in, and stilled.

Lizbeth moaned, though certainly not from pain, as heat and sweet pleasure infused her to the bottoms of her feet. Her toes curled of their own accord as all thoughts of the past and promises and dreams and classes were forgotten, replaced with a need for this man to once more move within her. Pressure built from the inside out, and all that existed in Albrath was her body and Adan's, joined together.

She opened her eyes and watched him watching her, waiting for her answer. She couldn't help but smile when he winked and grinned. He truly was magnificent, this barbarian husband of hers. From his golden, bedraggled hair, hanging in his ever-changing, deep blue eyes, to his aristocratic nose, full lips made for kissing, and strong cleft chin, he was every inch a prince.

Lizbeth lifted her hips, ground them against his pelvis, and was rewarded with his eyes closing and his nostrils flaring. Still, he held himself rigid, the strain of his effort showing in the creases of his forehead. She was humbled by his tenderness.

Lifting her face the short distance between them, Lizbeth brushed his lips lightly with hers. "Perhaps I'm not so very tender, after all, and I've merely allowed you to believe you're the one getting your way when, in fact, it's my bidding you are doing."

She wasn't sure if she heard his sigh of relief or felt it against her skin as his body began to move. Over and over, his cock powerfully thrust in and out of her pussy, and she strove to match his rhythm.

His lips found a particularly sensitive spot on the side of her neck and nuzzled while his fingers teased an already firm nipple to complete alertness. Spirals of pleasure leapt from every area he touched and pooled in the very core of her being until Lizbeth could do little more than hold onto Adan and breathe.

Faster and deeper, he thrust, and even the act of breathing was forgotten as what had begun as a steady, throbbing need where their bodies met morphed into an all-out necessity, essential for her continued existence.

She knew herself truly lost when she gazed into his eyes and begged, "Please, Adan, fuck me fast. Fuck me hard."

Lizbeth didn't get the chance to utter another word as Adan's arms wrapped around her hips, his eyes glazed over, and the speed and depth of his thrusts doubled. It was like lightning on a stormy night as sparks of delight shot through her and landed squarely in her belly and lower. Tiny spasms racked her body, leaving her quaking in its aftermath.

Her pussy thrummed happily along as Lizbeth answered his thrusts with her own. Her nails scored his back as her legs squeezed tight about his waist. Holding on tight, wanting to make the moment last as long as she possibly could.

His cock stretched her and filled her, throbbed within her and overflowed her heart. Tears of joy stung her eyes as his balls slapped against her ass, and his lips nuzzled her neck.

Pressure built deep in her pussy, and her clit throbbed. *Not yet*, her mind begged as she fought for control. It was much too late, however, as Adan slipped a finger between the folds of her pussy and stroked her swollen nub. Spasms shook her, and she exploded.

Lizbeth screamed her pleasure, but Adan probably didn't hear her as he was also in the throes of his own release. Hot liquid coated her insides while the pulsing of his still deeply embedded cock rocked her gently back to Albrath.

Rolling onto his side a moment later, he gathered her into his arms. "You're nothing like I thought you were, Lizbeth. You amaze me." He kissed her forehead.

She smiled into the darkness. "Remind me

sometime to show you what I learned in my Adan Hammerstrike classes. Then you can tell me if I amaze you or not."

The sound of his chuckle, then his relaxed snores, lulled Lizbeth once more back into her memories. They should have been good memories, especially considering the experience she'd just had, but they weren't. Lying here in Adan's arms brought back other memories, dark memories she would rather forget. Memories of Adan's mother the queen and the special Adan Hammerstrike classes Lizbeth hoped to never again remember.

Queen Allanna Hammerstrike. Even thinking her name was an unpleasant experience. Not as unpleasant as being in her presence, however. Lizbeth's mind flooded with scene after scene she wished she could forget.

She'd always understood why her parents were so taken in by the royal house of Hammerstrike and hadn't held it against them. After all, to be the poor relatives of the King, then to have their only daughter chosen specifically by him from the moment of her birth to be the future wife of his only son and the next queen of the Barbarians must have been a great honor. However, her parents had never truly been privy to the side Queen Allanna saved just for Lizbeth, and she was glad they hadn't.

Her father, fifth cousin twice removed from the king, Lord Lonhiem Soulenticer, and his wife, Lady Liszt had been kind people. He, a hulking barbarian who loved to laugh and hunt and tell stories, and she, a wood-elf who would rather spend her days collecting mushrooms in the forest and digging in the rich soil than in a parlor sipping tea, had been wonderful parents but easily impressed.

Lizbeth had made a promise to herself they'd never know what the private instructor Queen Allanna brought along to give special lessons to their young daughter was really like, and they hadn't. She wasn't even sure the Queen herself truly understood the lengths Master Seiger had gone to. But it didn't matter whether Queen Allanna had known or not. It was still the Queen who had brought him to Lizbeth's home and, in the end, it was the Queen who had defended his actions.

Always, the morning after the Queen and her entourage arrived for their yearly visit, the classes would begin. Hour after tedious hour of sitting completely still and reciting over and over the virtues of the Hammerstrike family as Master Seiger saw them and all the reasons Lizbeth was lucky she'd been the chosen one. Every year the list grew longer. Every year she would forget at least one small fact no matter how hard she studied, and that's when the *memory lessons* as he called them began.

Lizbeth lay very still, crunched her eyes closed, and forced her breathing to remain steady. Why were these dark thoughts invading now? She didn't want to think about them this morning. She didn't want to remember. But it was already too late. The blackness she fought overtook her, and once more, she was back in the classroom staring at the white trunk and dreading what was to come next.

White. How she hated white. Every time the Queen made an appearance at their small castle, she always came with an entourage of servants all dressed in white and was accompanied by Master Seiger with his chalk white skin, long white beard, wrinkled white fingers, and spotless white robe.

Sometimes, the Queen's family came with her, and sometimes, they didn't. She always arrived in a white coach driven by eight white horses. She always wore a gown of sparkling white, and upon her head was a crown covered with white pearls. She even wore white slippers upon her feet. But, worst of all, she always, always, always brought along six white trunks of varying sizes.

The very first *memory lesson* had occurred when Lizbeth was five. She'd actually been as excited to see the beautiful lady everyone called the Queen as anyone else had. She'd even been thrilled at the prospect of a new instructor.

The excitement had quickly turned to horror, however, while during her very first session with Master Seiger, she'd forgotten the name of Adan's favorite steed. Master Seiger had taken her by the hand, walked her over to one of the pristine white trunks, opened it, and placed her inside. He'd told her bad little girls should either be beaten or fed to the dragons. But future queens must not be allowed to have marks on their skin. So, instead, they must lose their air. It would help them learn to be obedient and not ever to forget their lessons again.

Then he'd closed the lid.

Lizbeth wiggled out from under Adan's arms, grabbed her discarded clothing, and rushed to the window. As soon as she managed to get it open, she collapsed to the floor, gasping.

It was always like this when she remembered. The

trunk closing, the sound of the latch clicking, the weight of Master Seiger sitting upon it so she couldn't escape. The muffled consequences he threatened her with if she dared tell.

Threats of her parents losing their home and its pretty, forested grounds they so loved. Threats of no longer being the chosen bride of Adan Hammerstrike and the disgrace that would bring upon the heads of her family. Even threats of what would happen to the people she loved and to herself.

Lizbeth could still hear his scratchy voice just as clear as if he were right there whispering in her ear. *"You'd better not tell anyone, little girl. You'd better not tell. Remember what I said about the dragons. For by darkness of night, wings take flight. And seek out the naughty to devour by next light."*

Then total blackness would envelope her and she would no longer be able to move in the suffocatingly small space. It had frightened her to the point she would sometimes lose control and wet herself, or worse. By the time the air became stale and thin and there was none left to breathe, she'd welcomed what she knew would come next. The terror and finality of darkness and oblivion overtaking her was longed for, considering the alternative was the trunk opening and being forced to face Master Seiger once again. For facing Master Seiger once more meant the process started all over again.

Year after year, this had gone on until Lizbeth was too big to easily fit in even the largest of the white trunks. It had finally stopped when she was eleven.

She remembered the incident precisely. It had been the day after Adan had killed Horatio. Lizbeth had decided she didn't want to be his queen, after all, and it didn't matter anymore if Master Seiger carried through with his threats. She would never willingly be put in any small space ever again by anyone.

That was the time she hadn't gone willingly. That was the time she'd fought back. That was the time she'd demanded to speak with Queen Allanna and exposed Master Seiger for the monster he was.

Queen Allanna had called her an ungrateful little liar and told her how lucky she'd been to be chosen in the first place. The Queen had let her know in no uncertain terms she would be sorry for causing trouble.

Then, the Queen, the King, Adan, his sisters, and the Queen's entourage, including Master Seiger, had left and never come to visit again. It had also been the first and last time she'd ever seen her mother cry.

Within a season, both her parents were dead.

A horrible sickness had spread like wildfire all across Albrath and taken her parents as two of its first victims. Lizbeth always wondered if it was her fault, her punishment for telling.

It didn't alleviate her guilt even a little when she'd promised both of them as they lay dying that she would carry out their wish and make them proud of her by becoming the Barbarian queen they'd always wanted her to be.

Although King Alfred Hammerstrike and the queen's mother, Grandmother Ava, had made a token appearance, the Queen hadn't had the grace to attend Lord Lonhiem and Lady Liszt's funerals.

Queen Allanna hadn't even bothered to attend her own son's wedding ceremony of the day before. After she'd sent the hideous white gown she demanded

Lizbeth wear, she made an excuse about being too distraught over Adan's loss in the arena at Yulemass and the recent weddings of her four daughters to attend Adan and Lizbeth's ceremony.

In truth, Lizbeth was grateful her new mother-in-law hadn't been there.

Slowly, Lizbeth stood, slipped her tunic over her head, and ran her hands down her sides, straightening wrinkles as she went. Then she threaded her fingers through her hair until it was tangle free. Silently, she slipped on her traveling pants and closed the window. She gave herself one final moment to school her countenance and put back in place the mask she'd learned long ago to hide behind, one of indifference.

When she turned, her eyes darted involuntarily toward Adan, and she was relieved to see he still slept. As quietly as possible, she gathered her valise and slipped away.

**\*\*\*\***

Adan watched the door close behind Lizbeth. Who was this strange, lovely creature now his wife? She certainly wasn't the mindless little chit he'd been led to believe. The woman who'd sparred mentally toe to toe with him, then given as good as she'd gotten in his arms was no chit. No, she was vibrant and beautiful and intelligent and more than a little troubled. The question was, what was troubling her, and what, if anything, could he do about it?

Had she been aware he slept little more than she? Did she have any inkling he'd held her all through the night and felt her fears and doubts as real as if they'd been his own?

He'd noticed every startle when he stroked her

back, every gasp when she tried to prevent a tear, and every time she'd sighed. And then, just as dawn approached and right after they'd once more made love, something had frightened her. So much so that she'd run away without so much as a word.

Would Lizbeth be happy to see him at the Academy when he arrived later today? Or would she be angry and resent him, thinking he'd followed her?

Adan sat and scratched the stubble along his jaw as he stretched muscles that had gone stiff during the night. If he'd been the one who spent his entire life having every trivial fact about her shoved down his throat day and night, wouldn't he want a chance to spread his wings a little? Wouldn't he want to see what else was out there in the big wide world before he settled for what would most assuredly be a routine, boring life?

How long had he been aware of the restrictions he and his family lived under? Always watched, always judged, and never having a moment they could be sure was private. Being part of a royal family might seem glamorous to the outside world, but with power and privilege came great responsibility and, ultimately, boredom.

Could he blame Lizbeth for wanting the opportunity to see something beyond the forest she'd grown up in and the castle walls of Alaria? Could he deny her the chance to make her own friends, her own decisions, and her own mistakes? He knew he couldn't.

But that didn't mean he wasn't going to go back to The Academy himself. And if being at The Academy awarded him the chance to be close to his pretty little wife, all the better.

## Chapter Four

Though the trip through the portal from Alaria to The Academy had been a short one, it had left her strangely dizzy and disorientated. Her head pounded, nausea threatened, her muscles ached, she was tired, and the first class of the day had more than a half turn of the hourglass to go before it was over. Lizbeth wasn't sure she'd survive this first class let alone the entire day.

She couldn't begin to fathom the enormity of an entire four-semester enchanter program, but she was determined to give it her best shot. Even though she felt like the walking dead this morning and probably looked even worse, she was excited beyond belief to finally be at the famous school.

The Academy of Magical Arts was amazing.

Housed within a series of towering castles with spires so high they touched the clouds and baileys so wide they took the better part of a turn of an hourglass to traverse, the Academy was an entity unto itself. Surrounded by fields and gently rolling hills with a backdrop of mountains to the west, it was situated in a northwestern section of the left lower quadrant of the continent of Landis.

The Academy easily boasted a population to match, if not exceed, most small realms. Its ceilings were high, its hallways drafty, its students as varied as they could possibly be, and it was wonderful.

Lizbeth glanced around her Spells and Spirits class and smiled. Even though it was still early, there weren't many empty seats. Six elfin girls of various genealogies sat together one row in front of her, and two dwarves with their long red beards, big noses, and scruffy robes sat directly in front of them.

Lizbeth couldn't tell which of the dwarves was female, though she knew from their voices one had to be.

The instructor, a dark-elf with indigo-blue skin and snow-white hair named Mr. Neoseraph, had taken the roll at the beginning of class, and one of the dwarves had definitely answered with a high-pitched female ring.

There were also four halflings, three gnomes, a single troll, two other half-elves like herself, and half dozen full-blooded high-elves scattered about the room, plus five dark-elves sitting together in a clump.

Mr. Neoseraph cleared his throat, and Lizbeth sat at attention. So far, his lecture had been confined to what textbooks and supplies would be needed and the lecture as opposed to lab schedule. She listened avidly, glad something of real interest was about to be imparted.

"Before I start doing any in-depth lectures, I would like to ascertain your levels of expertise. Is there anyone in class who isn't a beginner? Anyone who has moderate or advanced spell-casting training?"

He then pointed directly at the high-elf females who had started giggling. "And before you raise your hands and waste my time, by moderate or advanced, I mean something beyond your daily PDUP spells and such."

Lizbeth didn't hear another word Mr. Neoseraph said. Her ears began to ring, and her mouth suddenly went dry. How could she have been so stupid? How long had it been since she had worried about casting her daily PDUP spell? Protection from Disease and Unwanted Pregnancy wasn't something she had needed to worry about for quite some time. Being betrothed to the prince of the barbarians had meant after her sexual practices and theory classes were completed, she'd lived a life of celibacy.

She hadn't been reminded by her instructors to cast the stupid spell for more than a year now. And her brothers…Lizbeth had no doubt they'd taken for granted she would automatically cast whatever she needed to cast when she was supposed to. Just like brushing her teeth or taking a shower or eating her vegetables, not because she didn't like them but because they were good for her.

Casting the PDUP spell was expected. It was part of every female's normal daily routine even before the time they were old enough to begin their cycle of the moon and bleed. Which was something, she had no doubt, her brothers would rather not think about.

What had she done? She hadn't intended to have sex with her husband last night. As a matter of fact, it had been her intention to do just the opposite and leave him sitting in his cold, white castle high and dry.

Lizbeth sighed. It was yet another thing she'd failed at.

Her hand involuntarily went to her flat stomach. Could she be? What would she do if she were? She couldn't be. After all, it had been just one night. God

Draka couldn't be so cruel as to let her get pregnant after just two times. Could he?

She didn't want to be. It would ruin everything. How could she finish the enchanter program if she were with child? She couldn't. Adan would lock her away in his castle. He'd want his heir safe.

And the Queen, oh my God Draka, the Queen would want to oversee the birth. She would expect to be involved. She'd want to pick the child's instructors when it was old enough.

*Little girls lose their air when they're bad.*

Bile rose, and Lizbeth rushed from the room. She barely made it through the doors, down the hallway, and into the stall of the ladies room before what little food she had broken her fast with came back up. Splashing cold water on her face and wiping it dry with a towel, she finally said the spell she should have said the day before. She hoped with all her heart it wasn't too late.

Turning and heading back out the door, Lizbeth's mind was spinning. Did the PDUP spell work right away? She couldn't remember. And did she need to say a series of them before she was sure she was protected? If so, how long did she need to wait before it was safe to once more do the things she and Adan had done? Not that there was going to be an opportunity to do any of those things with Adan miles and miles away.

Heat flushed her face, and Lizbeth cringed. How could she be thinking such things, and why couldn't she recall even the most basic principles of the PDUP spell? It was almost as if thinking about the man placed her under a magical spell.

A smile involuntarily curved the corners of

Lizbeth's lips. What had transpired in the circle of her husband's arms had certainly been magic.

Even though he was miles away, Adan's face the way it had looked this morning, with passion burning in his eyes and her name on his lips, invaded her mind, and she blushed even hotter.

Deep in thought, she headed back toward class. She hadn't taken more than a handful of steps before someone warm and solid stopped her forward progression. Two strong arms enveloped her, and Lizbeth slowly looked into the last face on Albrath she'd expected to see again this morning.

For a moment, excitement filled her to her toes, then she groaned. "What are you doing here?"

The rumble of Adan's laughter grated on her already stretched thin nerves. "I may very well be a barbarian, Lizard, but I'm a well-educated one. I've been taking classes for sometime now, as you well know, and even teaching a few. So see, you aren't the only one with outside interests, and since you did lose the bet, I don't have to leave you alone. As a matter of fact, I spoke with Headmistress Seychelle, and we now have an entire suite of rooms all to ourselves. What do you think of that?"

Lizbeth closed her eyes and counted to ten, then counted to ten again. What was she going to do? The warmth of his arms was already wreaking havoc with her senses, and it hadn't been but a few moments since she'd finally cast her PDUP spell. She couldn't do this, even if he did smell faintly of wood smoke and lust and even if his arms were a safe haven. She wasn't going to give in. She couldn't. It would ruin everything.

Lizbeth glanced into Adan's eyes and knew

without a doubt her hopes and dreams would fall to the wayside if she gave in to his wishes, and she wasn't ready to chance that. There was only one thing she could do. She took two deep breaths, looked him straight in the eye, and denied her own desires.

"First, don't call me Lizard," she said. "I don't like it. Second, of course, I know you've been taking and giving classes here. I know *everything* about you. Third, go away, Adan. I don't want to share a room or anything else with you. I paid the price for the bet I lost in full. One night only, remember? And lastly, I have a perfectly good cot in my dormitory. I have no need nor do I want to share your bed."

Lizbeth Hammerstrike turned and walked away.

Thank God Draka, Adan didn't follow.

****

"What the petrified jam between the toes of a troll trollop tap-dancing on a keg of stale beer were ya thinking, lad? She's ya wife, ain't she? Ya gotta show her who's boss. Go get her, take her ta yare room, and have ya way with her. It'll put a smile on her face. Trust me, I know women."

Adan stared at his almost-bald gnome friend with the bulbous nose and overly large ears. "You have a blow-up doll tucked under your arm, Leeky. Forgive me if I'm just a tad leery about taking advice on my love life from you."

Leeky Shortz blustered. "Ya can think what ya want about me and Miss Bunny here, but I'm not the one having lady troubles. Miss Laycee Titwilder is more than willing ta be sharing my bed. Even if it does get a bit crowded once ya throw my very talented Miss Bunny and Laycee's useless Tug McGroin doll inta the middle of it. If ya ain't gonna take her ta yare room and do her, then at least buy her a present. All lasses like doodads, no matter how stubborn they are. I even have a couple suggestions for ya if ya want."

Adan shook his head. "Oh, no, thank you. I've seen your idea of gift giving, remember? You gave Laycee a cucumber when we were leaving on Sarco's quest last year and told her to use it on herself as some kind of sick sex toy and then eat the disgusting thing in her salad when it started to get mushy."

Adan shuddered. "I've known Laycee practically all my life, remember? She was governess to my sisters before they wed. It was a very disturbing sight when you gave her that…that vegetable. I'd rather not scare Lizbeth more than she already is until we've been married at least a week or so, if I can help it."

Leeky had the grace to pinken. "Well, Laycee liked her cucumber, and there's nothing wrong with a gift that keeps giving."

The sound of choking coming from the other side of the desk didn't concern Adan. Instead, he scowled at his brother-in-law. "Trust me, it's not that funny."

Sarco wiped a tear from his eye, coughed, and smiled. "It's pretty funny, you've got to admit. Didn't you tell me just a week ago Lizbeth was going to be like putty in your hands? Pliable, that's what I believe you called her. Oh, and wasn't it Lackluster Lizbeth you nicknamed her?"

Sarco grinned. "I distinctly remember you complaining about being saddled to a woman with no personality and how you'd never have another moment's peace with her following your every footstep and catering to your every whim. Now you can't even get her to share your bed? It seems the mighty prince of the barbarians isn't the great lover he boasts of being, after all."

Adan threw up his hands. "Where did you say my sister went? I need to speak with an intelligent adult."

Sarco Sunwalker continued to smile. "Lark is setting up a wizard's class for me right now. My wife is also my apprentice, remember? Some people actually work for a living around here. I'll be sure and tell her you wish to speak to her about how to get your lackluster little wife under control when she gets back."

Sarco almost fell out of his chair laughing.

Adan didn't think it was funny. He closed his eyes, folded his arms, and shook his head.

The sound of Sarco clearing his throat caught Adan's attention, and he opened one eye. Though his friend still had a wide grin on his face, there was also sincerity shining in his eyes. "I truly am sorry for your trouble, Adan. The biggest problem I see is your relationship with your wife has no middle. You said yourself you hadn't seen her for ten years before yesterday. You met as children, went your separate ways, you married, the end. Where is the romancing and falling in love part? Where is the excitement? Women like that kind of thing. They tend to feel cheated without it."

His smile faded. "Even a woman who was forced to learn what you do with your toenail clippings wants to be pursued. Maybe even more so because of that. And what do you know about her? Do you even know what her favorite food is, or color or places to be kissed?"

Adan sighed. "I shouldn't have to woo my own

wife. Arranged marriage means you get to skip that part. She knows I'll do my duty by her. I know everything I need to know about her. I know we've been promised to each other all our lives, and I know it's our responsibility to live together and produce an heir."

Sarco chuckled but the sound of it held no humor. "If all you want out of marriage is the fulfillment of a cold, loveless contract, then you're right. You don't need to get to know her or romance her or sweep her off her feet. But if you want her to want to be in your bed and love you the way only a woman can, then trust me, you've got to work at it. It's up to you, my friend."

It was Adan's turn to laugh. "I'm a Barbarian, remember? Romance isn't my strong point. We tend to stomp in, wield really big swords, take what we want, and stomp back out. I don't have the first clue about this wooing stuff."

From across the room Leeky Shortz cackled. "Then it's a good thing ya've got us ta help ya, lad, now isn't it?"

Adan groaned.

****

Lizbeth couldn't concentrate. The headache that had been developing even before she'd seen Adan earlier had gotten worse as the day wore on.

After Spells and Spirits class had come Channeling with none other than Briarlarn Dragonheart as the instructor. Even if Briar hadn't been the wife of one of Adan's closest friends, and an amazing healer, Lizbeth would have still been jealous.

Beautiful seemed a dull word to describe Briar, but beautiful she was. Hair all the shades of red, like a roaring fire, and she wore it in a long braid swinging gently to her waist. Intelligent eyes the exact green of the moss on the forest floor and ears just slightly pointed complemented her pixy-style nose and full lips.

Quick to smile and friendly, Mrs. Dragonheart was even quicker to explain how channeling worked and how, in the end, not everyone was cut out to be a channeler and some wouldn't be able to do it at all. Channeling required intense concentration to allow magical energy to flow through fingertips and into an object.

What were the chances Lizbeth would be magically gifted enough to channel? And if she wasn't, would she be considered an embarrassment to Adan since Briar was obviously gifted beyond belief?

Lizbeth regretted not speaking more than five words to the woman yesterday after the wedding ceremony when she'd had the chance. She'd simply been too out of place to talk with anyone, let alone the great healer.

In hindsight though, it would've been nice to ask Briar her opinion on whether she sensed Lizbeth had enough talent to be in her class and also what was the half-elf instructor's thoughts on arranged marriages.

There had certainly been no censure in Briar's gaze yesterday or today, only open friendliness. But then, Briar was a woman who was well aware of her own powers, and her marriage had been a true love match, not a cold, calculated arrangement. She probably hadn't given Adan's marriage more than a passing thought, expect perhaps to pity him.

Even though Lizbeth had come from a small village, she'd heard the stories of the deep love between the healer and her paladin Uthiel Dragonheart, and how, because of their great love, they'd saved a young dragling and solved the riddle hidden in a nine-hundred year old fable. All of Albrath had heard the tale.

Lizbeth hoped she and Briar would someday become more than simply student and instructor, possibly even friends. And, since Briar was a healer, perhaps she'd be able to ask her about the effectiveness of PDUP spells the morning after the fact and count on her discretion. Or even more importantly, could the healer ascertain if she were now with child? Only time would tell.

The day dragged on and on.

Midday meal had been uneventful, and though Lizbeth couldn't bring herself to swallow much more than a crust of bread, that alone helped settle her stomach and ease the persistent ache in her head.

Then had come the second half of her first school day and Wizard's class. Why had she even signed up for Wizard 101 with Sarco Sunwalker? She didn't want to be a wizard. She wanted to be an enchanter. The only reason to take wizard class was so she'd become familiar with the implements she'd be trying to imbue with magic. All the staffs, rods, swords, daggers, and wands.

Lizbeth sighed, sorry yet again she hadn't thought her plan through as completely as she should have. Couldn't she have accomplished basically the same thing with a few extra hours in the library without exposing her lack of knowledge of all things magical to, of all people, Adan's youngest sister Lark?

She shuddered, and in her own defense knew when she'd selected the wizard's class, she'd had no idea

Sarco Sunwalker even knew Lark, let alone had been about to go on a dangerous quest to win her hand in marriage. It was all very romantic when the minstrels sang about it but, again, it meant Lark probably wouldn't understand Lizbeth's reservations about her own wedded unbliss.

Exquisite, intelligent Larksong Sunwalker, fledgling wizard in her own right, powerful Spirtmaster from birth, was apprentice to her husband, wizard instructor and heir to the Lordship of the Elves, Sarco Sunwalker. A newlywed herself, Lark was now destined to be Sarco's lady when he took over the rule of the elfin kingdom from his father one day.

She was a beautiful woman with a curvaceous body, hair the color of warm amber, a mind quick as lightning, and piercing gray eyes that Lizbeth could swear saw directly into her soul. The notion didn't frighten her as much she thought it would. As a matter of fact, it brought her a strange sense of comfort. And, by the time wizard class finished, Lizbeth had relaxed and enjoyed it.

Then, finally, she sat in the class she'd been waiting for all day. Lizbeth pinched herself to make sure she wasn't dreaming. Even her persistent headache couldn't distract from the excitement. She was actually in Basic Enchanter class with none other than Headmistress Seychelle as her instructor.

Lizbeth shook her head as she sat staring. She'd heard rumors about the headmistress but thought they must have been exaggerated. They weren't. Headmistress Seychelle could only be described as coldly beautiful, a true ice princess.

Well known as not only the headmistress of the

Academy, but also as a powerful enchantress in her own right, Seychelle certainly looked the part.

Dressed from head to toe in black leather, she was a sight to behold. Tall, even for a high-elf, her skin was so pale as to be almost translucent. Her emerald green eyes slanted upward and were fringed in cheek-touching black lashes. Her red lips curved in an almost cruel smile, and when she spoke, her voice, though not loud, held power and demanded obedience. Her crisp, perfectly-pointed ears peeked through a waist-length mass of black, riotous curls.

The only thing off kilter about Headmistress Seychelle in any way was the strange creature she called Ray, who followed her every footstep.

He was human, or at least had once been. Now he was just a pathetic pet on the end of a golden chain. Wisps of dull brown hair covered most of his head, and a yellowed tunic covered his skinny body. What was truly disturbing about Ray, though, was what he carried between his teeth like a puppy's well-loved toy.

No matter from what angle Lizbeth looked at it, there was no other explanation…it was a dildo. And, not just a dildo, but the biggest, gaudiest, knobby orange rubber example of a dildo she'd ever seen.

Just when Lizbeth thought the little man couldn't possibly get any stranger, he walked straight over to her, plopped the slimy dildo right into her lap, got down on all fours, grinned at her with his tongue lolling from the side of his mouth, and yelled at the top of his lungs, "Ray loves cock."

Lizbeth jumped so quickly her chair toppled with a loud thud. Her heart beat fast and hard, and she almost missed what Headmistress Seychelle was saying because Ray chose that moment to once more scream, "Ray loves cock."

The enchanter instructor didn't even bat an eye. She simply raised her voice and exclaimed louder, "Oh, look, very first day of the semester and Ray has already picked a favorite playmate, our one and only half-elf half-barbarian. Isn't that precious?"

She clasped her hands at her waist. "For those of you who don't already know, Ray was once my very capable assistant before I loaned him out to High Mystic Purrell. One week with that man, and he hasn't been the same since. All anyone can figure is he must have suffered some kind of traumatic shock. So I take care of him."

The headmistress beckoned to Lizbeth. "Go on. Be a good girl now and give him cock, sweetie."

Ray jumped up and down, shouting. "Ray loves cock. Ray loves cock. Ray loves cock."

Class was abruptly interrupted when, a moment later, Lizbeth not only lost the crust of bread she'd eaten for lunch, but then some.

## Chapter Five

She wanted sleep. Mind-numbing, no-dreaming, time-stopping, at least seven-turns-of-the-hourglass, undisturbed sleep.

Lizbeth hadn't gone to the cafeteria for her end of the day meal or even back to her dormitory to enjoy the camaraderie of her roommates. Instead, she'd gone straight to the library and stayed there hiding and studying until forced to leave because its doors were closing. Food and friendship could wait until tomorrow. Peace was more important. Her stomach growled its displeasure, and she ignored it. She wasn't willing to face anyone or anything else today.

The last couple of days had been more than a little trying. First the wedding and the night spent in Adan Hammerstrike's arms. Then, this morning, she'd remembered she hadn't cast her PDUP spell and might well be pregnant at this very moment. Not to mention running smack into said potential father here at the Academy where she'd forgotten he might be. It should've given her a clue as to how the day was going to go.

And then to make matters even worse, throwing up in front of her entire enchanter class, and directly on poor Ray's head, had just put the topper on her first day of classes. How was she to have known he just wanted to play fetch with the disgusting thing? The sound of her fellow students laughing still rang in her ears.

Hiding away until tomorrow might well be the coward's way out, but Lizbeth had already gone though her entire week's allowance of courage. Inside her dormitory, in the middle of her small cot, tucked under the covers, in the dark of the night, was the safest, most normal place in all of Albrath for her to be, and she couldn't wait to get there.

Rounding the corner, the faint echo of a familiar laugh reached her ears, and with dread, Lizbeth followed it all the way to her dormitory door. Glancing inside, she cringed and, for a moment, wished she could be anywhere else. There, seated upon her cot, was the very last person she wanted to see tonight, her husband, Adan Hammerstrike. And, he wasn't alone.

The prince was surrounded by all eleven of Lizbeth's dormmates, and the women were gazing at him as if he were a gift straight from God Draka and they couldn't wait to rip off his wrappings and expose the treats waiting beneath. He at least had the grace to pinken when he looked up and she was standing in the doorway.

He jumped to his feet, almost knocking over two of the women who'd been practically sitting in his lap. "Lizbeth, my little lizard, there you are! I've been waiting for you. Your friends were just entertaining me with all sorts of stories. I thought I'd check and see if perhaps you'd changed your mind about staying here. These beds are kind of small, and the room is cramped. There's a lot more space in my suite."

Eleven women sighed in unison. Four high-elves, two dwarves, three humans, one gnome, and a dark-elf.

Lizbeth didn't sigh. She was too angry. A moment

later, she got even more upset when the dark-elf female spoke. "Oh, don't go yet Pooksie-pie, unless you mean to take us with you. We're just beginning to get to know each other."

The indigo-blue-skinned woman with the snow-white hair, who Lizbeth remembered was called Dylin and was here studying to be a healer, licked her full, red lips suggestively.

Lizbeth glared at Adan. "Pooksie-pie?"

The pink in Adan's cheeks turned bright red as he shrugged his shoulders. "It wasn't my idea. They all just kind of nicknamed me. Girls. Go figure."

Lizbeth brushed past him and made her way to her cot. Tears threatened, but she swiped them away. Dropping her books upon her bed, she turned and faced her husband. "I haven't changed my mind, and I'm too tired to fight with you tonight, Adan. Just go, please."

The stubborn man stood there staring at her as if he couldn't believe what he was hearing. Lizbeth rubbed the pounding ache in her temples. It was worse now than it had been all day. She took a deep breath and tried again. "Can we talk about this tomorrow? I really am tired."

Adan folded his arms. "I don't see what there's to talk about. You're my wife. You should be in my room, in my bed, not in some dormitory."

Eleven women collectively sighed once more. Lizbeth had no doubt that this time it was due to the fact any one of them would have been more than glad to take her place in his bed. She told herself she didn't care.

"I don't wish to discuss this right now, Adan. And I especially don't wish to discuss it in front of an audience. Please leave."

Neither of them got a chance to say another word as a brand-new, high-pitched voice interrupted.

"Adan Hammerstrike, what are ya doing in my dormitory harassing one of my lasses? I know for a fact ya were taught better than that. Don't be thinking ya're too big ta bend over my knee, little mister. I was right in the middle of an important game with Leeky, and it was my roll when I heard a commotion coming from up here. Had the Tug intercom running. Bet ya forgot about that, didn't ya?"

The female gnome with an ill-fitting blonde wig upon her head, an unusually large nose, even larger ears, and dressed in a black and white cow costume sat the strange-looking blow-up doll she'd been carrying beneath her arm on the floor. She placed her hands on her hips and glared at the barbarian while tapping her foot.

Lizbeth almost smiled as she watched Adan's transformation. His arms unfolded, his shoulders drooped, and he shuffled his feet. "I'm not harassing anyone, Laycee. You know I would never do that. I was just trying to collect my wife."

Adan pointed in her direction. "Miss Laycee Titwilder, meet Lizbeth Hammerstrike. And what do you mean *your* dormitory?"

The gnomes face lit like a candle, and a smile spread all the way across. "With all my vast experience being governess ta ya sisters, Headmistress Seychelle made me the new dormitory matron for first years." She then turned toward Lizbeth. "So, ya must be that little half-wood-elf lass Adan's been promised ta for so long. My, how ya've grown since I last saw ya. Finally married him, did ya? Well, congratulations ta the both of ya."

Then she glared. "So, what ya doing in my dormitory instead of in his bed? He's had plenty of training I can promise ya. Saw ta the picking of his very first seducer personally. Wanted it done properly. The lad won't have a problem keeping a smile on ya face all night long if ya know what I mean."

Laycee's face gentled, and she winked. Lizbeth wanted to climb onto her cot and cover her head with her pillow. Instead, she took two long breaths and blew them slowly out before answering. "I don't wish to be in his bed right now. I wish to be here in the dormitory. I don't want to talk about it. I simply want to go to sleep. I can do that, can't I?"

Laycee Titwilder gave her a motherly smile as she reached up and patted her on the hand. "Had a falling out already, did ya?" She shook her head. "Barbarian men, I swear. Barely house-trained, if ya ask me. Of course, ya can stay here, as long as ya like."

The gnome dorm matron walked to Adan and poked him with a finger in the kneecap. It was as high as her three-and-a-half-foot tall frame could reach. He jumped backwards as if struck by lightning.

"The lass says she wants ta stay here, so off with ya. And don't think ya're gonna be sneaking back in the middle of the night either. I'm gonna set the Tug alarm."

Adan groaned and shook his head as the female gnome picked up the plastic blow-up doll that was at least twice her size with its brown, patchy berber chest hair and painted-on smile.

"Not the doll, Laycee, anything but the doll," Adan

whispered. "I'd really rather Lizbeth wasn't exposed to Tug quite yet. There are things she doesn't know about our family."

Laycee Titwilder opened the doll's tunic and pushed two buttons where nipples would have normally been and placed it directly in front of the door while pulling it almost closed behind her. With only a sliver of doorway still open, she had a few final words for Adan Hammerstrike.

"A Tug McGroin is nothing ta be ashamed of, and ya well know it since he was a birthday present from ya yareself a few years back. He's a lean, mean, multitasking, plastic machine with interchangeable parts, and the best intruder alarm ever made. Not ta mention his talents as a vacuum cleaner, margarita shaker, and, well…other functions. Now get on back ta ya own room and don't let me find ya lurking around these hallways anymore tonight or I'll sic Leeky on ya."

Lizbeth's eyes met Adan's right before the door finally clicked shut. She'd expected to see stubbornness, but she didn't. She even expected to see anger, but she hadn't. What she did see confused her. Adan's eyes filled with sadness and disappointment, as if a good friend had just let him down. Even though she didn't understand why, it made her sad, too.

****

"I won't do it."

Adan stared at his sister trying to decide on a new tactic. Reasoning with her certainly wasn't working. "Why not?"

Lark shook her head. "It's not my place to tell your wife she should be sleeping in your bed and not her own. There's a lot more to marriage than sleeping together. Didn't anyone ever tell you it's not wise to get other people involved in your relationships? Never ends well."

Adan shook his head as his sister droned on.

"Anyway, she's not going to be in much of a mood to listen to anything I have to say after wizard's class today. Sarco has this exercise he does at the beginning of each semester to determine who has wizard potential and who doesn't. He throws fireball after fireball at his students until there is only ten left standing. I'm his apprentice, and I'll be there with him. I seriously doubt Lizbeth will make it through the class without getting hit so I doubt she'll be in the mood to speak with me for a while, let alone take my advice."

Adan drummed his fingers on the desk in Sarco's office, glad he had finally found his sister alone so he could speak freely with her but frustrated that it wasn't going as he wished. "Is there any way you can make sure she doesn't get hit?"

Lark shook her head. "Short of asking Sarco to not aim any of them at her, I can't think of a thing. I still feel guilty about using my abilities last semester to keep myself in Sarco's class. I swore I'd never interfere again."

Adan rubbed his chin. "Well, if you won't talk to her and you already think she's going to get dropped from the wizard class and you won't help her with that either, then would you consider a little mind control just to make her more agreeable to my wishes? You know, some of that Spiritmaster stuff you inherited and I didn't."

The shoe she aimed at his head barely missed. "And you wonder why Lizbeth doesn't wish to share your bed? I won't use mind control on my own sister-in-law, Adan. It isn't right. Why don't you take Sarco's advice and simply give her time to get to know you? Spend time getting to know her. Women have a need to be romanced. It makes us feel desirable."

Adan shook his head. "She already knows me better than any other living soul. She's been studying me all her life. That's the problem. She knows every boring detail and can't stand the sight of me. It's driving me crazy. Everyone likes me, they always have, or at least, I thought they did. Do you think they were just being nice to me because I'm a prince?"

Lark came around the desk and gave her brother a hug. "No, I think people like you for who you are. I know I do. You say she knows everything about you, but there are things books can't teach. I'd bet anything she doesn't know the man who sat for nights on end in a stable nursing his sick steed until it was back on its feet. Or the man who hunts to fill the coffers of widows and the elderly before he'll put a single scrap of food on his own table. And she certainly doesn't know the barbarian champion who suffered his only loss ever to Sarco Sunwalker, when he could've easily won, just because he wished to see his sisters happy. That's the man you need to show Lizbeth. Become her friend, Adan, the rest will fall into place."

He tweaked her nose and smiled. "I didn't lose just to see my sisters happy, that was a bonus. I lost to Sarco because it was the right thing to do. He needed to fulfill the prophecy, and the only way to do that and get the woman he loved was to complete his quest and win the right to choose you. It was the honorable thing to do."

Lark laid her head upon her brother's shoulder.

"See, that's the Adan Hammerstrike Lizbeth needs to meet."

Adan gave his sister a squeeze. "Well, if you won't help Lizbeth during today's class, let me at least go to the arena with you and cheer her on. Maybe if she sees me watching, she'll realize I'm on her side. Then, when she does get hit with a fireball and needs comforting, I'll be there to step in and be the hero."

\*\*\*\*

Being a sore loser about the sleeping arrangements was one thing, but this was beyond ridiculous. It was bad enough Adan Hammerstrike was standing nonchalantly in the entrance to the arena, watching the entire proceedings. But then, to have him involve his own sister and brother-in-law in his despicable plan to get her tossed out of a class was unforgivable. It was obvious to anyone with eyes he wanted his bride to fail and be forced to return to his cold, white castle. Well, it wasn't going to work.

Lizbeth dove sideways to avoid yet another fireball and cringed as muscles and bone came into jolting contact with the solid ground. The persistent nausea she'd had since arriving at the Academy reminded her once more of its presence, and she swallowed down the rising bile. There was no way she was going to embarrass herself again like she had in enchanter class yesterday.

As quickly as she'd fallen, she jumped back up and glared in Adan's direction. Again, he grinned at her and even flashed a thumbs-up. Then he folded his arms across his fancy golden-tunic-clad chest, crossed his legs, leaned back against the door, and smiled arrogantly. Lizbeth seethed.

Did he really think for a moment she didn't know he was in on this sick game with Sarco Sunwalker? Had even probably put Sarco up to it? No instructor would intentionally throw real honest-to-goodness fireballs at his students. Even if he had given the class the lame excuse of weeding out the weak. Someone might get hurt.

Another ball of fire whizzed a mere inch from Lizbeth's nose, and she smelled the singeing of her own hair as she tripped over a dwarf in her haste to get out of the way. With an *oomph,* she landed hard on her backside. Standing, she dusted herself off, determined Adan wouldn't see the tears threatening to escape from between her lashes.

Anger at the injustice of being singled out quickly replaced any pain, and Lizbeth turned away from her husband and faced her instructor. If her brother-in-law was going to kick her out of his wizard's class by hitting her with a fireball, then he was going to have to do it while looking her straight in the eye.

Lizbeth noticed the second of hesitation in Sarco's eyes right before the spinning ball of blue flames left his hand. She didn't think. She simply reacted. Raising her own hand, palm out, she meant to shield herself from the blow, but when the fireball was a few inches from its target, something entirely different happened. With a loud pop, the ball of flames reversed direction and landed with a resounding thud directly in the middle of Adan Hammerstrike's chest. The look of surprise on his face made the entire absurd game almost worth it.

The floor of the arena shook when his greater-than-seven-foot frame finally came to rest. Then there was complete silence for a total of six heartbeats. Slowly, Adan sat, shook his head, and looked in her direction.

Lizbeth grimaced as she met his gaze. Though the same arrogant smile still graced his handsome face, his eyes didn't look quite right, they were glassy even from this distance. A moment later, she understood why, when Adan raised one hand as if he were about to speak. He got out three words, "How did you—" then toppled over in a dead faint.

Everyone else in the arena ran to the barbarian prince, but Lizbeth didn't. She took the time to send a quick prayer upward to God Draka in the hopes she hadn't done any permanent damage before making her way to him.

## Chapter Six

Lizbeth winced.

When he woke, Adan wasn't going to be pleased. His golden tunic with the fancy stitching and rich material was obviously beyond repair, and a singed hole the size of her fist in the middle of it left little doubt as to how. She stood on the outskirts of the group circling her husband and stared. What had happened?

Though she'd dreamed all her life of having inherited magical abilities, none had manifested before. Why now? Her mother had been a wood-elf, and though a wonderful person and a half-decent druid to be sure, there was no real aptitude for magic in her family. And her father? Barbarians were certainly big and strong, but magic wasn't their weapon of choice. Swords and daggers were.

So why then? Why did the fireball meant for her turn and strike Adan? Lizbeth knew without a doubt she was responsible for it doing just that. The moment she'd raised her arm and opened her hand, energy had coursed through her. Not unlike the definition of channeling Briar had given the class again, just a few turns of the hourglass ago.

Had she channeled?

It had been the strangest sensation. Her fingers still tingled from it, and her arm was heavy. It had been a self-preservation reaction. Something entirely beyond her control.

Adan's eyes fluttered open, and there was no more time to think about the why as his gaze cleared and found her. Lizbeth braced herself for his anger and was completely caught off guard when, instead, he laughed.

"It's been a very long time since I've been knocked flat on my arse by a lass. How did you do that, by the way?"

She made her way to his side and knelt, allowing her hands to quickly ascertain his wounds weren't serious. "You deserved it, but I didn't do it on purpose. I have no idea why the fireball turned the way it did or why it struck you. That's what you get for putting Sarco up to throwing them at me in the first place and then for standing there grinning while I was trying my best to avoid them."

Adan shook his head. "You have it all wrong, Lizard. Sarco does this exercise at the beginning of every semester, with every class. Ask anyone, and they'll tell you. And I was smiling because I was proud of my wife. All around you, others were dropping, but not you. Oh, no, you were magnificent. A true barbarian queen if I've ever seen one."

Warmth crept into Lizbeth's cheeks. "Don't lizard me, Adan Hammerstrike. We both know you don't want me here, and you're doing everything in your power to make things hard for me so I'll be forced to leave."

She didn't want to meet his eyes, but the touch of his hand, warm and gently stroking her own, drew her gaze to his. Then, he had the audacity to wink.

"You couldn't be more wrong, Lizbeth. I want you anywhere I can get you, and if here is where you wish to be, then here will do just fine. Though, I would prefer the privacy of our room. And as far as making things hard for you, aye, I can think of one thing in particular I wish to make hard."

Lizbeth swatted him on the shoulder, and Adan playfully grasped both of her hands in his own as he spoke once more. "In all seriousness, there is something I would ask of my bride. Would you give me one turn of the hourglass each day, Lizbeth? Just one shifting of the sands for us to really get to know each other? I promise you won't regret it."

Where once there was simply warmth at the point their hands touched, the tiny circles Adan made with the pad of his thumb against Lizbeth's palm turned to tingles of unexpected pleasure. Tingles that traveled up her arm and straight to her brain, making it difficult to concentrate and even harder to breath.

"There's no need, really. I already know all there is to know about you. And as for me, there isn't anything of importance you don't know."

Lizbeth took in three deep gulps then held her breath. She tried to look away from the piercing, stormy blue eyes that saw too much. But then he smiled at her and she couldn't. The challenge in his gaze held her entranced.

Adan chuckled. "I doubt a lifetime of studying you could tell me *all* there is to know about you, Lizard, but we must start somewhere, mustn't we? Did you not bet me that you knew me better than I know myself? Shouldn't I be afforded an equal opportunity to learn?"

Lizbeth's cheeks burned with heat as she whispered her answer. "You know very well why I took that bet. You also know I lost it, so I suppose I don't know you as well as I thought I did. It's very ungentlemanly of you to remind me of it though. Especially in front of your sister, her husband, who happens to be my instructor, and my entire wizard's class."

Those same classmates began all speaking at the same time, and Lizbeth wasn't sure if perhaps Lark and Sarco's voices weren't somewhere in the mix.

"Give the lad a chance, what can it hurt."

"I bet she doesn't."

"I'll take that bet. Just look at how she's staring at him. She's already more than halfway lost her heart to the lad."

"Naw, my money's on her. Don't believe for a minute women are the weaker sex. They've had us by the willies since time began."

"For God Draka's sake, move away and give them a moment's privacy please."

The same thumb that had been stroking her palm traveled her wrist. The rough calluses formed from hours of brandishing a sword stoked a fire in her belly. This was no weak man. This was a barbarian warrior, and he was asking permission, not taking as was his nature. Still, she hesitated.

Adan grinned. "I could find a suitable chaperone if it would make you more comfortable. Say yes, Lizard."

Lizbeth laughed. "I don't need a chaperone. I can handle you just fine on my own, Adan Hammerstrike. And how many times must I tell you not to call me Lizard?"

Adan's hand roamed the inside of her arm until it grazed the outer edge of her breast. He grinned lecherously. "I was thinking it was I who needed the chaperone's protection. I can't help but notice how very aggressive you look when you gaze upon me. But if you insist on having me all to yourself, who am I to argue? You will be gentle with me though, won't you? After all, Lizard, everyone here has just been witness to you trying to do me great bodily harm."

She swatted him on the shoulder once more as she rose. "You are incorrigible, Adan Hammerstrike." But she couldn't quite contain the smile that threatened the corners of her mouth or the fluttering of butterfly wings in the pit of her gut. "One turn of the hourglass a day and that's all you'll get. Now leave me alone, you daft barbarian. I have classes to attend and studying to do."

Though her mind was still befuddled and tiny sparks of pleasure continued to course through her, Lizbeth couldn't help but wonder how she had let Adan win once again, and so easily. Shaking her head, she grinned, turned, and walked away. She still had enchanter class to get through today, and hopefully an enchanter class without Headmistress Seychelle's pet Ray in it. She would just have to save dissecting her reactions to a particular barbarian for later.

****

"Quit fidgeting and leave it alone."

Lizbeth reluctantly stretched both hands straight out in front of her and allowed Adan to lead her. "Why must I be blindfolded to go wherever it is you are taking me, and what is the blanket for? This is ridiculous. It better not require more than the one turn of the hourglass you've been allotted to get there and back."

Adan chuckled, but his relaxed pace didn't change. "I've already told you where I'm taking you is a surprise. It won't be a surprise if you can see the destination. Now will it? Be patient, Lizard. We're almost there. As far as the blanket, it's simply to sit upon, and as I told you, I'll bring you back before the last grain of sand has a chance to fall if, at that time, you still wish it."

She heard the soft hum of the portal stone a split second before its vibrations strummed beneath her feet. Lizbeth caught herself hesitating to move forward. It wasn't as if she minded traveling in this manner. After all, it was a common practice, and portal stones made transversing great distances in a very short period of time not only possible, but also quite efficient. What she did mind, however, was stepping through an abyss blindfolded, without any idea of where she'd be when she reached the other side.

Three simple words, "Lizbeth, trust me," whispered against the very edge of her ear calmed her fears enough to allow tiny quivers of pleasure to shoot down her spine and get her feet moving forward once again.

As they exited the portal and the thin scrap of material Adan had used to fashion the blindfold slipped away, Lizbeth gasped in amazement. Before her stretched a sandy beach the color of warm cream surrounded on three sides by towering craggy cliffs. Blue cloudless skies kissed the watery horizon, as churning froth playfully danced to and fro along the beach's edge.

The sun filtered down warmth upon her skin as at the same time gentle ocean breezes fought to cool her. The smell of salt and sea saturated her nostrils, and the sound of birds in flight and waves crashing close by upon rocks filled her ears.

Spinning around, trying to take it all in, excitement and the need to be heard above the song of nature raised her voice a few octaves and filled it with awe. "Are we really where I think we are? Is this *the* ocean?"

Adan grinned and nodded. "Yes, Lizard, this is the Great Ocean of Albrath. I was hoping you'd enjoy this outing. It's one of my favorite places in all the world. I come here often when I need to think or simply wish to be alone. It's the complete opposite of my kingdom. Here, there's no ice or snow or cold blustery winds."

He gazed intently into her eyes, and it made Lizbeth nervous.

"Surely you've been here before, haven't you, Lizbeth? I mean, everyone's been to the Great Ocean at least once in their lifetime, right? Every main portal is linked to some section of it."

Heat that had nothing to do with the sun worked its way up her neck until Lizbeth's cheeks burned to the point she was forced to fight the urge to fan herself. How was she to explain her life to this man without giving him the wrong impression?

"I haven't been anywhere except the forest I grew up in, your kingdom of Alaria when we wed, and now the Academy. Oh, and the one day trip to that town on my eighteenth birthday to see you in the arena. Though, I didn't actually get to see you then."

Her voice trailed off, and Lizbeth shuffled her feet. She kept her eyes down and took a deep breath before continuing. "I'm sure I could've come here if I'd asked. I guess I just never thought to. I always had classes to attend and chores to see to. I didn't wish to be more of a burden to my family than I already was."

Once more, she looked up at Adan, willing him to understand. "My brothers are good men and they were very kind to me after my parents died, really they were, but they're always busy. It's just...they're so much older than I and have their own children and wives and crops and worries and duties to deal with. Don't think they didn't care for me, though, for they did. They always saw to my basic needs. I never lacked for food or shelter, truly I didn't. And I had lots of instructors and servants to talk to. Most of the time, anyway."

Lizbeth shook her head and rubbed her hands together. "Oh, never mind, I'm making a horrible mess of this. No, I've never been to the Great Ocean or the other two lesser oceans as far as that's concerned. Field trips weren't part of my curriculum."

Adan stopped her speech with a single finger held lightly against her lips. "I wasn't trying to judge. I was simply curious."

He dropped his hand, and the warmth of his fingers intertwining with hers did more to calm Lizbeth's nerves then any words could have. Adan led her along a well-worn path between the boulders below the cliffs, and she followed.

Rounding a corner, Lizbeth once more stopped and gaped in awe. There, nestled in a small, secluded cove, was paradise. Two weather-worn palm trees swayed lazily in the breeze while waves crashed on the nearby rocks. The large yellow sun dipped a little farther down toward the surface of the water, and in the distance, lemon-feathered birds soared effortlessly through the afternoon sky.

"It's beautiful, Adan."

He squeezed her hand, and tiny ripples of

excitement scampered up her arm. "Take off your tunic and slippers, Lizbeth, feel the sand and surf upon your body and between your toes. Last one to the other side of the cove grants the other a wish. Deal?"

Lizbeth laughed. "Deal."

She did as he asked and pulled off her tunic and kicked off her shoes, leaving them without a second thought lying in the sand. With a freedom she hadn't known since she'd been a child, Lizbeth ran.

Though Adan won the first round, back and forth they scurried the edge of the water, laughing as they went and stopping frequently to pick up and examine a shell, play in the surf, or romp in the sand until exhaustion forced them to seek rest beneath the trees.

The wool blanket Adan laid out was still warm from the sun and Lizbeth gratefully collapsed onto it giggling as she stared at the man who had brought her to this magical place. "I'm pretty sure we've been here more than a single turn of the hourglass, Adan."

He nodded but didn't come anywhere near having the grace to look guilty as he placed a hand over his heart and responded, "Aye, Lizard, you're correct. But I'm having so much fun I must admit I don't want it to end. Forgive me?"

A gleam lit Adan's eyes. "Oh, I won the first race, remember? And you lost. You owe me a wish before we head back to the Academy."

Lizbeth gazed into the handsome face of her husband, and even to her own ears, her voice sounded breathy. "Your wish is my command, my lord."

Adan leaned and caressed her lips with his own so gently she was left wondering if they'd even touched at all. Yet at the same time, shivers of excitement shot through her, telling her in no uncertain terms, they had. When a moment later he whispered against her lips, those same shivers exploded with heat.

"I wish only for the opportunity to know you, Lizbeth, all of you, in every way imaginable. Grant me a lesson."

She sighed against his warmth and inhaled the intoxicating mixture of man and sea air. "What do you wish to learn?"

Adan chuckled as he kissed first her forehead, then her cheek, a spot behind her ear, and the curve of her neck, before burying his face between her breasts. He lifted his head and met her gaze. "The tastes and textures of every inch of your body."

"Oh!"

That was the only word Lizbeth uttered before Adan drove away her ability to think, let alone speak, and replaced them with ecstasy.

His lips captured hers, but this kiss was different from any he'd given her before. Gone was the gentle plying she'd come to expect. Gone was his slow, teasing pressure as he deepened his possession. Gone was any hint of softness.

No, this kiss was barbarian through and through, raw and lust-filled, hard and fast, punishing, yet imparting such sweet, hot pleasure it brought tears to her eyes. It was pure breathtaking, life-giving, soul-shattering need. She answered his need with her own, and the world ceased to exist.

The kiss might have lasted the space of a minute or an entire turn of the hourglass, she didn't know and didn't care. All that mattered was Adan made her feel things she'd never felt before.

Not even in her sex and sensibility classes had she experienced this level of emotion. She wanted to laugh and cry at the same time, and she had the desire to submit to him completely one second, while the overwhelming urge to be the one to dominate the next.

He slid a little ways down her body and captured a pert nipple between his teeth and tugged. Shockwaves of pleasure rippled from her core outward. She leaned up, nipped the very tip of his chin, hard, and growled.

Adan laughed. "Quite the little barbarian yourself, I see. I like that in my women." His eyes were smoky and heavy laden, full of passion and possession. "But can you keep it up, or will I have you begging for mercy before we're through?"

Lizbeth laughed, but it was no girlish giggle. It was deep, full, and raw. "I can give as good as I get. As a matter of fact, I can give even better. I'll not only keep up with you, but it'll be you who loses control first."

Adan's eyes widened. "Another challenge, Lizard? You do remember who's won the last two?"

She stared her barbarian husband in the eye, nipped his chin once more, then slowly kissed it all better. "Not only will you beg me for more, but you'll orgasm before I do. I'm the one who's had all those boring Adan Hammerstrike classes, remember? I know exactly what makes your eyes cross and your cock gush. By the way, I passed that class with an A plus."

Adan suckled a nipple, and Lizbeth couldn't hide her quick intake of air. His eyes twinkled with the knowledge she wasn't the least bit immune to his touch, and he taunted her with his words. "So, Lizard, what does the winner get when *he* makes you come first?"

Lizbeth shook her head. "Let's not worry about the

winner. *She* will be quite content with the fact *she* bested her barbarian husband. How about, the loser has to walk back through the Academy portal and all the way to *his* room butt-naked. Deal?"

Adan chuckled. "Oh, you are so on. Deal."

There was no more time for words as Adan slid all the way down Lizbeth's body and spread her thighs. He was a breath away from capturing her clit between his teeth when she suddenly scooted away.

Rising up on all fours, Lizbeth shook her head, wagged her finger at Adan, and grinned. "Oh, no, you don't. If you think for a moment that you're going to get the opportunity to torment me into an orgasm without me tormenting you right back, you better think again."

She shoved him onto his back, straddled his face, and eagerly lowered her pussy to his awaiting lips. She leaned over the length of his body, captured the very tip of his cock in her mouth, sighed with contentment, and sucked.

The wet heat of Adan's tongue suddenly laving her clit was almost her undoing, but Lizbeth closed her eyes and concentrated.

She tested the weight and feel of him as she slid her mouth along his shaft, taking in as much of his cock as she could. He was big and thick and hot, pulsating with an energy that matched the throbbing between her legs.

He tasted of salty, ocean spray and warm, male musk, and he smelled of sunshine and passion. The beat of his heart pounded through his coursing veins, and the head of his cock tickled the back of her throat.

He chose that moment to nip her clit, and Lizbeth's

eyes crossed with pleasure and she almost forgot her task. His chuckle and his "Oh, I see you really like that, Lizard" reminded her, this was a competition. One she had no intention of losing.

She concentrated on remembering her Adan Hammerstrike lessons and redoubled her effort. Up his cock she sucked, stopping to tease the tender skin below and around the head. Her tongue played, darting in and out of the small hole on top one moment, only to lap, lick, and swirl about his shaft the next. One hand cupped, squeezed, and toyed with his balls, while the other held his cock captive.

He squirmed beneath her, his breaths no more than quick pants. The muscles of his abdomen contracted, and his toes curled. She had him now. Victory was no more than a handful of heartbeats away.

His tongue delved deep into her opening, followed quickly by first one finger, then two. Sliding them in and out, he stroked her. Latching onto her clit as if it were his lifeline, he sucked, and Lizbeth forgot to breathe. Pressure built to an almost impossible level, and her hips thrust back and forth of their own accord. She tried to concentrate, really she did. She lapped and sucked for all she was worth.

Adan's cock spasmed, and hot liquid flowed down her throat at the same time her own world exploded. She drank her fill of him while he devoured the last drops of her juices.

Once the last spasm abated, she rolled off Adan and with total contentment snuggled into his arms.

They looked in each other's eyes, smiled, and at the very same time said, "Tie."

Lizbeth giggled once more.

## Chapter Seven

"Fine, forget about food then. What's your favorite color, my lady?"

Lizbeth gazed into Adan's smiling face, and her lips curved upward in response. "I don't have a favorite color, my lord, anymore than I have a favorite food. I'm afraid I like them all."

Adan chuckled. "This is our third...date...Lizbeth. Yesterday shouldn't even count. All you allowed me was to walk you to your dorm room. How am I ever supposed to get to know you if you insist on being so evasive? I can see I'm going to have to come up with consequences since you continue to avoid answering my questions."

His right hand slipped up the edge of her tunic and came into contact with the skin of Lizbeth's left side. Warmth infused every inch his fingers touched. Then he began tickling, and with a shriek, Lizbeth squirmed and tried to scoot away to no avail.

"Stop." She giggled.

"Not until you tell me." Adan doubled his efforts.

The last golden rays of sunlight filtered through his wheat-blond mane and silhouetted his bronzed skin. He had taken her once more to the beach, and its golden sand reflected exactly the warmth in her heart.

Lizbeth longed to draw his head down to hers and run her fingers freely through his fair hair as her lips sought to memorize his face. Instead, she squirmed once more below him.

"Yellow," she squealed. "Today my favorite color is yellow."

"Now, was that so difficult, Lizard?" Adan whispered against a particularly sensitive spot right below her left ear.

Even though the ocean breeze blew steadily against her heated skin, suddenly there wasn't enough air to be found to breathe deeply. Lizbeth tried taking in large gulps of the invisible stuff while doing her best not to think about the tremors of excitement his touch had elicited. Shivers rushed down her extremities and left tiny chill bumps of pleasure in their wake.

"I think we should be going. It's getting late." Her voice sounded far away and unconvincing, even to her own ears.

Adan nuzzled her neck once more. "Answer just one more question for me then we'll go. I promise."

Lizbeth smiled. "It depends on what your question is, Barbarian. I'm beginning to think you brought me here in the hopes of simply having your way with me once again."

His eyes gleamed with mischief, and heat flooded her middle, spreading upward all the way to the roots of her hair before spiraling down. Her pulse quickened, her breath came in quick little pants, her mouth went dry, and her cheeks burned as if on fire.

"Ah, my lady, you wound me. Having my way with you could never be considered a simple task. I put much thought into my lovemaking. Though, the idea of you beneath me here and now on the sand is quite appealing. Perhaps later if there's time." Then he winked.

Lizbeth shook her head. "You are incorrigible, Barbarian. Ask your question so we may be on our way."

Adan cupped her chin and stroked her cheek, the warmth of his fingers causing further havoc on her already sensory-overloaded brain.

"Why do you wish to be an enchantress, Lizbeth?"

Of all the things she thought he might ask, why she wanted to become an enchantress hadn't been one of them. His question caught her off guard, and for a moment, all Lizbeth could manage to do was stare at him. Finally, she took a deep breath, compiled the same list she'd given her brothers, and answered.

"It's been a dream of mine since childhood. I think I could be good at it. It would be a useful skill if you ever need a weapon imbued with magic or a talisman forged. It would be my way of contributing. And I believe one should never stop learning new things."

She held her breath, hoping Adan would let the subject drop. He didn't.

"But why an enchantress? Why not strive to become a druid like your mother? That could prove handy. Druids dabble in simple magic, but you only need a spell book to do what they do. Growing plants, healing sick animals, and such." He scratched his head.

"Enchantresses on the other hand come from predominantly magical races like high-elves or dark-elves, some humans or even the occasional gnome. I don't think I've ever seen a barbarian enchantress. We barbarians aren't usually the magical type, Lizard. We have talents, but it's our brawn we are most famous for. So, just what are you trying to hide?"

Clouds rolled in overhead, and the air became chilled, yet heat warmed her cheeks. This time, however, it wasn't from passion.

"Your own sister, Lark, certainly has more than her share of magical abilities and she's as much a barbarian as I am."

Adan chuckled, but there was nothing remotely funny about the sound of it to Lizbeth's ears.

"Lark is half-human, remember? That's where she gets her magical abilities. We have Spiritmasters on my mother's side of the family, as you well know, and she took after them." He reached over and tweaked her nose. "You, my sweet, aren't any more magical than I am."

The wind picked up, and Lizbeth hugged her arms about herself as she sat up and scooted to the far side of the blanket. "Then how do you explain what happened with the fireball? These past few weeks, since I've been at the Academy, I've changed deep inside my very soul. I'd always hoped I would develop magical talent, and I think I have."

Adan reached over and patted her on the shoulder as if contending with a troublesome child, and Lizbeth had an almost overwhelming urge to smack his hand away.

"There's no need to try and explain the fireball incident. I thought it would be obvious to you by now. One of the other students in Sarco's class must have diverted the ball of fire just to make you think you did it. It was a trick, Lizard, nothing more."

He chuckled. "Now, if it had been Uthiel's wife, Briar, who hit me with a fireball, then I would've known it came from her. She's magic all the way to her toes. Or even Lark. She certainly has more than her share of magical ability. But you? You've never shown any indication of such things, Lizbeth, and though I'm sure your talents are vast, there's nothing magical about you.

"Forget this silly enchanter stuff before you embarrass yourself. You have nothing to prove. You're perfectly acceptable just as you are. Queens don't need to be magical. My mother isn't."

The first fat drops of rain fell as Lizbeth jumped to her feet. Tears stung her eyes as she fought to control the shaking of her limbs. "Embarrass myself? Is it really me you're worried will be embarrassed if I fail? Or are you afraid I'll embarrass you? And...and since your mother doesn't have magic abilities, I shouldn't strive to hone mine?"

Her voice cracked, and Lizbeth swallowed twice as she took a deep breath. She clenched and unclenched her fists over and over again. "Well, I can't be like her, and I won't. I couldn't care less what your opinion of me is, and I don't need you to believe in me, Adan Hammerstrike. You just watch, though, I'll prove to you I have magic in me. I'll become the best enchantress you've ever seen."

She picked up her tunic, spun on her heels and headed toward the portal. A moment later, she turned around and faced her husband. Adan was quickly gathering his own clothing, the blanket, and heading in her direction.

Lightning flashed across the angry sky and thunder rolled in the distance. Rain pelted the sand, and Lizbeth shouted above the wind. "Don't follow me, Barbarian. I don't like you, remember?"

\*\*\*\*

The wind rattled the windows of the dorm room so hard Lizbeth was afraid they might break. She huddled further under her thin coverlet, hugged her arms about herself, and rocked back and forth. The blockhead, the barbarian blockhead wanted her to be more like his mother? For at least the hundredth time since she'd arrived back at the Academy a few turns of the hourglass ago, Lizbeth was glad she hadn't told Adan the real reason she wanted to become an enchantress. Not only wanted, but needed to. It was their only hope for a future together.

She punched her pillow and shoved it back under her head as she fought a losing battle with her tears. He would never understand even if she did dare tell him. Not only would he not understand, he wouldn't believe her any more than her brothers had.

It wasn't as if they'd been cruel on purpose, for they hadn't. Since their parents' deaths, Lionel, Leonitis, and Levi Soulenticer had provided a solid roof over her head, clothing on her body, and food in her belly. They had also a provided a fine, if slightly one-sided, education.

She knew she had no reason to complain because they considered her nightmares to be simply the ravings of a hysterical female. What had always bothered her though, was the fact they wouldn't even consider the possibility her fears could have any real basis. Not only wouldn't they consider it, but they had adamantly refused to hear another word about it years ago. So, since then, when the nightmares threatened, she had taken her comfort from the book.

Lizbeth peeked out from under the cover and

glanced around the dark dorm room. Not a single person stirred. Slowly, she leaned over the edge of her bed and slid her hand beneath the frame until her fingers came in contact with old leather. The familiar rush of warmth she got whenever she touched the volume infused her, and she sighed. Pulling it close up against her heart, Lizbeth quickly lit a small candle, said a protection from fire spell, and huddled once more in the center of her bed with the coverlet over her head to hide the light.

Goelz's *Study of Enchantments.*

Lizbeth ran her fingers lovingly over the faded, gold-lettered title of the book. Written by the greatest enchanter Albrath had ever known, Horatio Goelz, the man she'd named her bunny after, had long been her hero. The book was her most prized possession. It was old, very old, and probably had been even the day she'd found it in the basement of her parents' castle when she was but a small child.

It had been dusty and discarded, and left to decay. Finding it had been her salvation, for within its pages, lay not only hours of escape from the nightmare of Master Seiger, but magic and the solution to all her fears.

Adan had asked her why she wanted to become an enchantress, but would he really want to hear the answer? Probably not. She needed to become an enchantress because of his mother the queen. Because she'd always known that someday she would have to do her duty and marry Adan Hammerstrike. She'd always known she would have to go live in his castle where the Queen, and probably even Master Seiger, would still be in residence. And she'd always known she'd have to give him heirs. Heirs the Queen and her evil instructor would have access to.

She had to protect her children. Never would they be stuffed in a trunk. Never would they be told *don't tell*. Never would they lose their air. That was the promise she'd made to herself. It was the only way she could convince herself to go through with the marriage contract.

Lizbeth flipped the book's cover open and the smell of old ink and parchment was as comforting as the aroma of a feast to a starving man. She closed her eyes and inhaled deeply, allowing the peace of it to seep into her soul. Outside, the winds calmed.

Again, like so many times over the years, she searched the pages, stopping at the ones that were special to her. Pages that held very particular spells. Like the spells for Talisman-of-Protection, so no one would be able to so much as touch the person who wore it unless the caster wished it. Spells so powerful their magic could cover an entire castle or a space no bigger than the head of a pin. Spells that could reach across great expanses and affect many people and spells so precise they could single out one heartbeat from another. But they all had one thing in common. They could only be spoken into power by an enchanter.

They weren't like the normal everyday spells such as the PDUP, the Protection-From-Disease-and-Unwanted-Pregnancy spell. Or even the Directional-Compass so you never got lost spell. Let alone the routine Protection-from-Physical-Harm spells children were taught before they could even walk. No, these spells required much more. They required specific ingredients, intense concentration, the ability to wield magic, and most important of all, the strength of character to believe in oneself.

Lizbeth yawned, blew out the candle, and carefully closed the book. She wrapped her arms about it as if the power between its pages could ward off nightmares, and closed her eyes. "As God Draka is my witness I will not fail us," she whispered into the darkness. "Even though you don't understand, Adan, I will become an enchantress, for you, for me, and for our children. We will not live in fear."

Thunder rumbled once more.

\*\*\*\*

"You said what to her? Did growing up with four sisters teach you nothing about women?"

Adan jumped as lightning streaked across the night sky and thunder shook the room. "Will you please stop doing that? I honestly don't understand what I did wrong. One moment we were lying on the beach laughing and talking, then before more than a smattering of grains of sand could get the chance to sift through the hourglass, Lizbeth jumped up, and stomped through the portal. All I asked was why she wanted to become an enchantress. She's hiding something, I just know it."

Lark glared at him. Adan closed his eyes and rubbed his temples.

"Don't blame the weather on me tonight, dear brother. Sometimes a storm is simply a storm. Whether she's hiding something from you or not, telling your wife she is certain to fail at her chosen profession because she couldn't possibly be magic enough to succeed, especially compared to me, your sister, and your friend's wife, Briar, is a little more than simply asking her why she wants to be an enchantress. Then to make matters worse, you all but directly compared her, unfavorably I might add, to our lunatic mother. That alone is tantamount to marital suicide."

Even with his eyes closed, he could tell his sister was not only pacing, but building up a head of steam that was near ready to explode. Adan sighed as she continued her rant.

"Of course she's hiding something. She's female, isn't she? We all have…things we like to keep to ourselves. But when you ask your wife a question, unless it has something immediate to do with the defense and safety of your family and castle, your duty as a husband is to keep your mouth shut, nod vigorously, and smile at her answer."

Adan ran a hand through his hair. His head hurt, his stomach growled, and his bones ached with weariness. "So, how do I make this right?"

A knock interrupted the discussion, and Lark headed toward the door. "Sarco must have forgotten his key again."

When the door swung open, however, it wasn't his sister's husband standing there.

Adan groaned. He'd always had a soft spot for the female gnome who'd once been governess to all four of his sisters, but tonight he wasn't in the mood for whatever business brought Miss Laycee Titwilder to Lark's door. Especially considering her large, watery brown eyes had lit up like twin torches the moment they caught sight of him.

"Adan, oh good, ya're here, too. Now I won't have ta hunt ya down." She carefully held up two identical manila envelopes as if they were made of the purest gold. "As I'm sure ya've both heard, my dear brother, O.T.T., is here at the Academy, giving a series of lectures this semester on his specialty—historical artifacts."

She grinned from ear to ear. "Leeky and I are throwing a party tomorrow evening in his honor, and we'd consider it a huge favor if ya and yare spouses would attend. I know it's been a long time, but ya two remember O.T.T., don't ya? Ta think, the assistant ta the assistant of gnome and ogre affairs, came all the way from the other side of the world just ta give lectures and visit with me. I'm so proud."

Adan looked longingly at the door. Not that he had anything against Laycee's brother. He just had bigger problems on his mind right now, the least of which, gnome parties.

Laycee folded her arms across her more than ample bosom. "It'll be the party of the season. Everyone who is anyone will be there. Even Headmistress Seychelle has agreed ta stop by. And Briar, of course, will be in attendance." For a moment, a crease furrowed Laycee's brow. "Though not Uthiel, I'm afraid. He's still rebuilding that drafty old Castle Kuropkat and can't make it."

As quickly as the crease across her forehead formed, it was gone, and a smile once again graced her chubby face. "Oh, and just wait until ya see the special outfits I've been fashioning for me, Tug, and Leeky. Been working on them all week. Sometimes I amaze myself. By the way, since it's almost the start of Samhain, the theme is end of autumn, beginning of winter, so dress accordingly."

Laycee Titwilder turned, and back through the door

she scurried. Over her shoulder, she gave one last departing message. "Party of the season, I tell ya. Starts at sundown, don't be late."

Even before she opened her mouth, from the gleam in her eye and the smirk on her face, Adan knew he wasn't going to like whatever Lark was about to say. Then she giggled.

"You really want to know how to make things right with Lizbeth? I say take her to Laycee and Leeky's party. Trust me, compared to what she's bound to hear there, she'll think anything that comes out of your mouth to be pure poetry."

Adan wasn't amused.

## Chapter Eight

What was he up to now?

Lizbeth glanced once more through the open doorway of her enchanter class and, just as he'd been for the last half-turn of the hourglass, there was Adan Hammerstrike, directly across the hallway, pacing back and forth like a caged animal and starring at her. Did he honestly think since he'd failed to talk her into throwing away her dreams yesterday, he could intimidate her today and get her to quit? Well, it wasn't going to work. All his antics were likely to accomplish was to make her even more determined to stay and prove him wrong.

Finally, the bell tolled the end of class, and Lizbeth took two deep calming breaths and prepared to face her husband. Even though she had hugged her precious book close to her chest all night long, she hadn't slept well. She was tired, grumpy, and hungry, and at the same time, a little nauseated. Her breasts were tender even though her cycle of the moons wasn't due for a few more rotations of the sun, every muscle in her body ached, and her head pounded. To make matters worse, the entire day had been cold, gray, and drizzly. If it was a fight the barbarian wanted, then a fight was what he would get. She lifted her chin, straightened her spine, and prepared to meet Adan.

Before she could get within verbal sparring range,

he held up both hands.

"Truce, my lady? You look near ready to do battle, and it's not my intention to fight with you this day. I admit, at times my mouth gets ahead of my brain, and I'm truly sorry about what was said yesterday. Forgive me, Lizbeth? I'm here only to inform you of an invitation we have received, nothing more."

For the space of a heartbeat, she was disappointed he didn't wish to fight. All day, a nervous energy had flowed through her and she'd found herself looking forward to the chance to dissipate some of it with a shouting match. Instead, she settled for answering his question with one of her own. "An invitation for what?"

Though Adan smiled, it didn't reach his eyes and there was no joy behind it. "A gathering this very evening, Lizard. Laycee has requested our presence at a party in her brother's honor. I realize this is short notice, and if you don't wish to attend, I'll understand. After all, I'm sure you have better things to do than sit around a boring, stuffy dinner party for a gnome you don't even know. On second thought, don't give it another thought. I'll be more than glad to give Laycee and Leeky your regrets."

He turned to go, and Lizbeth knew without a doubt he didn't wish her to be present at the party with him. Was he really so ashamed she was his wife that he didn't want to be seen with her? Or was there something or perhaps someone else behind his reluctance? Anger hot and sudden bubbled forth.

"I don't suppose my dorm-mates, your Pooksie-pie club, will be there, will they? After all, since Laycee is giving the party, I doubt she'd single me out and not invite them. Is that the real reason you don't want me to be there with you, Adan? Since I'm not begging to share your bed, you'll take your pleasure elsewhere?"

His mouth gaped, but for long minutes, no sound came out. Finally, just as Lizbeth was beginning to realize she'd most probably misjudged him, Adan spoke. "For all your complaining about the years of endless classes where I was the main subject, your lack of understanding even my most basic characteristics never fails to astound me. Your low opinion is undeserved, my lady. It truly was your best interest I had at heart. Now, however, I insist you grace me with your presence. After all, you do owe me my one turn of the hourglass this evening, and nothing teaches a better lesson like firsthand experience. The theme is end of autumn/beginning of winter/Samhain, so dress accordingly. I'll pick you up at sunset."

He leaned in close and whispered against the ridge of her pointed ear. "Oh, and Lizard, it's just a suggestion, but if I were you, even though there will be food served, I'd eat before you get there."

Adan chuckled, but instead of making Lizbeth smile, it sent cold shivers down her spine.

\*\*\*\*

She had insulted him without reason and knew it. Not only did she know her words had been unjustified, but if the sour, stiff look on Adan's face was any indication, she was going to have a very long evening to regret them. Even her sincere "I'm sorry" had been met with nothing but cold silence when, good to his word, Adan had called for her promptly, just as the last rays of the sun were tucking the horizon in for the night.

Lizbeth tried to keep her eyes on anything other

than her husband as he led her through corridor after corridor and down first one flight of stairs to the left, then another to the right, until finally they were in the very underbelly of the Academy. She glanced at dusty pipes overhead and slabs of plain, reddish stone that made up the floor below as they followed a winding trail.

She didn't want to notice how splendid he looked this evening, but she did. From head to toe, Adan Hammerstrike was every inch the barbarian prince. His golden mane curled seductively about the nape of his neck, and his anger at her only proved to add sparks of blue fire to his already strikingly azure eyes. The soft harvest-gold suede of his snug-fitting tunic and breeks kissed and caressed his tall, muscular frame, teasing her senses with what she knew to be hidden beneath.

Shaking her head, Lizbeth let out a breath. What was wrong with her today? One moment she wanted to flay him alive and the next all she could think about was running her fingers through his hair while her tongue licked every inch of his body.

Suddenly, Adan stopped before a plain wooden door and Lizbeth didn't have any more time to analyze her emotions as he turned toward her. What she did notice, however, was the anger was gone from his gaze. For the first time since he'd picked her up, she relaxed enough to smile.

"I thought not to warn you about the situation we are about to find ourselves in, but, in good conscience, I can't do that. Though, you would deserve no less for being so disagreeable earlier."

Lizbeth had the grace to blush as Adan tweaked her nose and granted her a smile.

"I don't know if there is any way to prepare you for what you are about to see and hear, my lady, but I'm obligated to try. Leeky is a friend of mine, and I'd lay down my life for him without reservation just as he would for me, and Laycee…well, she's family and has been for as long as I can remember, but never forget for a moment, they are gnomes."

He gestured with his hands as if trying to come up with an adequate way to describe what he meant. Finally, Adan simply shrugged his shoulders. "Whatever you see or hear, just smile and nod, and whatever you do, don't eat anything. Most importantly of all, don't ask questions. Trust me, you won't like the answer whatever it is. That being said, I think the best advice I can give you, even though you don't believe much of what I say, is stay close and I'll keep you safe. We'll make our presence known, greet the guest of honor, and then I'll get us out of here as quickly as I can."

Lizbeth laughed. "Adan, stop it. You're just trying to scare me. I told you I was sorry about how I acted earlier, and I am. Leeky and Laycee's party can't possibly be as bad as you're making it out to be. After all, they're just two very sweet, little people."

Adan shuddered, took two deep breaths, then knocked.

She wasn't sure what she'd expected to see when the door opened, but a red-faced gnome with a wreath of purple and pink flowers askew on his balding head, a half-empty mug of ale clenched in his stubby, puce-gloved fist, and a filmy white toga-looking garment haphazardly draped over his pudgy, short body, wasn't it. Lizbeth stepped back behind Adan.

"What the chewed-on toenails of a troll trollop dancing third from the left in the chorus line of a Caberet are ya doing out there, lad? Get on in here." He turned his head and yelled over his shoulder. "Laycee, Adan's here with his lass."

Leeky Shortz leaned in close to the couple. "Have ya ever had your thong ride up the crack of your hiney? Miserable, I tell ya, simply miserable." He turned and tugged at something as he led the way inside.

Even though Adan gently pulled at her elbow, Lizbeth hesitated a moment longer before following him.

It might have been located in the very bowels of the Academy, but one thing about it, it was the most colorful apartment she had ever seen. The walls of the entry area were a creamy buttercup yellow splashed with lavender and orange speckles, while the red stone floor was scattered with multi-colored braided rugs. The overstuffed couch and chairs looked more like weird works of art than furniture, and even the lampshades, curtains, and tapestries on the walls were fashioned from the most unusual combinations of materials.

Green polka-dots and bright red flowers adorned the same pieces as blue stripes, yellow stars, and various animal prints. Not only were the patterns unique, but so were the fabrics themselves. Lace was mixed with velvet, and leather was right alongside cotton and silk. It was as if a child was let loose with all the discarded textile scraps in Albrath and told to sew them together. Lizbeth ran her hand along the arm of a chair, lost in its unique composition.

"It's about time ya two showed up. O.T.T. should

be here any time now."

Lizbeth turned toward the sound of the familiar high-pitched voice of her dorm matron, and even though she'd already seen Leeky and expected Laycee to be attired much the same way, it was all she could do to hide her shock.

Naked! Well, not entirely naked, but as close to it and still technically covered as Lizbeth had ever seen the little gnome. Like Leeky, a wreath of flowers set atop the ill-fitting blonde wig on her head, but that was where the similarities ended. Laycee's toga was almost as transparent as air. White gauzy material so thin, the gnome's nipples could be seen bouncing up and down with every breath she took, no more than scant inches above her pudgy little belly button. The only thing that concealed anything of consequence at all was a pair of bright purple granny-style panties matching the flowers in her hair.

Heat crept up Lizbeth's neck as she realized Laycee had been speaking to her and she hadn't heard a word the gnome was saying. It took all the courage she could muster to look her dorm-matron in the eye and listen.

"Guess I should be glad ya and Adan made it at all tonight. Being newlyweds and all, ya probably can't keep ya hands off each other. I still remember when he was just a lad and didn't know what ta do with his willy. Is he half as good between the sheets as I told ya he'd be?" Laycee beamed.

Beside her, the sound of coughing and choking told Lizbeth she needed to say something, anything, to change the topic. She grasped onto the only safe topic she could think of.

"Laycee, your apartment is so…so different. Did you decorate it yourself?"

If Lizbeth thought the gnome was smiling before, there was certainly no question of it now. Her eyes lit up, her cheeks pinkened, and every tooth in her head sparkled, her grin was so wide.

"Yep. Made all this myself from thousands of pairs of pilfered panties. Just ask Lark. She, her sisters, and even Briar helped me sort 'em out. Bet ya haven't heard about my Leeky yet, have ya? What am I thinking? Of course, ya have. He's a world-famous rogue, after all.

"He's been the resident panty thief here at the Academy for more than twenty years. He's probably even filched a pair or two from ya by now."

The thought was more than a little disturbing to Lizbeth, but she concentrated on keeping her expression neutral as Laycee continued talking.

"First time I walked into this apartment there were panties piled all the way ta the ceiling. It was all ya could do ta even get around the stacks. It's taken me a couple of seasons ta put them all ta good use, but I've done it. Go on, sit down and see how comfy that chair is for yarself."

The last thing Lizbeth wanted to do was sit on a bunch of other women's panties. She searched for a polite way to refuse, but lost her concentration when Adan leaned in close to her and whispered. "Didn't I warn you about asking questions?"

Lizbeth didn't get a chance to respond.

"Where's my manners? Ya young folks come on into the dining area and get yarselves a nice big mug of ale. It's a special brew, Leeky made it himself."

Laycee turned and Adan and Lizbeth had little

choice but follow.

If she thought the apartment's entry space was unusual, then she didn't know what to think about the dining area. As bright and unusual as the other room had been, this one was just as bizarre. A red table, with what Lizbeth now had no doubt were panty placemats on it, sat in the middle of the room. It was loaded down with a large ceramic crock, an array of bowls and spoons, trays of vegetables and fruits, and mugs. The walls were light green with blue splotches, and like the entry area, the floor was scattered with braided rugs.

It was the sound of something bubbling over in the corner surrounded by a small crowd of people that really caught her attention. Lizbeth recognized a group of her dorm-mates off to one side, and Leeky, Lark, Sarco, and Briar standing directly in front of it.

Most of the guests were attired in robes of rich fall hues, reds, browns, and golds. For a moment, Lizbeth felt self-conscious and drab in her plain, faded orange tunic with its matching pants. It had been the only remotely end-of-autumn-like outfit she owned.

Suddenly, the crowd parted, and she got a glimpse of what they were standing around, and all thoughts about the inadequacy of her garments fled.

It was Tug McGroin, or at least she was pretty sure it was Laycee's blow-up doll. But one thing was for certain, she'd never seen Tug like this before. He had short, little horns on the top of his head and a wide, plastic grin on his face. Both hands held a small wooden flute to his lips as if he were playing a tune.

His berber-haired chest was bare, and what looked like a garter belt cinched around his waist held up a set of shaggy, white fur leggings that ended in hooves matching his horns.

Most disturbing of all, however, was a steady gush of foaming yellow liquid pouring out the end of the biggest, gaudiest-looking, plastic penis Lizbeth had ever seen. The stream flowed continuously into a white, ceramic pool the shape of a huge water lily at Tug's feet.

She forgot herself, and the question slipped out of Lizbeth's mouth before she even realized she'd asked it. "What's he supposed to be?"

Laycee cackled. "A Satyr, of course. Ingenious, don't ya think? What better ale dispenser can ya think of for an almost-Samhain party than a Satyr peeing into the pool of eternal youth? My Tug's multi-functional, don't ya know, and handsome ta boot. That's why Leeky and I are dressed as Wood Nymphs. After all, a Satyr needs followers."

The female gnome motioned toward something standing back in the corner behind the Tug beer fountain. It looked to be a dead tree with a flat plastic face sticking out of its middle. Lifeless blue eyes stared out at the crowd, and its red-lipped open mouth made it appear surprised at its surroundings. Three pathetic little leaves clung precariously to its otherwise bare branches.

"Took me quite a while ta come up with an idea for Leeky's good-for-nothing Miss Bunny over there, but I think I found a job even that airhead can handle. Worked more than two turns of the hourglass ta make her presentable and useful."

The little female gnome clapped her hands together in glee. "Ya can't have a Satyr and Wood Nymphs without the woods, now can ya? Why, that'd be like having a sky without any stars." Laycee chuckled. "Now, don't be shy. Get on over there and grab yourselves a mug. My Tug will be more than happy ta fill it up for ya."

## Chapter Nine

Lizbeth stood in a corner tucked behind the table, along with Adan, Lark, Sarco, and Briar. With her eyes scrunched tightly closed and a death grip on her husband's hand, she silently sent a prayer upward to God Draka.

Over and over, she kept telling herself Laycee's brother would knock on the door any minute and they would pay their respects, say their goodnights, and then this nightmare would be over. They'd finally be allowed to take their leave of this place. He had to get here soon, he simply had to. She couldn't take much more.

If she'd thought the bizarre furniture, the gnome wood nymph costumes, and the satyr-Tug-peeing-ale-fountain traumatic, then how would she categorize the last three turns of the hourglass since they'd first arrived? Beyond disturbing and nightmare inducing didn't seem to even come close.

The offer of ale had been quickly followed by a rousing game of ingesting copious amounts of chili as fast as possible by Leeky, Laycee, half her dorm-mates, and a couple of ogres whose names she couldn't even pronounce.

If that sight hadn't been bad enough, what came next was much worse. An extensive burping and farting contest with Leeky Shortz declared the unanimous winner after thankfully only three rounds. A noxious cloud still hung heavy in the air.

Then, the really alarming activities began. She, Adan, and their little group declined to participate, even though taunted to do so, but there was no way to completely avoid observing what proceeded.

Lizbeth had never even heard of Strip Charades before this night and hoped fervently to never see it played again. The site of pasty white bottoms scampering to and fro, combined with various saggy body parts trying to act out scenes, was permanently etched in her mind.

Right after charades, there had been a moment she'd thought the nightmare was about to end. Like manikins, all movement in the room stopped when a loud knock sounded at the door. To Lizbeth's chagrin, it had only been Headmistress Seychelle, thankfully minus Ray and his toy.

The arrival of the Enchanter instructor, however, sparked a whole new round of even more terrifying events. There was the Pin the Penis on the Dwarf game, with Seychelle supplying not only the pink rubber dildo used as the penis but the poor unsuspecting Dwarf himself.

The only remotely pleasant thing about the entire evening so far had been a short conversation with Lark. Her new sister-in-law had promised to have lunch with her sometime during the next week so they could become better acquainted.

The thought of lunch had made Lizbeth's stomach growl, and the sight of the vegetable trays still on the table before her had caused her mouth to water. She'd almost picked up and munched a slice of cucumber.

Almost. That was before Sarco had gasped, Lark had lunged toward her, and Adan had plucked it right from her fingertips as he not so nicely admonished her, "Didn't I tell you not to eat anything here? You have no idea where it might have been."

That had been a good half turn of the hourglass ago, though, and this was now. Now consisted of large bowls of whipped-cream being passed around, along with jars of chocolate sauce, sheets of plastic, riding crops, and lengths of rope. Lizbeth's appetite faded as chills of dread ran down her spine.

Her worst fears were realized moments later when Laycee spoke. "This next game is called Greased Piggy, Greased Piggy, Who Can Ride Their Greased Piggy. Lark, Adan, grab yare spouses and join in. Briar, ya can be Leeky's piggy, and I'll be the scorekeeper. Ya can't be stick-in-the-muds the entire evening, ya know."

Leeky grumbled somewhere in the background. Something about not wanting to take the chance of getting his eyebrows burned off by Briar.

Laycee didn't seem to notice. "The rest of ya pair up as ya will, and whoever catches and rides their piggy first gets ta lick 'em clean. So, when I say go, lather that whipped cream on yare partner and douse them good with the chocolate sauce. Then, they'll have them take off running. When ya catch 'em, tie 'em up with the rope, ride 'em over ta yare plastic sheet, and lay 'em down. First one ta get their piggy flat on their back gets ta enjoy their dessert! Okay, get ready, get set…"

A knock at the door prevented Laycee from finishing what she'd been about to say.

It was Leeky's "Where the watery crossed eyes and green snotty nose on the chubby face of a dwarf dandy standing bow-legged in a field of purple pansies have ya been, lad? Yare party's more than half over." That let Lizbeth know the guest of honor had finally arrived. She silently offered up her thanks to God Draka.

Laycee's brother wasn't anything like she'd imagined he'd be. Where Laycee was more than a little on the flamboyant side, O.T.T. was quite plain looking. Tall for a gnome but still less than five foot, he had a completely bald head, a pencil mustache that twitched with a nervous tic, and round wire-rimmed glasses. Even his attire was ordinary. He wore a dull brown tunic and trousers that looked a size too big, and his elfin shoes could've used a good brushing.

What did come as a surprise, however, was the volume of his voice. For being a gnome, the high pitch of his accent held none of the normal rumble she had come to expect from those of his race. It almost made her ears hurt to listen to it as, the further O.T.T. came into the room, the louder and more excited he became.

"I was unavoidably detained by Gnome-Ogre Affairs, and it was all very hush-hush and important. Work comes before play, I always say. After all, I am the assistant ta the assistant ya know. Now, where's the ale and the food? I'm hungry and parched." The gnome headed for the dining area.

Adan squeezed Lizbeth's hand, and she glanced into his smiling face. "It shouldn't be long now, Lizard. I doubt he'll even remember me, so this will be quick. Let me do all the talking. I'll simply greet him, say our goodnight, and we'll be on our way."

O.T.T. didn't look at, acknowledge, or address anyone in the dining area until he had collected a mug from the table and filled it to overflowing from the Tug ale fountain. After downing its contents, belching loudly, and filling it once more, he finally turned back toward the table and its spread of food. It was then the gnome's eyes lit up at the sight of Adan.

"Is that little Adan Hammerstrike all grown up? It is, isn't it? Has it really been that long since I've seen ya, lad? If I remember right, last time I visited Laycee at Alaria, ya were just beginning ta get pubic hair around ya itty-bitty willy."

The shocked look on Adan's face and his quickly pinkening cheeks almost made coming to the party worth it for Lizbeth as he faced her and tried desperately to explain. "Skinny-dipping. He caught me skinny-dipping in a pond once, just once, and it was a very cold pond. There was shrinkage. I was only twelve, for God Draka's sake."

She tried her best to avoid giggling. Luckily, that moment, O.T.T. distracted Adan once more as Laycee's brother wiped a tear from his eye, ran over, and wrapped his free arm tightly about Adan's left leg.

It was all the huge barbarian could do to pry the gnome loose. Lizbeth couldn't help but giggle at her husband's bright red face and unsuccessful attempts to completely extracate himself. Finally, he simply gave up.

"O.T.T., it's good to see you, too. It's been a long time. Might I introduce my wife?" Adan gestured to his right. "Meet Lady Lizbeth Hammerstrike, and Lizbeth, my lady, this is Laycee's distinguished brother, O.T.T. Not only is he a well-known diplomat in his own right, but an expert on historical artifacts to boot."

She wasn't sure what to say to the gnome as she bent and placed her free hand in his, so Lizbeth said the first thing that came to mind. "It's nice to meet such an important man. That's a very unusual name, O.T.T. What do the initials stand for?"

It was as if time ground to a halt. The fingers of her hand were being clamped in a vice grip, and there was no mistaking the plea from Adan being whispered in her ear. "You didn't really ask him that, did you? Please tell me you didn't."

From somewhere behind, Lizbeth heard Lark's voice. "Adan, you didn't warn her?"

The entire room went dead quiet. Not even the sound of a breath being taken could be heard. Then the sobs and the story began.

"Oh, they stand for something, that's for sure, lass. They stand as a symbol of my deep shame. Been known ta everyone as O.T.T. for years now. It wasn't always so. I used ta be known far and wide as Thaddeus Tobias Titwilder, only gnome ta ever be appointed ta the Diplomatic and Preservation of Historical Artifacts core at the same time. That was a whole 'nother life ago, though. That was before I was stationed for a tour of duty in the troll city of Karza, and that was before I met and fell in love with Karla."

O.T.T. sniffed loudly and wiped his nose on the sleeve of his tunic. "It's a sad story, ta be sure. I'm the victim of lost love and missing body parts."

Lizbeth gasped. Missing body parts? She got her first true inkling she probably didn't really want to know the origins of O.T.T.'s name, after all. It didn't matter. She had asked, and now it was too late. The gnome just kept on talking.

"Karla was the only daughter of the troll magistrate. Big, green, and mean as the day is long, but

I tell ya, it was love at first sight. How can any man my size be expected ta watch a more than seven foot tall troll lass stroll by daily, swinging her hips, and not become completely infatuated? It's not possible, I tell ya, and Karla was more troll than most. Why, I'd bet there was more meat on that woman's backside than you'd find on a full-sized Tambian water buffalo. Her arse alone was a virtual oasis."

Lizbeth gulped.

The gnome downed his mug of ale, filled it once more from the Tug fountain, and continued. "Even now, when I close my eyes, I can still see her matted, black hair, her big nose with that cute little wart on the end of it, her thick, sharp, yellow tusks, and those voluminous, greasy red lips of hers. What wasn't there ta love?"

The gnome hesitated and it looked to Lizbeth as if he were waiting for her to agree with him before he spoke again, so reluctantly, she nodded.

"At first, Karla didn't notice me. I must've thrown myself in her path a good twenty times before she finally fell for me. Skinned her knee and I suffered a few broken ribs and a concussion, but after that, we were inseparable."

O.T.T. got a far away look in his eyes, downed his ale once more, quickly refilled it, and continued. "We went everywhere together. Ta the market and ta the opera, ta church, out ta eat, and even ta the artifact dig site. Life was good."

Lizbeth watched as the gnome's smile faded and a shadow crossed O.T.T.'s face. "I didn't pay any real attention ta what the other guys said. I thought my fellow core members were just jealous of my vast expertise with women when they'd walk by, snicker, and call her Camel-Toe Karla, then wink. After all, trolls don't wear shoes often and I'd seen her toes plenty of times. And though I have ta admit, they were big, green, smelly, and had cracked, ingrown nails, they looked pretty normal ta me, for a troll anyway."

Lizbeth wasn't sure if it was the fact she hadn't eaten all day or O.T.T.'s descriptions that was making her nauseous, but something was. Her stomach grumbled its protest, and she closed her eyes and prayed the story would end soon.

The mug met his lips once more, and O.T.T. gulped down its contents in fast order. Returning to the Tug fountain, he didn't even bother with his container. He leaned back, positioned his mouth under the stream, and drank his fill.

Just as Lizbeth was beginning to worry the gnome would drown himself, O.T.T. came up for air, belched twice, farted once, and shook off the excess like a wet puppy. Refilling his mug, he went on. "Then tragedy struck. We'd been dating a little more than a phase of the first moon when we decided it was time ta take things ta the next level. Karla invited me over for dinner, and after her Papa fell asleep, she snuck me up ta her room. In my defense, I've never been able ta see well without my glasses, and well, her kisses had them all steamed up so I took em off. Then we began getting undressed so we could get down ta doing the nasty."

O.T.T. shook his head as if trying to decide how best to proceed. "You've gotta understand. Troll women are naturally well endowed and, well…hairy. So in retrospect, what I said ta her was perfectly reasonable at the time."

He got a far away look in his eyes as if watching the scene unfurl within his mind. "After I shed my clothes and freed all three and a half—I mean, seven inches of my Russell the Love Muscle, I turned, ready ta finally get a glimpse of my naked troll beauty. It was then I made the biggest mistake of my life."

Lizbeth braced herself and held her breath, instinctively knowing, whatever was to follow was going to be very disturbing.

Tears glistened in the gnomes eyes. "For a moment, I couldn't understand what I was looking at. There was something long and brown and hairy hanging right above me at eye level, and its sides were flapping back and forth as she walked toward me."

Once again, O.T.T. drained his mug. This time, however, he didn't bother to refill it. He didn't even look up at his audience as he continued. Lizbeth knew he was too lost in his own story to care about who was listening anymore.

"I looked up into my Karla's sweet face and said without blinking an eye, 'Ahh, now I see what the guys all meant by camel-toe.'"

He broke out in sobs. "That's when she got a lot closer ta me very fast. Just before her fist connected with my face, I finally realized she didn't consider camel toe ta be a compliment."

It took a moment for O.T.T.'s words to sink in, and when they did, all Lizbeth could manage to do was hold onto Adan's arm as if it were a lifeline and stare at the gnome with what she knew to be her best fake smile plastered in place.

O.T.T. sat down heavily on the floor. "That's the last thing I remember. Woke up three days later in the desert with a VoT of a sunburn, two black eyes, a busted nose, and missing not only my clothes but one of my favorite testicles ta boot. It looked ta have been chewed clean off. There was a scrap of paper attached ta my chest by a safety pin pierced clear through my left nipple. The note read, 'Don't ever come back ta Karza, or I'll bite off the other one, too.'"

He looked up into Lizbeth's eyes, and the pain in his made her almost want to hug him. Almost.

"So, now ya know my shame, lass. That's how I got the nickname One Testicle Thad, or O.T.T. for short."

Lizbeth couldn't think of a single thing to do but nod and pat the gnome on the top of his bald head.

\*\*\*\*

Adan slipped an arm about Lizbeth's shoulder on the pretense of safely guiding her through the maze of hallways when in reality, his whole purpose for touching her was to assure himself she was, at least, physically okay. Mentally was another matter all together. He doubted, after this night, she would ever be the same again.

Though her breathing did seem calmer and the pulse visible on the side of her neck no longer pounded erratically, she still occasionally shuddered as if sleepwalking through a nightmare. Not one word had passed between them since leaving Leeky and Laycee's apartment, and if the glassy gaze in Lizbeth's eyes was any indication, conversation of any kind for the rest of the evening was going to be sparse. Perhaps that was best.

Adan sighed and mentally kicked himself. Why had he taken her to the gnome party in the first place? It wasn't as if he'd wanted to. He'd even tried to talk her out of it.

As usual though, Lizbeth had misjudged his motives, and instead of being the bigger man and seeing to his wife's wellbeing, his pride had gotten in the way. He had wanted her shocked to the very tips of her pretty little toes so that the next time he told her not to do something, perhaps she'd listen to him. A little shocked was one thing, but even Adan had been surprised at the depth of gnome depravity he'd witnessed this night. He couldn't blame her if she chose never to speak to him again.

They reached the hallway leading to Lizbeth's dormitory, and as gently as possible, he nudged her in that direction. She turned and grasped hold of his tunic with both hands as she fisted her fingers into the material.

"Let me stay with you tonight, please Adan, I'll do whatever you want, I promise." Her voice held more than a hint of desperation and hysteria. "Just don't make me go back to the dorm. Laycee will be bringing Tug with her when she makes her rounds. I know she will. She might even bring O.T.T. and Leeky. I simply can't face any more gnomes this evening. Please, I beg of you."

As gently as possible, Adan lifted his wife into his arms and cradled her securely against his chest. "I would be honored if you'd stay with me, my lady. My bed and I are at your service anytime you wish."

He smiled and softly whistled a tune as he turned and carried Lizbeth toward his room. If it got his reluctant wife into his bed, perhaps the gnome party hadn't been such a horrid idea after all.

## Chapter Ten

After a long night filled with the sights and sounds of thunder, lightning, steady rainfall, and nightmares filled with white trunks, gnomes, trolls, and dragons, the streaks of early morning sunlight filtering through the windows of the tower room were more than welcome. Lizbeth finally mustered the courage to open her eyes. For a moment, she couldn't remember where she was or why she was naked. Then weight shifted somewhere on the other side of the bed, and a strong, long-fingered hand slid about her waist, pulling her snug up against its owner's warm, well-defined, equally bare body.

She smiled and stretched, breathing in the familiar essence of her barbarian husband. The tingle his lips induced as they lightly grazed her ear and the sound of his words being whispered against her skin sent shivers of pleasure scampering down her spine.

"Good morning, my lady."

Lizbeth marveled. However had Adan made a whisper sound so like a hungry growl? Yet, somehow, he had. Instinctively, she knew the hunger she heard in his voice had nothing whatsoever to do with food. Her body reacted with a craving of its own as she wiggled her bottom suggestively against the soft skin of his rapidly hardening cock. Immediately, her nipples responded in kind, and her pussy began to throb.

113

"Good morning to you, my lord." Even to her own ears, her voice sounded breathy with anticipation. Never had she felt so wanton, so powerful, and yet at such a loss as to how to come right out and tell this man what she wanted, desired, needed.

The next growl she heard certainly wasn't whispered as Adan quickly flipped her to her back and straddled her. A heartbeat later, they were nose to nose, and her husband wasn't smiling. His face was taut and serious.

"You little tease! All night long, you've been my tormentor. You've allowed me nothing but to share with you the warmth of my bed. Not even a taste of your lips did you offer. You have exactly the space of a single grain of sand falling through the hourglass to tell me you don't wish my attention before I ravish you to my heart's content. My patience is at an end, wife."

Lizbeth tilted her chin, grinned, and gazed into Adan's eyes as she slowly closed the short distance between them. Lightly, she brushed his lips with her own. "There's your taste. Now, what are you waiting for, husband? I'm sure at least one grain of sand has fallen by now. Ravish away."

The startled look on Adan's face would have been laughable if his lips hadn't chosen that very moment to capture hers. And what a kiss it was. All thoughts of laughter or anything other than the feel and taste of him quickly disappeared from Lizbeth's mind. He was fire and ice all at the same time. Ambrosia, cool and sweet, mixed with spices, hot and wild. Where he ended and she began, she wasn't even certain anymore. The only thing that mattered was her desperate need to get even closer.

Time slowed, and Lizbeth's surroundings became almost dreamlike as Adan's lips journeyed lower, first to her neck, then her collarbone, until finally latching onto the nipple of her right breast. Shock waves of pleasure undulated all the way to the tips of her toes, and of their own volition, her toes curled inward. She fisted her fingers in Adan's hair and held his head firmly in place. Taking deep breaths of tangy air mixed with the sweet smells of morning dew and lustful Barbarian, she tried powerlessly to slow the pounding of her heart.

Not wanting to give in to the urge to beg him to take his kisses even lower, Lizbeth turned her head to the side in hopes of finding something, anything to distract from the persistent, ever-increasing throb between her legs. She concentrated on watching the sheer curtains at the window billow inward with a loud hum, and even the streaks of sunlight made a sound all their own. Somewhere in the distance, Lizbeth could've sworn she heard mewling moans and gasps, then suddenly realized they were coming from her own lips. Of all the men in Albrath, why was it this particular man who held the power to turn her body to jelly and her mind to mush with no more than a touch?

In the space of another heartbeat, he flipped her over as if she weighed no more than a feather and positioned her straddling his face and looking toward his feet. As his tongue flicked out and captured the tiny pulsating nub between her folds, no more questions came to her mush of a mind as it melted into liquid sensation right along with the rest of her body.

The remainder of the room faded away, and all Lizbeth's eyes could see was Adan's glorious body stretched out before her and his huge, proud cock beckoning her forward. Tentively, she leaned toward it, flicked out her tongue, and tasted the very tip. The moan she heard resonating from its owner only served to spur her on. She wrapped both hands around the girth of its base, gloried in the power of the blood coursing beneath her fingers, opened her mouth, and with glee, took as much of his magnificent cock as she possibly could deep within and sucked.

She tried to concentrate and remember her lessons, really she did. How many hours of Adan Hammerstrike classes had focused on this one simple task? Lizbeth knew without a doubt her barbarian husband thoroughly enjoyed oral satisfaction, and now that she had the opportunity to once again show him how skilled she truly was, she couldn't keep her mind on the undertaking long enough to bring it to fruition. And to make matters worse, it was all his fault.

She tried swirling her tongue around the ridge just under the head and then nibbling the tender area where the shaft began as she'd been shown, but just as her tongue touched the skin above the vein that ran the length of the back of his cock, Adan nipped at her clit. Her eyes crossed, her thighs quivered, and a jolt of pleasure exploded outward and upward until even the roots of the hair on her head zinged with an electrical charge. It was all Lizbeth could do to remain upright and conscious.

"Oh, you do so like that don't you, Lizard?" His words, murmured against her already over-stimulated membranes, as well as the deep rumble of his laughter had her panting as if she'd run a very long race.

Lizbeth tried to think of a witty retort, something to

take the smugness out of his voice, but all she could manage to do was squirm against his mouth and bite her own lip so she wouldn't scream her joy to the rafters.

He nipped her once more, a little harder than before, then slid his hot, wet tongue along her pulsating opening. Adan's smugness became the last thing on Lizbeth's mind. She never knew she was capable of it, but it was as if something inside her snapped and a completely different woman burst out and took over. One who was brazen and wild, one who knew what she wanted and wasn't afraid to take it.

She sat up as straight as she could, threw her head back, grabbed hold of Adan's cock with both hands, and stroked.

A breath and a half later, she found herself flipped over and around again. Her hands and knees met the coolness of silken sheets, and Adan's thick, hard cock impatiently prodded the opening of her pussy. Lizbeth wiggled her ass, teasing, tempting, anticipating.

His warm breath caressed her cheek. "What have you done to me? I have a powerful need of you, Lizbeth. A hunger I can't seem to sate no matter how many times I have you." He kissed her neck and nibbled the lobe of her ear. "I need to bury my cock deep within that sweet pussy of yours and plunder. I need to feel my balls against that scrumptious arse of yours. I need to fuck you until your pussy clenches around me and you scream my name. I need...I need..." With one quick, decisive thrust, he entered her and Lizbeth forgot to breathe.

Her pussy clenched tight about him. Ripples of pleasure followed along the path his cock took. Every inch of her sheath tingled and quaked at the intrusion.

Harder and harder, he thrust, his cock pounding her pussy unmercifully as his balls slapped her ass, lightly stinging in a way that brought a smile to her lips. Lord God Draka, he was good and kind and loving and everything in between. The sound of his harsh quick gasps and the feel of his sweat mingling with her own fueled the already out-of-control spiraling of her heart.

For a moment, she almost froze. God Draka, was it possible? Was she actually in danger of falling in love with her husband? She couldn't. Not now. It was too soon. There was too much yet to accomplish.

Then he bellowed, and she knew he didn't care if all of Albrath heard. "Tell me what you want, Lizard. What you need. Command me, for I am yours, now and forever."

All other thoughts but one fled her mind. He was hers. For better or for worse, for richer or for poorer, in all things, he was hers.

Lizbeth didn't recognize the woman she became as she shouted, "More, faster, harder, there. Yes, right there." And she didn't care who might hear as long as each demand was met with immediate and thorough compliance.

Throbbing centered around her swollen clit and deep within the recesses of her pussy. It grew in intensity until it pounded in her ears. A warmth spread deep in her belly and flooded her pussy at the same time Adan's cock pulsed and he shouted her name. Hot cum shot forth coating her. Before she could let out her next breath, spasms shook her body and shooting stars of pleasure exploded behind her eyes. As if in slow motion, she fell forward and her face came to rest on the silken sheets.

The rumble of his laughter proceeded his arrogant "Ah, yes, I do believe my little Lizard liked that very much too."

She didn't have the energy to respond. All she could manage was to grin like an idiot and nod. He lifted her gently, turned her in his arms, and tucked her in beside him, close to his heart. Lizbeth couldn't prevent her eyes from fluttering shut and the world from slipping away.

She woke with a start as the sting and the sound of a loud whack upon her ass startled her. If Adan hadn't been grinning so adorably at her, she would've smacked him back. Instead, she couldn't help but return the smirk as she teased, "I see you've come by the title Barbarian quite honestly, husband."

Lizbeth found herself flat on her back again a heartbeat later, with her legs spread wide and that selfsame barbarian between them, pressing his still rock-hard cock against her pussy. He leaned down and nuzzled her neck. "Oh, I have every intention of showing you just how much of a barbarian I am, wife."

Then he thrust forward...again.

\*\*\*\*

Lizbeth sighed with contentment as she nibbled the last morsel of a piece of toast before pushing the tray away. She snuggled once more beneath the warmth of the thick coverlet on Adan's bed and smiled. Outside, the sun shone brightly and the day had long ago started, but she didn't care. There were no classes today, no gnome parties to attend, not even any unfinished studies to worry about, and after the wondrous lovemaking session with Adan a little while ago, she needed a day of rest.

Lizbeth giggled to herself. Her body completely relaxed, lethargic, and heavy. She smiled, knowing it would require more energy than she had left to raise her hand once more. Yet, at the same time, certain nerve endings still zinged with excitement.

Her nipples puckered and hardened as they rubbed against the thin linen of the shirt she'd borrowed from Adan, and her center still hummed with a steady rhythm matching her heartbeat. Even though it was now more than a turn of the hourglass since he'd ordered her breakfast in bed and then promptly fallen back to sleep, she could still feel his presence against her skin.

Adan. She shook her head and grinned at his sleeping form. Who would've ever guessed such a big powerful brute could be such a wonderful lover? Lizbeth wrapped her arms about herself and laughed. The man she'd made love to this morning had been much different than the one of her wedding night. Not that making love with him on their wedding night hadn't been an eye-opening experience, for it had. But that night had been more of a getting-to-know-each-other kind of lovemaking. Even then, Lizbeth could tell he'd been holding back, being gentle, gauging her reactions.

She wouldn't describe him as gentle today. Not that he'd inflicted pain upon her person, for he hadn't, but his forceful thrusts certainly had been anything but gentle, and his strong grip had possibly left a bruise or two. And then there had been his lips, they'd been demanding, and at times punishing. Her blood still boiled with the memory of it. Making love with a lust-mad Adan Hammerstrike had been much like a sparring match with both of them coming out as the winner.

When the man told her he meant to ravish her, he hadn't been kidding.

Not that she minded. On the contrary, Lizbeth was no delicate little flower. Though only half barbarian by birth, she knew herself to be truly barbarian at heart, and just like her barbarian ancestors, she could give as well as she got.

She licked her swollen, well-kissed, lips and marveled that she could still taste him upon them. A thought occurred to her, and no longer was it a kiss she tasted. It was the rise of bile.

Clouds began rolling in, and Lizbeth jump out of the bed and began pacing. Oh, God Draka, what had she done? How could she have forgotten her daily PDUP spell yet again? Once more she'd failed to say the words before they made love. Nausea threatened, and she swallowed hard.

There was still time, wasn't there, there had to be? What if she said it now? Would it work? Quickly, she mumbled the words she'd learned long before she'd ever had need of them. *"Protect my body, protect my soul. Let not the specter of disease be bold. Protect my body, protect my soul. Let not the spirit of a babe take hold."*

Lizbeth sat gingerly on the edge of the bed. Not wishing to wake her slumbering husband. Outside, the clouds darkened and rain began to fall. What was she going to do if she really were with child? How would she explain to Adan how careless she'd been?

A cold shiver ran the length of her spine, and Lizbeth pulled the coverlet around her shoulders and took deep breaths. She didn't have to panic yet. There was still the possibility she was worrying over nothing.

There were more than a dozen rotations of the sun left before the end of the second moon phase, and her cycle wouldn't really be overdue until then.

Lizbeth's hands went to her flat stomach of their own volition. With all the excitement of the first week of classes, she'd managed to dismiss the possibility of pregnancy and put it from her mind. She certainly couldn't do that anymore.

Hers had always been a second moon phase cycle. A single tear slowly made a path down her cheek as she remembered her very first cycle of the moons. She'd hoped to be a first moon phase like her mother or a third moon phase like her favorite sister-in-law, but it wasn't to be.

First moon women were known for their extraordinary beauty, and third moon females for their quick minds. Second moon women were the most common, and for the most part, ordinary.

Even though she'd ended up being a second moon phase female, her eleven-year-old self had been more excited than anything as she'd rushed headlong into her mother's room to tell her the news. That was the same day her parents' illness had begun, and before Lizbeth's first cycle had ended, both her parents were dead.

Her tears fell in rhythm with the raindrops, and a coldness matching the winds blowing outside the tower room filled her soul. Lizbeth shuddered, and hugged the coverlet closer. She wasn't even sure why she was crying. It had been years since she'd come to terms with her parents' deaths, and even though she missed them dearly, she rarely cried for them anymore. So then, were the tears because she was afraid she was with child, or were they because she feared telling Adan and being forced out of school and back to his mother's castle? Or perhaps a combination of both?

Something else suddenly occurred to her, and Lizbeth shook her head wondering why she hadn't thought of it earlier. The heaviness in her heart lifted, and outside the clouds cleared away as streaks of sunshine decorated the walls of the tower room. There was more than a good possibility she'd been worrying for no reason at all.

How many times had she heard of women who'd been through stressful situations or life-altering changes, skipping an entire moon cycle or flipping to a completely different one? That must be what was happening to her. It made perfect sense.

In the space of a single cycle of the moon, she'd left the only home she'd ever known, gotten married, started enchanter classes at the Academy, and been exposed to some truly traumatic sights and sounds.

That would be enough to make any woman skip a cycle. It was certainly enough to shift her cycles to the third moon. Lizbeth twirled around and around the room. Her wish had come true, and she was becoming a third moon cycle female like she'd always wanted. After all, she had been using her mind a vast amount lately.

Another thought occurred to Lizbeth, and she felt like singing. She didn't have a thing to worry about. All was well with her and Adan, and she couldn't be with child. By now, being a third moon cycle female, she wouldn't have even ovulated yet. Life was good, wasn't it?

Lizbeth glanced over at her still sleeping husband and frowned. If only she could trust herself to remember to say her PDUP spell daily. Until then, one thing was for certain, if she wanted to make sure it was only her mind doing the further expanding and not her mid-section, she'd have to find some way to avoid being alone with Adan.

Dressing quickly, Lizbeth headed back to the safety of her dorm.

**** 

Adan paced back and forth between the door and the far wall of Sarco's office and threw up his hands as he turned toward his sister and her husband. "I give up. I'm completely out of ideas." He closed his eyes and hung his head. "I honestly thought that after the night we shared Lizbeth would've stayed with me, but she didn't. She purposely waited until I fell asleep and snuck back to her VoT of a dormitory room. What am I supposed to do now?"

Lark sighed. "So, what did you do this time? Did you go all bossy barbarian on her? Or perhaps compare her to mother again? You must have done something. Lizbeth is one of the most reasonable women I know and she wouldn't have left without a good reason."

"Do wrong? Me!" Adan roared. "Why would you automatically assume I'm in the wrong? Lizbeth's the one with something to hide, something that keeps her running away from me. I can feel it."

Lark glared at him, and even though Adan knew he had no reason to, he felt guilty. He crossed his heart. "I swear, sis, it wasn't me this time. I was so sweet to her after the gnome party, I'm surprised she didn't go into a diabetic coma on the spot."

Lark's mouth softened, and she smiled. "I have to admit. You can be charming when you want to be."

Adan shook his head. "Thanks, but that doesn't help me figure out how to fix this mess."

"Just keep on romancing her, Adan," Sarco said. "Give her time and presents and lots of love every chance you get. Trust me, she'll come around. And if she doesn't, then go all barbarian on her ass and show her who's boss."

Lark punched Sarco right in the breadbasket, and the elf bent double. For the first time since Adan had awoken to find Lizbeth missing from his room, he smiled.

## Chapter Eleven

There was no denying it, Lizbeth was in love. Completely, totally, hopelessly in love. She didn't shout it from the rooftops, and she didn't sing it to the masses. She hadn't dared utter the words out loud yet for fear of jinxing it, but she knew to the very depths of her soul she was definitely head over heartstrings, irrevocably, mindlessly in love with her husband.

Not a single day had passed since the night of the gnome party that Adan hadn't met her for their agreed-upon dates at their agreed-upon times. He'd held her tenderly in his arms, whispered sweet words of his desire for her in her ears, and, on those days when she'd actually remembered to say her PDUP spell, he'd made passionate love to her until the wee hours of the morning.

And that had just been the nights. Their days had been filled with laughter, joy, and playful banter, for the most part, any way. That is, until their conversations in the evenings turned to magic. On the subject of her obsessive need to learn magic, they would probably never agree. As a matter of fact, when the word magic came up at all, the fight was on. But no matter how late into the evening they might bicker and disagree, when the sun rose, they began anew.

Each morning for the past seven weeks, she'd been greeted with some small token of his affection on her pillow in her dorm room. How he had managed to place it there, she'd never asked, though she suspected Laycee was in on it. She enjoyed the mystery of it, the romance.

One day a beautiful, rare, yellow flower tickled her nose while the next morning, yards of assorted, rich fabrics—always yellow—covered her from head to toe. Then there had been the necklace with the small heart-shaped locket of yellow gold dangling from its golden chain, and the yellow silk and lace thongs that made her blush.

Lizbeth giggled. She didn't have the heart to tell Adan yellow wasn't really her favorite color, and that she in fact preferred shades of blue most of the time. If the man wanted to give her yellow things for the rest of her life, that was fine with her.

She grimaced, wishing that not telling Adan yellow wasn't really her favorite color wasn't the only thing she was keeping hidden from him.

Outside clouds began obscuring the sun and thunder rumbled somewhere in the distance. The warmth of a hand upon her arm, and the sound of Lark's voice close by startled Lizbeth. "Are you all right?"

She plastered a smile on her face and looked around the lunch table at Briar and Laycee. "Of course, I am." Heat crept up her cheeks. "I think I'm just a little tired today. Now, what were you saying?"

Laycee cackled. "I'd be tired too if I had a big ole barbarian betwixt my legs every night. Didn't I tell ya my Adan could do a right proper job of doing ya?"

Lizbeth continued to simply smile. She had no idea what to say to the gnome. Luckily, Lark saved her from having to respond.

"We were discussing the upcoming end of the semester finals and the beginning of the Yulemass celebrations. Have you and Adan made any plans yet? I'm pretty sure Sarco and I are attending the yearly ball. Being the Wizard instructor and heir to the elf lordship, it's kind of expected of him."

Briar chimed in. "I can't wait. Uthiel will be here by then, and I've been working on my dress every spare moment I get. It seems like an eternity instead of just eight weeks since I've been with my husband, and I want to make sure his eyes pop right out of his head when he sees me in my gown."

Lizbeth relaxed a little. "Adan did mention the Yulemass ball, and yes, we plan to attend. I have this beautiful material he gave me, and I would love to make something out of it, but I'm afraid sewing was something I never had the patience for. Perhaps I still have time to hire a seamstress."

She started to pop another piece of Alarian mountain pheasant in her mouth when Laycee's next words stopped her midair.

"If you're gonna hire someone ta make ya a dress, ya better slow down on the eating, lass. Looks like you've put on a little weight ta me. Even your boobies look ta be getting bigger. But then love does do that ta ya. Makes ya fat and happy. Look at me and Leeky. Why the buttons are near ta popping on almost everything we own."

Outside lightning flashed across the sky and fat drops of rain began pelting the cobblestones of the bailey.

Lizbeth wanted to crawl under the table and hide.

She wanted to disappear. She had gained a little weight, her middle was slightly thicker, her tunic a tad tighter, and she couldn't help but notice her breasts were indeed becoming larger by the day, a fact Adan was very pleased about.

What she wasn't prepared to do, however, was explain why to these woman. Not only had the second moon phase come and gone, but so had the third, and still no cycle. There was no way she could deny it any longer. She was, without a doubt, with child.

Chatter continued on all around her. She even registered the fact all three women volunteered to help make her dress, and she gathered her wits long enough to nod in agreement, but for the most part, Lizbeth once more became lost in her own thoughts.

How was she going to tell him? She knew Adan Hammerstrike well enough now to know he would be totally thrilled with the news. She also had no doubt when he learned of the child, he would try and demand she return to his castle home where she and their unborn child would be surrounded by guards constantly to ensure their safety. They would also be trapped in the presence of the queen. Lizbeth shuddered.

One other thing she knew without a doubt about her husband, she had to tell him about the baby before anyone else found out. Though Adan was a kind man and hadn't even demanded reasons why she still resided in the dormitory instead of his rooms, he was still a very proud barbarian and he would consider it a disloyalty not to be told first. Matter of fact, she doubted he would easily forgive such a transgression.

It wasn't as if she meant to keep the news from him much longer that he would become a father, and she had no intentions of it. She simply wanted to wait a little while. Just until after her class finals at the end of the week were over, through Yulemass, and into the beginning of the new semester. Then, she'd gladly tell Adan the news and together they'd work out the details of whether she would stay with him at the Academy and finish out the year or go to his castle in Alaria.

Until her finals were over and done with, however, and the new semester was well under way, any talk of a child was out of the question.

Though going slower than she would've liked, she had learned so much. Already she could imbue most weapons with frost or fire at will, and she could easily turn simple baubles into any number of different charms. It wasn't enough though. She still couldn't make the enchantments of protection work, no matter how many hours she tried. She needed more time; she needed part of another semester at least. Lizbeth closed her eyes and unconsciously stroked her still mostly flat belly. *Bad little girls lose their air.*

Outside the wind howled.

The sound of Briar's voice rising an octave above the others broke through Lizbeth's thoughts. "This weather sure is strange lately, don't you think? One minute the sun's shining brightly, and the next it's a full-blown storm. It kind of reminds me of last year when you were having all that trouble with your mother and Sarco and that quest. Remember, Lark?"

Her sister-in-law's sigh was so loud it could've been heard all the way across the room. "You sound just like my brother sometimes, Briar. Not every storm is caused by a Spiritmaster you know, and certainly not by this one. Sometimes a storm is simply a storm."

Briar almost looked defensive. "I wasn't trying to imply it was you behind the strange weather. Perhaps there's another Spiritmaster around who's upset about something, and you simply aren't aware of their being here."

Lark shook her head. "That's not likely. Though many Spiritmasters are secretive about their identity because some people fear their power, we're almost always aware of each other. It's a weird mental bond thing. I have no doubt, if there were another anywhere in the area, I'd sense it, and I don't sense anythin—"

Suddenly, Lark turned toward Lizbeth, and their eyes locked. Lizbeth got the strangest sensation her husband's sister was looking straight through her. No, not through her, inside her, searching, probing every inch of her being. It wasn't painful or even unpleasant. It was simply strange. What was even more difficult to understand was how she could hear Lark's voice so loud and clear when her sister-in-law wasn't even moving her lips.

"*It's you! No, not you precisely.*" Lark shook her head.

Lizbeth glanced around the table to see Briar and Laycee's reaction. The two women's discussion had turned back to the Yulemass ball, and they didn't seem to notice anything out of the ordinary.

Concentrating hard, Lizbeth tried to communicate back with Lark mentally. "*What's me? It's not me. It can't be. I'm not a Spiritmaster. Perhaps you're sensing my new enchanter abilities?*"

Lark stared at her so intently it became uncomfortable. "*No, that's not it.*"

Warmth flowed through Lizbeth's mind as her

husband's sister graced her with a beautiful smile. *"When were you and Adan going to tell me about my nephew?"*

It was Lizbeth's turn to startle. "It's a boy?"

Suddenly realizing her words had been spoken out loud, her gaze quickly shifted to Briar and Laycee who were now staring at her as if she'd grown two heads. Nervously, she fingered the golden locket around her neck. The shout of Lark's voice in her head brought her attention back to her sister-in-law.

*"Yes, it's a boy. Oh, and by the way, he's a Spiritmaster just like me, sorry. I'm not sure if it's the Alarian mountain pheasant you've been consuming that has him objecting at the moment, or if he's just being cranky, but he's upset about something. Now that I think about it, I'd bet he's the one responsible for all the strange weather we've been getting lately and probably even for knocking Adan down with that fireball a few weeks ago. It all makes sense now."*

A sense of excitement skittered along Lizbeth's nerve endings as Lark continued.

*"I was once told when my mother was carrying me, not only did we have the worst winter on record in Alaria, but mirrors broke for no reason and objects moved from place to place. I bet Adan's so proud he's going to be a father. I can't wait to speak with him, and to my sisters. I must send them all a missive immediately."*

Lizbeth grimaced. *"Adan doesn't know yet. Please don't say anything to him."*

Lark looked confused. *"He doesn't know yet? How is that possible? You two had to have discussed stopping your PDUP spell, didn't you? Don't get me wrong, I'd never dream of denying you the pleasure of telling your husband he's going to be a father, but you really need to tell him soon. I know my brother, and he's never been one to enjoy being on the outside of a secret. I'll just tell my sisters, and Briar and Laycee. That is unless you want to."*

Lizbeth almost screamed her *"No!"* out loud. *"You mustn't tell anyone, please. Adan can't find out yet. I need more time. I just want to get through the holidays and the beginning of the new semester before I spring this on him. We didn't discuss having a child so soon. It was an accident. I'm not sure how I could've forgotten to cast my PDUP spell a couple of times, but I did."*

Lark patted her hand. *"Fine, I won't tell my sisters, but you're going to have to tell Briar and Laycee. Not only are they sitting here staring holes in the back of your head, but in your condition you need to be closely followed by a healer to be on the safe side. Oh, and don't forget, Laycee was my family's governess for many years, so I have no doubt she'll have all kinds of helpful, motherly advice for you. Don't worry about a thing, you can trust the three of us to keep your secret."*

\*\*\*\*

"Shhh." Lizbeth flinched as lightning once more streaked across the sky and thunder boomed in the distance. She linked the fingers across her tummy. "You need to calm down before your father gets here, please."

She sighed. Who was she kidding? She'd been waiting in Adan's room for him to get home for more than a complete turn of the hourglass, and it wasn't the baby who needed to calm down. It was she. He was only reacting to her panic. Though it was still early evening, the sky had the appearance of blackest night and had since her midday conversation at lunch.

She tried once more to sooth her tiny Spiritmaster. "I'm going to tell him about you tonight before anyone else has a chance to find out, really I am. Everything's going to be fine, you'll see. We'll get it all out in the open, and I'll explain to Adan why I must stay here at the Academy for another semester at least. I'll tell him why I have to perfect the protection spells before I can even think about leaving here. He'll understand. I know he will. He has to."

Of their own volition, her hands sought the heart-shaped locket at her throat, and she twirled it between her thumb and index finger.

Walking across the room to the doors leading to the tower's balcony, Lizbeth threw them wide open, allowing the crisp, fresh breeze from the storm to wash over her. She tilted her face to the wind, closed her eyes, and took in deep, slow breaths. Before more than a handful of grains of sand had time to slip through the hourglass, the clouds parted, the rain stopped, and stars twinkled above while the shimmer from the three moons of Albrath shone down upon the landscape.

She didn't hear him enter the room. She wasn't even aware of his presence until his familiar arms wrapped about her waist and his head rested upon hers. She plastered a smile on her visage and braced herself for what she was determined to do. "I'm glad you're home, Adan. I have something to tell you." She squared her shoulders and turned to face her husband.

Her smile immediately faded. She had seen many expressions on her barbarian prince's face over the past few weeks, but never this one. He looked defensive and tired, yet at the same time, strangely excited.

"What's happened?"

He shook his head. "It can wait. What is your news, my lady?"

Lizbeth opened her mouth, but no sound came out. She swallowed hard, took a deep breath, and tried again. "No, really, you go first. Tell me what's happened. It must be important."

Adan sighed, then grinned. "If you insist."

He took Lizbeth by the hand and led her to the bed, motioning for her to sit, and she did. He ran his fingers through his hair, twisted his neck as far right as possible while rubbing the back of it with his other hand as if he were trying to work out a stiff knot, then he knelt before her and smiled widely though no humor was reflected in his eyes. "Did you bring a proper gown with you for formal morning dining by chance?"

Lizbeth slowly nodded. "It's not new, but it's the most beautiful thing I own."

"Do you remember all those boring classes you were forced to take on deportment and how to carry yourself in the presence of royals?"

A chill ran up Lizbeth's spine. "Of course I do."

"Well, you won't believe it, but it seems my parents have arrived unexpectantly today and they've decided to spend Yulemass...here...with us. We've been summoned to break our fast with them on the marrow. I really thought it would take my mother much longer to get over being angry with me for letting Sarco win in the arena last year. I know I shouldn't care, but they are my parents and I have sorely missed my father's company. We used to spar every morning in the lists."

"The Queen and the King are here at the Academy, this very moment?" Her voice came out as more of a squeak than actual words.

Adan grinned even wider as somewhere in the distance thunder rumbled and the sound of fat drops of rain hitting cobblestone competed with the ringing in Lizbeth's ears.

When she didn't immediately say anything else, Adan stopped smiling, stood, and began pacing. "She's really not as bad as people make her out to be, you know. She told me she feels horrible about missing our wedding and wants to make it up to us. I know Mother can be trying, but she is the queen and I am her son. I must show her respect. I admit, she can be a tad abrasive and, at times, hard to take, but I do remember hearing her speak fondly of you as a child. All I ask is, while they're here, try and get along with her. For my father's and my sake, if for no other reason."

Adan grimaced. "At least you won't have to worry about her considering you a freak. She doesn't have any reason to look down on you or to be hateful like she is to Lark. She refuses to allow my youngest sister into her presence. She's never forgiven her for being born a Spiritmaster, even though the gene is from her own side of the family. She considers Lark the family disgrace. I don't though. I love my sister in spite of what she is."

A knot formed in Lizbeth's throat, and it became difficult to breath.

"Whatever you do, Lizard, don't mention the word Spiritmaster in her presence, please. It's taboo. Also, my mother abhors anything she doesn't understand, and that includes magic, so let's keep the fact you're studying to become an enchantress between us for the time being. Now, what's your news?"

Lizbeth shivered though not from the cold. It was deeper, a shudder all the way to her soul. She placed a hand protectively across her abdomen and looked her husband straight in the eyes. "Lark, Briar, and Laycee have volunteered to help me make a gown for the Yulemass ball from the beautiful yellow silk you gave me. Isn't that wonderful of them?"

Outside the sky opened into a full-blown downpour.

Chapter Twelve

"Do sit up straight and don't slouch, dear. A future queen must be conscious of her appearance at all times. Isn't that correct, Adan?"

Her husband nodded without even looking up from his plate of boar's kidneys, baked and wrapped in grape leaves, and Lizbeth was sorely tempted to kick him. Anyone paying any attention at all would think it had been years instead of weeks since he'd enjoyed one of his favorite delicacies. Lizbeth, on the other hand, absently pushed hers around with her fork. The thought of trying to swallow anything right now, especially boar's kidneys, was more than she could imagine. Even the idea of it had her stomach churning and bile rising.

The last turn of the hourglass had been pure torture, and the third course hadn't been served yet. She'd managed so far to keep her responses limited to yes, Your Majesty, and no, Your Majesty, but was doubtful at the moment if she would make it through the entire meal without causing at least one serious breech of etiquette. Right this moment, she couldn't remember a single point of deportment.

Lizbeth tried to take her mind off the woman sitting directly across from her, but she couldn't. It was almost as if the last ten years hadn't happened at all and she was once again eleven. Queen Allanna Zanlynn Calista Hammerstrike was as coldly beautiful and just as intimidating now as she'd been back then, perhaps even more so.

Eyes the same blue as Adan's glared across the table at her. The color was where the similarity ended, however. The Queen's held none of the warmth Lizbeth had come to love when she looked into her husband's face. Then there was her mouth. Lips red as blood, slanting upward and ending in the same cruel smirk Lizbeth recognized from so many of her nightmares. Skin as creamy and wrinkle free as a young girl, and a petite figure any princess would be envious of. It wasn't fair. Not a single hair was out of place on her human, golden-locked head. Her curls were so tight, they wouldn't have had the nerve to droop.

Lizbeth fought back the sudden urge to giggle. She would bet those curls could withstand the ravishing damage of a thunderstorm and still come out bouncing. And storming outside the window of the royal suite it was. It had been all night without a moment's relief. Lizbeth's smile sobered as she rested a hand against her abdomen.

"Forgive me for asking, dear, but after your mother passed away, didn't you have anyone around to teach you how to dress properly? Or perhaps your family was too poor and couldn't afford decent apparel? That gown looks to be more than a little tight on your...umm...larger than average frame and it's dreadfully old-fashioned. If I'm not mistaken, and I never am, it's at least two seasons out of date."

The Queen then turned her gaze upon her son. "Adan, how could you allow your wife to be clothed so shabbily? Shame on you."

Adan frowned. "She looks fine to me, Mother. Stop

picking."

The queen bristled. "It's a reflection on all of us, and I won't have it. I'll speak to my personal seamstress this very afternoon and set up an appointment for measurements to be taken. Then we can get a proper wardrobe at least started. Though one must wonder where in this part of Albrath we'll find enough quality material to do one justice."

Lizbeth wanted to shout at her mother-in-law and tell her she preferred her plain gown to the white, frilly, monstrosity the queen was wearing any day of the week, but she didn't. She glanced toward her husband who was already back into a deep conversation with his father about arenas, sparring, weapons, and such, and didn't have the heart to do it. Lizbeth couldn't remember another time she'd seen him look so relaxed and happy.

So, instead of saying what she really wanted to say, she simply nodded, cleared her throat, and spoke softly. "Thank you, Your Majesty. That would be very kind of you."

Lizbeth ran her fingers caressingly across the soft velvet sash at her waist. She loved this dress. Bluish-green silk from head to toe with a tight, gathered bodice, velvet trim, and full puffy sleeves. Not the ordinary blue of the sky or the green of grass, it shimmered with all the multifaceted, deep blue and green hues of the ocean. It made her feel like a fairy princess whenever she slipped it on.

The dress had been a present for her birthday two years ago, and Lizbeth knew for a fact, all three of her brothers had scrimped and saved to buy it for her. That's why she took very good care of it and wore the dress only for the most special of occasions. Now she wished she had come to break her fast with her in-laws dressed simply in her school uniform of tunic and trousers.

Lizbeth heard the distinct sound of sipping, then fine crystal touching down on china and braced herself for whatever insult the queen had thought up for her this time. She didn't have long to wait.

"I had hoped you would've ended up taking after your wood-elf mother more when it came to looks, dear. Though not particularly bright, she was passably pretty. But I see that didn't happen. You're definitely your Barbarian father's daughter, in appearance and size. I still don't understand why Alfred chose you to be our son's wife. It's not as if there weren't an abundance of real princesses around to choose from."

Adan looked up from his conversation with his father, and the anger Lizbeth saw gleaming in his eyes bolstered her heart. "I said stop it, Mother. That's quite enough." He held out a hand to her and Lizbeth gladly placed her own within his grasp. "I happen to think my wife is very beautiful."

The queen sighed. "Not that it matters now, I suppose. After all, the vows have already been spoken. With any luck, and Lord Draka knows we'll need it, the grandchildren to come from this…arrangement will take after my side of the family. We humans are inherently superior to other less fortunate races."

Adan shook his head.

Lizbeth wanted to scream. She wanted to shake the woman and tell her that at least in one way she would be getting her wish. Her tiny, still growing Spiritmaster of a grandson had definitely gotten that particular gene from his grandmother, but she didn't. She would never insult her child by comparing him to such an evil person. And, Lizbeth knew without a doubt, if she so much as opened her mouth, even a smidgen, she would cry. There was one thing she'd promised herself long ago, and that was, as God Draka was her witness, Queen Allanna Zanlynn Calista Hammerstrike would never, ever see her cry again.

Adan patted her hand, smiling at her not only with his mouth but also with his eyes. "I hope all of our children look just like Lizbeth."

His words almost sent her over the edge. But it was the king himself who saved a rush of tears from developing.

With the same exact hand-patting motion his son had just used on her, King Alfred Zavier Caden Hammerstrike now applied to his wife. "Now, Allanna, you know perfectly well why I chose the lass." His voice was low and almost apologetic. "Her father, Lonhiem, was my favorite cousin. It was the least I could do to repay his loyalty. As you well know, he was willing to sacrifice his life to save mine when we were but boys."

The queen cut him off with a flip of her hand. "Say whatever you will, Alfred. Just because the man jumped in a pond once and pulled you out because you were too stupid to learn to swim doesn't mean you had the right to saddle your only son with something less than he deserves."

The Queen then looked directly at Lizbeth and smiled. "Not that it's any fault of yours, dear. I certainly don't blame you. After all, it's not as if you were given the opportunity to choose your parents."

Lizbeth stood and, for a fleeting moment, feared the shakiness of her knees would reveal the fact she wasn't nearly as calm as she'd hoped to appear as she nonchalantly tossed her napkin upon the table. She had little doubt the visible trembling of her hands and the heat of anger she could sense burning her cheeks had long ago given away her true feelings. She was beyond caring.

"I'll have you know, my parents were wonderful people and I'm proud to have been their daughter. They may very well have been nothing more than a lowly wood-elf and a poor barbarian to you, but they loved each other and their children with everything they had. Not everyone can be like you and boast of coming from the lofty loins of not only humans but human Spiritmasters, Your Majesty, so I suppose you'll just have to lower your standards in regards to daughter-in-laws."

Lizbeth smiled. "By the way, in case you didn't know, I'm studying to become an enchantress. I'm going to practice magic, lots and lots of magic. Perhaps I'll even learn how to turn a nasty old biddy into a wart-covered toad."

The queen shrieked, and the king patted her hand faster.

Lizbeth glanced fleetingly toward Adan with a twinge of regret. His face was as white as his mother's dress, and to say he looked stunned was an understatement. Silently, she lipped the words *I'm sorry* and pushed her chair out of the way. Turning without another word, Lizbeth stiffened her spine and stalked toward the door.

"Well, it seems breakfast is over." Adan stated.

Lizbeth hesitated a moment to hear anything else her husband had to say.

"Perhaps we can do this again some other time when you can be civil."

The Queen gasped. "Me?"

Lizbeth didn't turn and look at Adan's reaction even though she was dying to. Instead, she grasped the knob on the still closed door and opened it. The last words she heard as the door clicked shut behind her were, "Yes, you, and I wouldn't blame my wife for a moment if she did turn you into a toad."

Etiquette had not only been breached today, it had been completely shattered, and Lizbeth smiled.

\*\*\*\*

"Well, that certainly didn't go very smoothly, did it?" Adan stared at his silent wife, trying to understand. "I'd be the first to admit that Mother can be trying, very trying, but, threatening to turn her into a toad, really, Lizbeth? And what about our agreement? I specifically asked you not to mention Spiritmasters or magic, and you did both."

Still she remained silent and refused to meet his eyes.

Adan's frustration bubbled over. For as long as they'd been wed, he'd had an inkling she was holding something back from him. But he had no clue what it could be.

When she was in his arms and they were making love, she was the most responsive woman he'd ever held and she gave freely and completely of herself. But in the light of day, when they were face to face, discussing day-to-day issues, there was something…not quite right. Something he couldn't put his finger on.

Something she was hiding. Some secret she wasn't willing to trust him with.

Could whatever she wasn't willing to discuss have anything to do with the obvious animosity between her and his mother? Surly not. In Lizbeth's entire life, she and the queen had spent hardly more than the matter of a week or two every so often in each other's presence.

He had no idea what haunted Lizbeth or what traumas may have befallen her. What he did know, however, was if she wasn't willing to confide in him, there was no way they'd ever be able to deal with it. He wanted to know. He deserved to know. He was her husband, for God Draka's sake, and he was tired of her hiding from him.

"Say something, Lizbeth, anything. You can't tell me the exchange I just witnessed between you two was nothing more than a simple case of dislike. Did something happen that I should be made aware of? What are you keeping from me? And don't tell me you aren't."

She did look at him then, and Adan almost wished she hadn't. Her soft hazel eyes were filled with tears, and it was all he could do to not reach for her, enfold her in his arms, make love to her, and make the world all better. He couldn't though. There was a very important point he needed to get across.

Instead, he sat on the edge of the bed so he no longer towered over her and pulled her onto his lap. He nuzzled her neck. "Ah, my little Lizard, what am I going to do with you? Keep your secrets to yourself if you must but know that I'm proud of you for standing up for yourself today. I truly am. But at the same time, you will some day take her place as queen, and you must learn to do whatever you do diplomatically.

"Today was only the first of many times you and my mother will be forced to interact. If you carry yourself like a queen, perhaps she will, too. I hope you can someday be friends. But if that isn't possible, then at least try and not be adversaries."

He tipped her chin until she had no choice but to look him in the eye. "Like it or not, we're going to have to share that big castle in Alaria with her and my father, probably for a very long time. Our home can't become a constant battleground, Lizard. No one can live like that for long."

She shook her head. "First, don't call me Lizard. You know I hate it. And, I won't live with your mother, ever. I...I simply won't."

Adan sighed. "Why? You've never stated those sentiments before today. You've always known the castle is where we'd live. There has to be more to this...this...thing between you than what happened today."

Lizbeth lifted her chin a notch, stared him straight in the eyes, and adamantly shook her head no.

It was at that very moment Adan realized he'd fallen hopelessly in love with his stubborn little wife and would move God Draka's chambers and Albrath itself to make her happy. The thought was sobering.

Even tear-streaked, pursed-mouthed, sitting with her spine ramrod straight and ready for a fight, she was still the most beautiful, desirable woman in all of Albrath. He couldn't imagine life without her.

Telling her so was on the tip of his tongue and almost out of his mouth before he realized now was not the time. Now was for making his point. There would be plenty of time later to not only tell her but show her how very much she was loved.

"Fine, Liz—beth, have it your way, for now. But understand this. I will speak to my father about building us a castle of our own. Still, we may not have a choice but to reside with my parents at some point. At least until it's completed. You are my wife and you *will* go where I go.

"Soon, and I do mean soon, we need to start thinking seriously about producing the next heir. It's part of the marriage agreement, remember? And the moment you're with child, it's to the castle in Alaria we must go. Even if you fight me on this, Lizard, know that I'll always do what I think best to keep you and our children safe, even if you don't like it."

She didn't say a word, just nodded, but the set of her jaw spoke much clearer than any words she could've uttered, and Adan wondered if the little speech he thought would help ease her worries, hadn't inadvertently made matters worse.

****

Lizbeth rolled her eyes. "It really wasn't that funny."

The giggling reverberated off the dusty walls of what had to have been the tenth identical library basement they had searched. She tapped her foot and waited for her three companions to compose themselves.

Lark was the first to recover. "I would've paid a hundred platt to have seen my mother's face when you threatened to turn her into a toad. As a matter of fact, it would have been priceless. How can you keep from doubling over with laughter every time you think about it?"

Laycee cackled. "Not just a toad, ya know, but a toad with warts. Would've served her right if ya ask me."

Lizbeth shook her head. The last thing she felt like doing right now was laughing. "You don't understand. I did the one thing a future queen should never do. I lost my composure, and now there's a chance I've damaged beyond repair everything important to me."

She wrung her hands. "You weren't there. You didn't see Adan's face when I walked out of that room. Though he took my side, he looked so disappointed. I've apologized over and over, but all he says is I shouldn't have taken it so personally and to not worry about it. He swears he isn't angry, and that he understands. I can feel the difference in him, though. He seems...distant, and he's spending a lot more time in the lists with your father than he's spending with me."

She shook her head. "There's no way I can chance telling him about the baby right now. I doubt our relationship could handle any more surprises on my part. And he told me it's off to Alaria the moment I'm with child, so I really can't tell him right now. And...and...anyway, the Yulemass ball is tonight and I'm sure the Queen will be there and I'll have no choice but face her again. And let's not forget the enchanter finals are tomorrow. It's almost more than I can take."

Lark frowned. "You still haven't told Adan about the baby? What are you thinking? You can't hide it forever, Lizbeth. One way or another, he's bound to find out soon. He won't send you away. That's all bluster, and it would be better if it came from you." She sighed. "My nephew isn't going to just disappear because you don't wish to deal with the fact you're pregnant with a Spiritmaster. That might even be a big part of his distress. Babies can sense when they're not really wanted."

Tears formed in Lizbeth's eyes, and she fought them back while protectively covering her stomach with a hand. "I do want him, very much so, really I do. It's just complicated. Not only do I not know where I stand with Adan right now, but your mother talked Headmistress Seychelle into allowing her to sit in and observe the final exams. I have to successfully complete an enchantment I've never even read the spell for in front of not only my entire class, but also the woman who, if she didn't hate me before, surely does now. And I have to do it all with a smile while my unborn child continues to wreak havoc on the skies above. I promise I'll tell Adan everything after my final tomorrow, just not tonight. I really need this evening to be perfect, inside the ballroom anyway. I have no control over what the weather will be doing outside."

To accentuate her point, thunder so loud it was easily heard from the inner sanctum of the library basement, rumbled somewhere overhead. Lizbeth chose to ignore it as she continued.

"I'm so nervous about tomorrow's test I can barely think straight. The only thing I know about the final is, I'm suppose to find a piece of dragon scale down here in the bowels of the library and take it with me to class, and I can't seem to even do that right. I was told there's a whole box of them lying around here somewhere." She turned in a circle. "We've been down here for at least two turns of the hourglass and not one single

149

dragon's scale to show for it. And people wonder why I detest dragons." Lizbeth grimaced. "It seems I've dragged you, Briar, and Laycee down here for nothing. I'm sorry."

Briar awarded her a bright smile. "Don't be silly. You didn't drag us along. We wanted to come. And I don't believe for a moment you really detest dragons. They are wonderful creatures. And to tell you the truth, I'm glad you asked for our help. It's nice to get a minute away from my big strong paladin of a husband. I love Uthiel Dragonheart with all that I am, but since he's been here, he's barely let me out of his sight. He keeps saying the dragons back at Castle Kuropkat are restless, especially his favorite one, Carnelian, and it's making him really nervous. Dragons know things long before we mortals do. It's kind of spooky sometimes."

A sudden squeal of delight from Laycee had all three women turning in unison. The female gnome was bent over a dusty-looking, wooden box tucked in a corner across the room. Standing, the dorm matron held up a shiny, iridescent crystal. It was blue, veined with gold, oblong and thick. The entire piece was rimmed with what had to have been a metal of some sort.

"Looky here at what I've found. Appears ta be a mighty fine specimen of dragon scale, if I do say so myself."

Lizbeth sighed with relief. Finally, something was going her way.

****

She stood before the full-length mirror of Adan's bedchamber and fidgeted with the lacy yellow ribbon adorning her upswept, toffee-colored ringlets, even though it didn't need adjusting. Her other hand toyed nervously with the only piece of jewelry she wore, the heart-shaped locket on the thin gold chain about her neck. Perfect. It was imperative she be without flaw this night. Adan deserved no less from her, especially after the mess she'd made of breaking their fast with his parents a few days ago.

She took a deep breath and ran her fingers slowly down the front of the gown, straightening any unforeseen wrinkles. She had to admit Lark, Briar, and Laycee had certainly outdone themselves this time. The dress was amazing.

Golden silk, in the form of a low-cut, snug-fitting, strapless bodice pushed up her already abundant breasts, accentuating the fact she was more than a little voluminous. While, at the same time, the high empire waist and long flowing skirt hid any hint of the secret she wasn't quite ready to reveal.

Even the delicate slippers beneath the hem of her gown had been fashioned from the golden silk, and as Lizbeth twirled before the mirror for the first time in her life, she felt like the queen it had always been her destiny to become. Now all she needed to complete her outfit was the arm of her future king.

As if thinking about him conjured him, the door opened and the royal-purple-and-gold-plaid-kilted, strikingly handsome barbarian prince of her dreams strolled leisurely into the room.

Her eyes met his, and he stopped in his tracks, mouth agape, staring as if he'd never really seen her before.

Lizbeth's heart beat so hard she could've counted each individual thump if she'd had the fortitude to concentrate enough to do so. She didn't. All she could manage was to stand waiting to hear her husband's opinion while trying unsuccessfully to swallow the dry lump in her throat.

Slowly, he smiled, puckered his lips, and whistled as a gleam of blue fire glistened in his eyes. His voice rumbled low and deep with a chuckle as he quickly closed the distance between them and took her into his arms.

"Who is this exquisite creature inhabiting my wife's body? I've always known you to be beautiful, Lizbeth, but tonight even a goddess would pale in comparison. Remind me to bring along my claymore and broadsword to stave off all the eager males groveling at your feet for a chance to sweep you around the dance floor." He rubbed the hardness of his cock against her. "Speaking of broadswords."

Lizbeth giggled.

Adan sighed deeply. He placed a hand across his heart and smiled. "You wound me, Lizard. I'm being completely serious. Every other man in the room will soon know what a greedy, selfish barbarian I truly am, for I cannot fathom being parted from you for even a short time. Mine are the only arms you will find yourself in this night."

Lizbeth laughed as she lifted a finger and gently stroked the cheek of the man she'd come to love. "Then take me...umm...to the ball, my lord. Hold me close and dance with me all night long. I happen to be quite fond of your arms." She winked. "And your broadsword."

He growled as he yanked up the edge of her gown and pushed her up against the wall. "I'll take you now, and then I'll take you to the ball. What do you think about that?"

Lizbeth gasped as he unbuckled his belt and allowed his kilt to drop to the floor. He lifted her legs, wrapped them snug about his waist, and with a single quick thrust, entered her. The world about them slipped away.

Outside, the three moons of Albrath shone down from a clear, star-filled sky, and the only sounds floating on the breeze were the songs of night birds and the strains of melodies sung by bards somewhere in the distance. But Lizbeth no longer heard them. All she could hear was Adan's pants of pleasure and the beating of her heart.

His hands gripped her hips, and his fingers bit deliciously into the delicate skin of her ass. The cold brick wall cooled her back while Adan's chest overheated her breasts. The sight of his muscled biceps flexing as he held her tight and drove himself in and out of her pussy had Lizbeth's breath coming hard and her insides tingling.

Oh, my God Draka, he was magnificent. His rock-hard cock slid along the walls of her sheath as if fashioned with only her in mind. He was thick and pulsating, filling her, touching her womb, touching her soul, driving her near insane. His balls slapped at the insides of her thighs with a delightful sting, reminding her that this barbarian, *her* barbarian, though civilized, could never truly be tamed. She liked that about him.

Lizbeth locked gazes with Adan. Loving this man, loving his possession of her, and trying to let him know without actually saying the words her heart could not deny. Knowing that once she actually said the words out loud, she'd never ever take them back. She would be bound to him tighter than even marriage vows could make them. Bound to him forever, heart, body, and soul.

Could she give him that much power? Could she really completely trust a Hammerstrike, any Hammerstrike with that much control over her?

He captured her lips with a kiss that rattled her brain and melted her heart. His thrusts became even more forceful, and her pussy zinged with the pleasure of it.

"I love you, Lizbeth, God Draka help me, but I do," he whispered.

Tears stung her eyes. She wanted to tell him she loved him, too. She wanted to scream it from the rafters, yet she hesitated, afraid to give him that much rule. Instead, she rocked against him hard and sighed against the tender skin of his neck, nipping, kissing, licking a path to his ear. "Fuck me, Adan. Oh, yes, just like that."

His tempo increased as he relentlessly pounded her pussy.

Lizbeth held on and gloried in the ride. Tomorrow, she would tell him she loved him. Tomorrow, she would take that leap of faith. But not now. Now, all she wanted to do was feel the length of him, the width of him, the strength of him deep inside her, pleasuring her, loving her.

There was much she knew she would worry about tomorrow, but she refused to dwell on it another moment this night. Her dragon scale was tucked safely away and ready for the enchanter final exam in the morning. The moment the test was over, she'd tell her husband about the extraordinary life growing within her and the love she had for both of them. Together, they would forge a future.

But that was tomorrow, and tomorrow wasn't here yet. For tonight, her husband was fucking her brains out and looking at her with love shining in his eyes. Life couldn't possibly get any better.

A moment later, she changed her assessment of better when spasms shook her body and sparks of excitement rocketed through her pussy. Her stomach clenched and her mind went fuzzy. A heartbeat later Adan shouted her name as his cock contracted and his seed shot up coating her.

For long moments, they stood that way, simply breathing, simply being. Then, slowly, Adan pulled himself out and allowed Lizbeth's feet to once more touch the floor.

She looked up into his eyes and smiled while she ran her hands over her gown straightening it. Tomorrow would just have to take care of itself. For the remainder of this evening, she would dance with her husband and be merry.

## Chapter Thirteen

Amazing! That was the only word Lizbeth could think of to describe the room stretching out before her. She'd never once doubted Headmistress Seychelle was a talented enchantress, but the way the woman had transformed her stranger-than-strange office into a ballroom worthy of the gods was so far above merely talented, Lizbeth was in awe.

She had only been in the headmistress's office once before during the first week of the semester when she'd had to change all her official documents over to her married name. That one trip had been more than enough.

When the door had opened that day, she'd stepped into an entirely different world. The floors were covered completely with snow-white fur and as white as the floors were, the walls were dark, reminding her of a medieval castle with cold, damp slabs of stone hung here and there with strange, torturous-looking devices. There'd appeared to be no ceiling, just the illusion of a night sky, complete with stars and a single full moon. Gray clouds had moved back and forth across the horizon as a gentle breeze blew. There had only been two stationary objects in the entire room. One, a small wooden desk against the far wall where a receptionist sat. The other, a huge black obsidian throne, complete with straps and shackles.

That was gone now, all of it, and in place of gloomy medieval torture-chamber decor was light and color in every form imaginable.

Enormous, intricately detailed crystal chandeliers hung from the high, ornate ceiling, evenly spaced to illuminate every inch of the room, bathing it in a soft, warm glow. The floors gleamed as only rich, smooth, marble tiles could, and the walls were adorned from floor to ceiling with panels of crimson silk.

Long tables with pristine white linens and multicolored runners, laden with dish after dish of scrumptious-looking foods sat along one wall. Against another, a band of minstrels and bards, attired in tights, peacock feathers, and little else, played and sang ballads while couples streamed by, smiling at each other and twirling about the elaborate dance floor. To Lizbeth, it was as close to a perfect romantic setting as she'd ever seen.

A moment later, her idea of perfect took on a horrifying aspect as all eyes turned toward her and Adan. The deep baritone voice of the Academy's Master Steward stopped the music and made the couple the center of attention.

"Hark Ye! His Majesty, Prince Adan Zeth Conner Hammerstrike, heir apparent to the throne of Alaria, and his princess and future queen, the Lady Lizbeth, have entered the hall. All bid them welcome."

A cacophony of applause and greetings from every corner of the room broke out. She tightened her grip on his arm and for a moment forgot to breathe.

"Relax, Lizard, this is something you'll get used to. It happens quite often." Adan's chuckle against her ear and his misguided assurance had her not only wishing she could escape, but actually glancing around for alternative exits. The applause died down, and for the count of a dozen heartbeats or so, there was silence, then the music began once more and so did the dancing.

Adan patted her hand. "See, just a formality. Shall we mingle?"

Almost everyone who was anyone was already there. Headmistress Seychelle, dressed tonight in skin-tight red leather with silver stud accents, held court in one corner of the room while her pet, Ray, lounged at her feet. Lark and Sarco stood off to the side, deep in conversation with Uthiel and Briar, while Laycee, Leeky, and Laycee's brother O.T.T. were busy helping themselves to the spirits and ale table across the room. Just as Adan and Lizbeth made their way past a table heavy with all manner of treats and appetizers, the Master Steward spoke once more.

"Hark Ye! His Royal Majesty, King Alfred Zavier Caden Hammerstrike, and his queen, Her Royal Majesty, Allanna Zanlynn Calista Hammerstrike, of the kingdom of Alaria, have entered the hall. All bid them welcome."

A shiver ran down Lizbeth's spine as she turned. Though the ballroom was already near to overflowing, Lizbeth knew it was her the Queen sought. Her mother-in-law's eyes bored into her, and the look she gave Lizbeth held no hint of kindness, only spite. Her stomach growled with dread for what she had no doubt was coming, and Lizbeth popped a small tart into her mouth to quiet her nervous tummy and help bolster her courage as she waited for the inevitable.

Just before the King and Queen got within hearing distance, Adan leaned down and whispered, "Please, my lady, for the sake of my relationship with my father, I beseech thee. I know my mother can be…more than a little difficult at times, but for this one night only, try and ignore whatever she says. It is my only request."

Lizbeth didn't know what to say or even how to feel about what he asked, and the Queen was almost upon them, so she simply bit her lip hard and nodded.

"Lizbeth, my dear, I see you're already eating this evening, or perhaps it's that you haven't stopped? And with your fingers no less. How unbecoming of you. Also, a girl of your…size, should really watch what and how much she consumes, don't you think? The wife of the future king of the Barbarians should care about how she looks at all times."

Lizbeth gulped, trying to swallow the delicate crust that refused to go down. Coughing and choking instead, her face reddened, and she knew she'd just made the situation worse.

Adan patted her on the back. "I like how she looks, and as far as I'm concerned, if she's hungry, she should eat. I don't ever want my wife to go without. If you'd bother to look around, Mother, you'd see she's quite petite for a barbarian female. If anything, she could use a little more meat on her bones."

The Queen sighed. "Don't make excuses for her self-indulgence, Adan. The girl has obviously never gone hungry a day in her life. But it's not her fault she's the way she is, I suppose. After all, she can't be held responsible for her upbringing. Although, God Draka knows, I tried my best to see that she was properly educated. Alas, it seems even poor, dear Master Seiger failed in his attempt to turn an Alarian boar's snout into a silk satchel."

She couldn't breathe. It was as if all the air had been sucked from the room and it had become a vacuum. To make matters worse, her hearing must've been affected, too, because she couldn't believe what her husband was saying.

"I'm not going to argue with you tonight, Mother. This is a social gathering and we *will* act civil or else. Now, as far as Master Seiger goes, how is that sweet old man?" He turned toward Lizbeth, his face aglow and smiling widely. "For his years of invaluable service, my parents awarded him a manor house on the castle property when he retired. Isn't that wonderful?"

Lizbeth had no choice but look at him, freeze what she hoped was a smile on her face, nod, and listen. It wasn't easy to hear anything but the pounding in her head and the ringing in her ears.

"I'd forgotten you met Master Seiger, Lizard. What did you think of him? Isn't he something? He was my favorite teacher when I was growing up. He used to read me stories every night and take me for walks, even taught me how to swim. My sisters didn't seem to overly care for him, especially Lark, and I never knew why. Guess he just related better to boys."

She didn't know what to say. She wanted to blurt out what the monster of an instructor had done to her, but this was neither the time, nor the place. At the same time, she didn't wish to lie to her husband.

"I'm afraid I'm going to have to agree with your sisters on this one." The words almost choked her, and she had to force them past her lips. "I didn't overly care for the man much myself. You're probably right though, he most likely did relate better to boys."

The Queen glared at her. "Perhaps it wasn't so

much Master Seiger related better to one gender as opposed to another in general, but that he has such a keen sense for true quality and intelligence that even the sight of those so low class and not very bright, like your family for instance, must've been horribly offensive to him."

Adan stiffened beside her. "That's entirely enough, Mother."

Lizbeth clenched and unclenched her fists, determined she would not shout from the rafters what a hideous creature the white-bearded, old instructor had been, but that the Queen herself was even worse. There would come a time when she would sit down with Adan and tell him everything, but not this night. This night she'd given her husband a promise she meant to keep, even though it had been given with no more than a nod. Silently she vowed, no matter what the queen might say or do, she wasn't going to give in to the temptation and verbally spar with her.

Instead, Lizbeth plastered on her face what she knew to be her most sickeningly sweet smile and curtsied deeply. When she rose once more, she batted her eyelashes, tilted her chin, and exclaimed in her sweetest voice, "Yes, Your Majesty, whatever you say, Your Majesty. I'm sure you know best, Your Majesty."

She had never seen, let alone felt, pure hatred pour from another being before, but she did now, as the Queen glared. Lizbeth shivered with a sense of foreboding as she recalled another childhood lesson she'd learned the hard way. If you tug on a snake's tail, it'll turn and bite you.

\*\*\*\*

True to his word, Adan's arms had been the only

ones she had danced within for the last two turns of the hourglass and that was just fine with Lizbeth. Within the captivating circle of those arms, she had almost been able to put not only the Queen, but tomorrow's exam, and even her secret little Spiritmaster, out of her mind and enjoy her very first Yulemass ball.

It was wonderful. Beyond wonderful, it was magical. Around and around, Adan twirled her about the ballroom floor to the strains of one melody after another. When the very last chord of the latest ballad faded, Lizbeth gazed lovingly into her husband's eyes. "Would you excuse me a few moments, my lord? I find myself parched and have need of a beverage. Lark, Briar, and Laycee are making their way to the refreshment table, and I would so like to speak with them. I wish to brag about my handsome barbarian husband's dancing abilities."

Adan chuckled. "Take all the time you need, Lizard. Just don't tell them how many times I've stepped on your toes this evening. That will be our little secret. I'll go and seek out their husbands. I've barely done more than greet anyone in passing so far this evening, and to tell you the truth, my feet, and most assuredly yours, could use the respite."

Carefully, Lizbeth made her way across the floor of the ballroom and through the crowd until, within moments, she stood face to face with her friends.

"From the way my brother has been looking at you all evening," Lark smiled and raised a brow, "and not letting you more than a few inches from his side, let alone out of his sight, I'd say we did well with the dress."

Lizbeth laughed. "I don't know how I'm ever

going to be able to repay you." She twirled around. "The dress is amazing, isn't it? It makes me feel pretty. Thank you all so very much."

"You certainly don't need a dress to make you attractive, Lizbeth," Briar interjected. "You're lovely just as you are, but we're glad we could help. It was enjoyable, except of course for the part where Laycee stuck me with a pin...twice."

The female gnome blustered as she placed her hands firmly on her hips. "Well, if ya had stood still like I told ya ta do in the first place when I was working on the hem, ya wouldn't have gotten stuck. Serves ya right if ya ask me. Lasses, these days, they just don't listen. Fidget, fidget, fidget all the time."

The sight of something adorning the edges of the refreshment table caught Lizbeth's eye, and she reached down and picked a section of it up. "Oh, look, mistletoe. I should take this and hold it above Adan's head and get my kiss." She sighed. "I haven't seen mistletoe since I left home. My mother used to hang it from every doorway in our small castle this time of the year in hopes of catching my father under it. It's just one of many Yulemass traditions I miss."

Briar snatched the sprig from her hand and tossed it back on the table. "No, you shouldn't be touching that *particular* species of mistletoe."

Lizbeth laughed. "Why ever not? Is it a protected plant in this part of Albrath? In the forest where I come from, you can find it growing on almost any tree."

Briar slowly shook her head and leaned in close. "Mistletoe normally is harmless and would have to be brewed and the tea drunk to have the effect that worries me, but not this *particular* mistletoe. You see, this variety is often used to, well, you know…get rid of unwanted mistakes when a girl forgets to say her PDUP spell. This is Tansian mistletoe, and it's very potent. Exposure to even a small amount of the oil found on the underside of its leaves can be enough to cause really strong cramping, and well…a miscarriage."

A cold shiver shot down Lizbeth's spine, and instinctively, she covered her abdomen with her hands as she quickly backed away from the table. "I would never knowingly do anything to hurt my child. I had no idea, I swear."

Lark smiled and patted the hands Lizbeth still had linked across her tummy. "Even if you have been putting off telling Adan, he's going to become a father sooner than he planned, and I have absolutely no doubt you would never do harm to my nephew on purpose. And, in all seriousness, I doubt the baby would allow something to happen. The little Spiritmaster seems to already have quite a strong will of his own."

Lizbeth was sick. She could've damaged him, and it was her job to protect him. For the first time since she had thought of the possibility she might be pregnant, Lizbeth knew true fear. Not the fear of telling Adan she was with child and possibly having to leave the Academy. Not even the fear of failing to become an enchantress as she'd dreamed. No, her fear was much deeper. It was a mother's worst fear, that of losing a child, her child. A child she hadn't even had a chance to know.

With sadness, Lizbeth realized how selfish she'd been. She hadn't so much as bothered to start thinking of names for him. To her, he was just the little Spiritmaster. But now, she couldn't help but wonder, would his hair be the same shade of golden wheat as his father's? And would his chin have the same stubborn tilt as her own? She hoped so.

These were the thoughts she was lost in when the sound of distress in Laycee's voice snapped her out of her daydreaming. "Lasses, I think we should take this conversation elsewhere. I really do."

Lizbeth turned, and that's when she saw her. Queen Allanna Hammerstrike stood close enough she could have reached out and touched Lizbeth if she'd wanted to. And the woman had a smile so twisted and evil, the sight of it brought back vivid visions of nightmares past. Just how much had she heard? The answer wasn't long coming.

"So, you carry within you an abomination, do you? I'm not surprised. To think someone of your low quality could produce a decent grandchild was folly."

The Queen then turned her smirk toward Lark. "I'll make sure she doesn't make the same mistake I did when I was forced to carry and bear you. If I'd known, I would've ended your life before you ever had a chance to draw your first breath."

Her eyes then found Lizbeth once more. "The disgrace of my father dies here and now. I'll be plagued by his heritage no more. I'll not be haunted through another generation, and as God Draka is my witness, I swear no filthy Spiritmaster will ever be heir to or sit upon the throne of Alaria as long as I have the ability to speak." She pointed a finger in Lizbeth's face. "And don't think for a moment Adan will support you in this. He may tolerate his sister, but I raised him and believe me when I say he won't welcome the creature you carry with open arms."

The Queen's face twisted with rage. "If you dare refuse to rid yourself of this spawn from the bowels of the Valley of Torment, not only will I tell my son, and anyone else who wishes to hear, what you've been keeping from him, but I'll also convince him to put you aside and find a suitable mate. One who knows her place and has the capacity to give him decent heirs. If you doubt my power, just watch me. After I'm through with Adan, you'll be lucky if he even allows you and your demon seed to reside in the dungeon."

Lizbeth didn't say a word as she balled her fist and let it fly.

Every eye in the ballroom looked upward in surprise as lightning flashed, thunder roared, and fat drops of rain began splattering the marble ballroom floor.

## Chapter Fourteen

Adan had no sooner taken his first gulp from the tankard Leeky handed him moments before, when his wife, whom he'd just been bragging to his friends about, punched his mother square in the nose. He coughed, choked, sputtered, and spit ale on all three of his companions.

Out of the corner of his eye, he saw his father make a mad dash toward his mother, who was now sprawled in the middle of the floor, and knew he had no choice but to react. His feet ran before his brain had a chance to register what he was doing. Then, as if matters weren't bad enough, an all-out downpour began right inside the ballroom. The marble tiles became slick, and twice he almost lost his footing. As carefully as he could, without slowing, Adan pushed forward.

Though he had to elbow his way through the gathering crowd more than once, with Sarco, Uthiel, and Leeky fast on his heels, it took more than a few grains of sand falling through the hourglass to reach the sight of the disaster.

And a disaster it certainly was. His mother held her nose and shook her head, her face more crimson than the small, red drops of blood spotting her snow-white gown. His father sat directly on the floor beside her, patting her hand and trying unsuccessfully to get her to lean her head backward to stanch the flow.

Headmistress Seychelle flailed her arms hysterically, her imperious voice mixed with a note of panic. "Give her room to breathe, people." Ray crouched at her side gleefully screeching, "Ray loves cock. Ray loves cock. Ray loves cock."

Two elfin dignitaries' wives fainted, and one troll debutant threw up.

Off to the side, as still as death, with her arms hanging limply at her sides and a look of total shock and disbelief on her face, Lizbeth waited. He wanted to go to her. He wanted to wrap her in his embrace and assure her all would be well. He wanted to take her away from here, away from all the prying eyes and wagging tongues. But he couldn't do that yet. He had to sort this out first.

Lizbeth stood beside Lark with both hands pressed firmly over her own mouth as if she were afraid what might escape if she let go. She glanced at him, her eyes wide with surprise, then she looked back at the scene before them.

Briar, on Lizbeth's other side, didn't seem to know anyone else was around as she mumbled to herself and frantically searched for something in the small medicine bag she always carried at her waist.

Laycee, on the other hand, jumped up and down, her horrid blonde wig flapping in the wind, her little fists pumping the air furiously, and yelling at the top of her lungs, "Hit her again, hit her again."

He didn't want to be his mother's son right now. He didn't want to be a prince or the heir to the throne. All he wanted to do right this moment was collect his wife and escort her safely back to his room. There was no one else who could deal with this situation with a clear head, though, so Adan took a calming breath and looked toward his sister. "Compose yourself and stop the storm, please, Lark. This situation alone is enough chaos to deal with, don't you think?"

Lark nodded. "I truly am sorry, Adan. This time the weather really is my fault." A moment later, the rain slowed then stopped completely.

Next, Adan made his way to his wife's side, leaned down, and spoke softly so as to not frighten her. "What happened, Lizbeth?"

She didn't even glance at him. It was as if she couldn't force herself to look away from the sight of what she'd done, and when she did finally speak, her voice sounded flat, and hopeless. "I hit the Queen."

Adan took two deep breaths and slowly blew them out, trying to be patent. If he wanted to find out what had transpired, he was going to have to take things slowly. "I see that. And why exactly did you hit her?"

It was as if that one simple question brought everyone out of their stupors, and all three of the other women began to speak at the same time.

"It wasn't her fault, Adan," Lark cried.

"She had it coming." Laycee socked the air once more as if practicing her own punch.

Briar looked up from searching her bag. "She really was being particularly horrid, even more so than normal."

His mother, however, ended any further comments with a voice that could have stopped a heard of Alarian wildebeests. "Your wife, and I use the term very loosely, was trying to prevent me from telling you what she's really been up to. It won't work, though. You're my son, and you have a right to know what you've been forced to join yourself to."

Queen Allanna swatted away her husband's hand and stood. "She's been hiding things, Adan. Very important things. Dark things."

Adan turned to Lizbeth and gently tilted her chin until she had no choice but to look him in the eye. "What is she talking about, Lizard?"

Tears pooling and slowly making paths down her cheeks as she shook her head was Lizbeth's only reply.

The Queen, however, didn't have a problem answering. "I'll tell you exactly what I'm talking about. She's been deceiving you. I bet you didn't know she's pregnant, and not just pregnant but pregnant with an abomination, a Spiritmaster. Everybody knows about it except you."

His heart soared. A child? His child? He was going to become a father? Could it be true?

He didn't dare believe his mother's words. "You're wrong. Lizbeth wouldn't keep such news from me."

The queen smirked. "Are you sure?

He looked directly at Lizbeth and saw the truth written on his wife's face. "You are? You really, truly are, aren't you?"

Lizbeth nodded. "I wanted to tell you, really I did. I've just been waiting for the right moment."

He looked at his sister, and she looked just as guilty as Lizbeth did. "You knew, too, didn't you?"

Lark grimaced. "Only for a short time."

Adan didn't even have to ask Briar or Laycee. Both of their faces were bright red and they refused to make eye contact with him. He turned toward his friends. "And did all of you know and not tell me either?"

"Lark let it slip a few days ago." Sarco was the first

to answer. "I would've told you, but I promised your sister I wouldn't."

Uthiel threw up his hands. "Don't look at me. I didn't know until this very morning. I swear."

Adan glared at the little gnome. "And you?"

Leeky shifted back and forth from one foot to the other. "What the pollinated pointer finger on a professional pickle tickler are ya thinking, lad? Of course, I knew. My woman would never keep secrets from me."

The Queen cackled. "See, I told you so. And she refuses to rid herself of it. I told her it wasn't acceptable. No son of mine would allow such evil to be born and someday sit upon his father's throne. Make her kill it. Make her kill it now before it gets too big and powerful. Do it for your people. Do it for Alaria. And if she refuses, then lock her away, discard her, and take another wife, one of your choosing. A wife who will bear you many fine barbarian sons, free of this one's taint. If you are to become King, it's your duty, your responsibility."

"Do what you wish with me, my lord." Though her voice was barely louder than a whisper, Adan heard Lizbeth's words loud and clear. "But I will not harm our child or allow him to be harmed by anyone. Not even you."

He wasn't sure he could get his own words past the emotion swelling his throat, but he had to try. He captured one of Lizbeth's cold hands within his own and faced his parents. "All my life I've been groomed to become King, to sit upon the throne and rule over our people. If you really believe I must have my own child slain to be worthy to do that, then someone else can have the honor. It's no fault of the child's that Spiritmaster blood runs through his veins."

He glared at his mother. "The days of fearing those whose powers we don't understand are over. Spiritmasters are respected now, Mother, not feared, nor shunned, nor hunted, nor punished. Look at your own daughter. She's an instructor at this very school and she's well loved. It's a legacy I gladly give my child, and one he has a right to be proud of. I'll be honored to call him my son, and you should be happy to call yourself his grandmother."

Adan started to turn with a hand firmly at Lizbeth's elbow but hesitated when his mother appeared to be working up for another tirade.

The Queen opened her mouth, but the King stopped her with his own words as he furiously patted her hand. "Now, now Allanna, calm yourself. You know what yelling does to your blood pressure. Don't say anything more you may come to regret later. After all, the boy does have a valid point. The Spiritmaster bloodline comes directly from you, and you should be proud of it. Why, you might even consider what he said to be a compliment."

She pushed her husband's hand away. "She thinks she's won because she's turned my son against me. Well, she hasn't. You'll see, you'll all see. Nobody disrespects my wishes the way that little usurper has and gets away with it. Nobody!"

How could he have been born from the womb of this woman? They couldn't be further apart in word, thought, or deed, even if they'd been complete strangers, let alone mother and son. Part of him felt sorry for her, knowing the story behind her own father's flee from injustice and her subsequent fears of being punished for what he'd been. But this time she'd gone too far. This time there would be no looking past her hate. This time he would choose his wife and his child over god, queen, or country.

This time when Adan turned with Lizbeth in tow, he didn't look back.

****

Adan was angry. It flowed from him and filled every crack and crevice of the room. Not that Lizbeth needed an oppressive feeling to tell her that.

Before they'd arrived at his high tower suite and the door had clicked closed behind them, she had known. She would have known even if he hadn't glared at her and whispered, "Not one word," as he firmly took her by the hand and walked her from the ballroom.

The stiffness of his posture, the tightness of his lips, the short snorts of air like a penned-up bull wanting to get out to pasture gave it away. Not to mention, she had always known he would not like being the last to find out about their child.

Because she did know this, it surprised her when the sound of Adan's hurt instead of angry voice startled her. "Why?"

Lizbeth closed her eyes and wished she were anywhere but face to face with her barbarian husband.

"What did I ever do, other than kill your stupid rabbit when I was a child, to make you trust me so little? And not only distrust me enough to refrain from telling me I'm to become a father, but then to put enough trust in everyone else in the Academy to tell them. What part of those actions did you think right, Lizbeth?"

She shivered though she wasn't cold. As a matter of fact, she was so warm, tiny droplets of sweat worked their way down her back. She took a deep breath and kept her eyes riveted on the small tic Adan had suddenly developed on the right side of his mouth. "I meant to tell you, really I did. It was just never the right time."

Adan shook his head, the tic becoming even more pronounced. "You're going to have to do better than that, Lizbeth. How far along are you, and how did you even get pregnant? I thought that spell you females say every day is supposed to prevent that."

She sighed. He really did have a right to know. What she wasn't sure she could do, however, was explain it adequately. "I probably got pregnant the very first time we were...umm, intimate." She held up a hand. "And before you say anything, yes, the PDUP spell usually does prevent that sort of thing from happening, but I didn't plan on sleeping with you that night, remember? And, well, I just plain forgot to cast it. As far as why I didn't tell you as soon as I knew..." Lizbeth hesitated, took another deep breath, then continued. "I was afraid you would send me away."

Adan got a confused look on his face and scratched his head. "Send you away?"

Outside thunder rumbled in the distance, and he shook his head once more. "I wish Lark would stop doing that, it's making me crazy. This evening has been difficult enough without a storm sweeping in."

Heat wicked up Lizbeth's neck until her cheeks burned with it. "It's probably not Lark this time." Her hand protectively slid down to her abdomen. "Our son tends to do that when he gets upset."

"Our son?" Adan's voice gentled, and his face relaxed a bit.

Lizbeth could once more see the little boy he'd been long ago. She wanted to go to him and hold him, but she still had a lot of explaining to do. She stiffened her spine, and her resolve. "I thought if you knew I was with child, you'd send me to Alaria, and I couldn't allow you to do that. It's very important I become an enchantress, Adan, for all of our sakes. I must stay here long enough to learn how to enchant all the talismans of protection."

He looked at her as if he were at least trying to understand. "You don't think I'm barbarian enough to protect us, Lizbeth? Have I really failed so miserably as your husband?"

"No, no, no, no, no, that's not what I mean at all." Lizbeth began pacing. "I have no doubt you can protect us from almost anything, but you can't protect us from evil you can't see, Adan. That takes magic."

Adan laughed, but there was no real humor to the sound. "What evil are you so afraid of? It's time to put away childish fears and grow up. There haven't been monsters for centuries now, and even the dragons you're so afraid of have become mostly docile these days."

He puffed out his chest and rested his hand on his claymore. "I have all the magic I need in the strength of my arm and the steel of my blade. I don't need your help to protect our family. You should be concerning yourself with the running of the household and leaving manly matters, such as protection, to me. Oh, and while I'm thinking about it, there will be no more going back to the dormitory for you. *My* wife and *my* child stays with me, and that's final."

Anger flared and though she should probably not provoke him if she wanted him to see her side, she simply couldn't help herself. "Manly matters? And stay with you? I think not. I've been betrothed to you all my life and not once have you ever protected me from anything. I'm safer in my dorm with virtual strangers. Not only have you not protected me, but you praise those who have done me harm."

For a moment, he looked surprised then his eyes narrowed. "Who has harmed you that I didn't protect you from? Your father? Your brothers? How was I to know if that was the case?"

She wanted to scream. Instead, she calmly looked her husband in the eye. "My father was a wonderful man, and so are my brothers. It was your mother and that horrible instructor you're so fond of, Master Seiger. Do you want to know what he's really like?"

She stiffened her spine and took a deep breathe. "He used to lock me in a trunk if I got an answer about you wrong, and your mother didn't believe me when I told her. She called me a liar."

Lizbeth wrapped both hands across her stomach, and hot tears coursed down her cheeks. She swiped them away. "No one will ever put my child in a trunk, not ever."

Adan's face crumpled. "He locked you in a trunk?"

Lizbeth nodded.

Adan shook his head. "I'd almost believe it of my mother. She's not a nice person, never has been, even to her own children. I've always thought it was a ploy she used to protect herself from being hurt. Her father was a Spiritmaster who was hunted down and executed right before her eyes, you know? She and Grandmother barely escaped and were forced to live in poverty for years. She fears and hates them. But Master Seiger? I know that man better than I do my own father. He'd never harm a fly, let alone lock a little girl in a trunk. Why would you say such a thing?"

He ran a hand through his hair. "Granted, I'm angry that you withheld the fact that we are to become parents, but don't compound your mistake with untruths."

She couldn't breathe. "You don't believe me?"

Again, Adan shook his head. "How can you expect me to believe such a wild story, Lizbeth? If there were even a grain of truth to it, you'd have told someone long before now. I've no choice but to doubt you. Your motivation is obviously an attempt to shift the focus from the fact you betrayed my trust. It's not going to work."

Anger bubbled forth and Lizbeth seethed. Outside lightning streaked across the nighttime sky and thunder boomed overhead.

Adan raised his voice an octave. "I'm sorry Mother has been horrid to you, and you're right, I haven't protected you as I should've. But making up stories about a feeble old man who isn't even here to defend himself isn't going to help the situation. A relationship must be built on trust if it's to survive. You didn't even trust me enough to tell me about the baby. How on Albrath can I trust anything else you have to say now?"

Lizbeth stared, so stunned she could hardly respond. "So, that's how it's to be? I finally gather enough courage to confide in you and you think I'm lying?" Tears burned her eyes and throat. "Well, then, if you don't believe me, why don't you just go ask him? He seemed very proud of his techniques at the time. I have no doubt he'd be glad to regale you with the tale."

Adan glared at her and Lizbeth forced herself not to cower.

"Perhaps I will do just that." Adan huffed. "God Draka knows I need to get out of here before we both say more we'll regret." He shook his finger at her. "But, know this, my lady, when I get back, we're going to sit down and have a rational conversation. I won't tolerate being betrayed, mistrusted, or lied to ever again, Lizbeth. I'd rather live alone."

He headed toward the door. "Perhaps a few turns of the hourglass alone is just what we both need. What's really important to you, Lizbeth? Your silly magic nonsense and keeping secrets or your marriage? If you can't trust me enough to take care of us without magic, if you can't trust me enough not to deceive me at every turn, if you can't trust me enough not to make up ridiculous stories, then this marriage is doomed."

He turned back toward her for just a instant. "Oh, and Lizbeth? If you know what's good for you, I'd better not have to go searching for you when I do get back. You better be waiting right here."

The door slammed behind him, but Lizbeth didn't care. She was too hurt, too angry.

Raising her voice to make sure he or anyone who cared to listen heard, she shouted, "Trust goes both ways, Adan Hammerstrike. And you just watch. I'll go wherever I please. I'll do whatever I want, and I'll be whatever I want to be. You don't own me."

## Chapter Fifteen

A darkness enveloped Adan that even the candles sprinkled about Master Seiger's manor house couldn't hold at bay. So it was true after all. Not that he had completely doubted his wife, for he hadn't, but nothing could have prepared him for the extent of the nightmare Lizbeth had lived through. She'd been telling the whole truth, and his beloved Master Seiger was a monster.

No, more than a monster. He was a demon straight from the pits of fire in The Valley of Torment. If the man wasn't so frail he was in danger of a strong wind snapping his bones in two, Adan would have choked the life from him with his own bare hands.

He sat stiffly, facing his old master and wiped unfamiliar moisture from his cheeks. Had really only a scant number of turns of the hourglass passed since he'd left her all alone in his room at the Academy and walked away? It felt more like a lifetime since he'd hurried to the stables, mounted his steed, headed for the portal to Alaria, and come to the only place he'd ever truly belonged—his home. He'd needed to see for himself if what Lizbeth had said was true, and now, he almost wished he hadn't.

Once more the white-haired old man laughed. "Ah, those were the days. The girl was hopeless, and not fit to be your wife in the first place. I'm not sure how the Queen expected me to be a miracle worker. After all, one must start with quality stock in order to produce anything near exceptional. The little half-elf brat couldn't even remember your favorite dessert most days, let alone the name of any new pet. She obviously wasn't very bright, especially for eight."

Adan fisted his hands in his lap and held himself rigidly straight. Knowing, that if he let his guard down for even the time it would take for a single grain of sand to sift through the hourglass, he'd smash the old man's face in. He couldn't do that...yet. He needed to hear this. He needed to hear it all.

"I wiped the defiant smirk off her face in short order, however." Master Seiger chuckled. "I made her stay in that trunk until I could no longer hear her incessant whimpers. On many occasions, she'd disgustingly wet and soiled herself, and even though the stench was horrid on my refined sensibilities, I refused to allow her to bathe until she could recite the entire Hammerstrike lineage without flaw."

Adan couldn't breathe, and if the man sitting before him didn't finish his tale soon, he wouldn't be breathing either.

"Perhaps I should've listened to the Queen and spent even more time with your little betrothed. As it was, it took more sessions than it should've even to begin to break her spirit and make her pliable to the Queen's wishes." The old instructor sighed heavily. "And in the end, I'm not sure I completely succeeded."

Master Seiger's eyes gleamed with insanity, and a twisted smile contorted his already weathered face. "But you were worth every moment I was forced to be in young Lizbeth's presence, my lord. I swore I'd not fail my future king and I didn't. No, my sweet prince, you deserved only the best efforts I could put forth."

Adan shuddered, unable to listen to another word. For him. Because of him. All the evil done to Lizbeth had been due to his mother and this crazy, wicked old man's misguided loyalty. No wonder Lizbeth didn't trust him, couldn't trust him. He was surprised she didn't hate him. VoT, she probably did. Would he ever be able to earn her trust, her love? He didn't think there was a grain of hope.

Pesky moisture dripped down his cheeks, and once more, he swiped at it with the back of his hand. Here he had gone and allowed himself to fall in love with his wife, and now it was all for naught. Lizbeth was more essential to his well-being than his next breath. And not just her, but now their child, their son. And their relationship was doomed.

He shook his head. Oh, God Draka, because of him.

No, he could no longer blame Lizbeth for not trusting him. And he certainly didn't blame her for seeking some kind of magical protection or for keeping secrets. He didn't even blame her if she never wanted to lay eyes on him again. He knew he'd have a hard time looking himself in the mirror come the new day.

He stood and straightened his tunic. Though morning was all but upon him, he had to get back to the Academy, back to Lizbeth as quickly as he could. He wouldn't let her down this time. Even if he arrived late, he had to be there when she took her end-of-semester exam. Then, he'd find a way somehow to begin making up for the injustices she'd suffered because of him. Even if it took the rest of their lives, he vowed he'd prove to her he was worthy of her trust and, hopefully, her love.

He looked one last time at the man he'd once so admired and a bone deep coldness filled him. "Don't be here when I return, or I'll kill you with my bare hands. I don't care where you go or what happens to you when you get there. Just make sure I never again set eyes on your face again."

Master Seiger gasped. "What? I don't understand. Why would you be angry with me? Everything I did, I did for you. You can't send me away. I have nowhere else to go."

Adan turned and tripped over the edge of a rug he didn't notice. Since when had Alaria become so VoT damp? Especially this time of the year. Usually by now, the entire countryside was frozen solid. Moisture once more dripped down his cheeks, and he wiped it away.

"For me? You did this for me?" Adan shook his head. "Perhaps that was your intention, but what you did, you did more because you and my mother are sick and you both enjoy torturing those too weak to defend themselves.

"I don't care where you go," he shouted. "I'd better never again hear your voice or see your face. For if I do, I swear, I'll shove *your* stupid ass into one of those fucking trunks and lock it down tight. The only difference being, that even after you shit and piss yourself, I'll be nice enough not to open it and let you out only to repeat the process over and over again. I'll simply bury your filthy carcass so deep, even a sick prick like yourself won't be able to claw his way free."

Adan's last thought before bounding up the stairs and heading back to the portal was *With as wet as this night has become, it's a good thing full-grown barbarian men don't cry.*

****

Her eyelids opened to the sensation of sandpaper scraping raw flesh. The bright sunlight burned her retinas, but Lizbeth forced herself to squint and face the morning anyway. Her head pounded, her throat hurt, her stomach threatened to empty itself, and every muscle in her body ached.

Sunshine, really? The windows of Adan's chamber were inundated with the bright stuff. How could the sun dare shine today of all days when cloudy rain filled skies would be so much more appropriate? As if to prove her point, tears flooded her eyes, spilled over her lids, and made a path down her cheeks. Somewhere in the distance, Lizbeth heard the first rumblings of thunder.

She sighed as dark clouds obscured the offending sun. With a hiccup and a groan, she gave in to her sorrow and allowed it to take her where it would.

After the evening before, Lizbeth was surprised to find she still had tears left to cry. Last night hadn't been the first time in her life she'd cried herself to sleep, but it had been the first time she felt truly and totally alone in the world.

She indulged her self-pity, and the tears fell fast and hard. Her parents were dead. Her brothers were miles and miles away, and Adan, no matter where he was, was now beyond her reach. He didn't believe her, he no longer wanted her, and he hadn't bothered to return to his room for a single moment since the door had slammed closed behind him. Even though in the end, she'd done as he asked and waited.

A fluttering like butterfly wings from inside

183

stopped the tears, and brought a small smile to her face. Lizbeth placed the palm of her hand across her slightly rounded tummy. "Guess I'm not totally alone, after all, am I? It's you and me, little Spiritmaster. Time to stop this foolishness, get out of this bed, and get on with our lives. We have an exam to take."

\*\*\*\*

She followed a group of frazzled-looking students up two flights of stairs and around a corner. Lizbeth had never been on this floor or even in this part of the castle. There had never been a reason before today.

The hallway was long and winding, the walls a warm butter-cream, the carpets below her feet a rich walnut. Soft, lilting music flooded her senses and, like a drug, filled her with the beginnings of serenity and contentment, calming for the moment her frayed nerves. Then, she saw the notices on each door, and her heart rate and breathing sped as if she were in a race. The doors were plainly marked. 502, Mystic finals. 504, Minstrel's finals. 506, Sorcerer finals. 508, Warrior finals. 510, Healer finals.

She hesitated for a moment between rooms 510 and 512, where Wizard finals were in progress, and contemplated going inside even though her own Wizard final wasn't scheduled until tomorrow. The thought of either Briar or Lark giving her a smile of encouragement, if nothing else, was almost irresistible. To disrupt another class's finals would draw even more attention to herself, however, and after last night, attention was the last thing Lizbeth wanted.

On down the hallway she went, and the further she walked, the harder her heart pounded. At room 514, where Rogue and Ranger finals were taking place, she broke into a sweat. By the time she walked the few steps to room 516, the Druid finals, she was ready to turn and bolt, but stubbornly put one foot in front of the other.

Finally, she stood in front of the door to room 518 and stared at the Enchanter finals placard for the space of seventy-four heartbeats and six breaths before she could tell herself, *I can do this*, and believe it. Then, she mustered her courage and stepped inside.

A moment later, she truly did almost turn and flee. At the front of the room, seated beside Headmistress Seychelle, was Queen Allanna Hammerstrike herself. A backdrop of floor-to-ceiling windows illuminated her every feature. Today, as was her custom, she was dressed in all white. A smirk hardened her features as her eyes met Lizbeth's.

The sight of Queen Allanna's impressively swollen nose told Lizbeth in no uncertain terms there would be VoT to pay. Shivers skittered down her spine. What retribution did the Queen have in store for her? For Lizbeth would pay, of that she had no doubt.

There was no more time to contemplate the matter, however, as the Headmistress spoke. "Welcome to Enchanter 101 finals, class. As you can see, four stations have been set up and you will be taking turns performing today's enchantment."

Lizbeth glanced at the tables, and her name was on the third one. She groaned. She had hoped to have been in one of the later sets of students. It would've been nice to have had the chance to watch at least one full group perform the spell before her turn.

The Headmistress's next words made her forget about turns. "Queen Allanna was gracious enough to come early and set out all the materials you'll need for today's exam, except of course for your dragon's scale. For doing this task for you, please show her your deepest gratitude when the exam is over."

Ray chose that moment to jump up and down with his tongue lolling to and fro, but luckily he didn't shout his favorite phrase. The class giggled at his antics, but sobered as Headmistress Seychelle merely patted him on the head and continued.

"One more comment before you begin. This enchantment recipe is very specific. When it says one pinch of this or a certain number of drops of that, it's extremely important you use only what is called for. As with all magic, there can be disastrous results if you don't follow the spell's directions precisely. And you will most assuredly fail this exam. It is imperative you pay attention to detail."

The Headmistress clapped her hands. "Come now, first group to your stations. Let's not keep the entire class waiting."

The smooth, wooden table was just a little higher than her waist, and Lizbeth marveled at the array of ingredients neatly situated on its surface. One by one, she examined them.

First, a small amber bottle with a label that simply read *Manna Oil* caught her eye. She picked it up, felt its warmth, and set it back in its place. Next, there was an olive green decanter labeled *Essence of Life*. She tipped it and shiny silver flakes floated into the palm of her hand. Lizbeth quickly put them back.

A small, dark, and intricate box sat next to the decanter, and she picked it next. Etched into its surface were the words *Blood of the Ancients*. She opened it and peeked inside. Small grains of what looked to be red sand shifted back and forth. She snapped it shut and put it down.

Finally, only one ingredient remained, and Lizbeth lifted the tiny burlap bag of *Spirit Herbs* into her hands and held it to her nose. The pungent smell of Bohe and Muxiang made her sneeze. She set it back in its place. Taking the midnight blue scale from the pocket of her tunic, she put it with the other ingredients.

Turning over the single sheet of parchment on the table, Lizbeth began reading.

*To Bring a Scaled Creature Back to Life.*

*1: Grind a small section of the creature's scale with your pestle until it is a fine powder and set it to the side.*

*2: Into the mortar, add—*

Lizbeth squinted her eyes. The parchment was smudged, and she couldn't tell for sure if it was three or eight drops of Manna Oil she was supposed to add.

*3: Mix in twenty...*

Lizbeth blinked twice and tried again but couldn't tell if the recipe called for twenty-three or twenty-eight grains of Blood of the Ancients. She looked toward her mother-in-law, and from the evil smile she was granted, Lizbeth had no doubt her recipe had been tampered with. She shivered though the room was extremely hot. How was she going to accomplish this task if she couldn't even read the spell? She coughed once and cleared her throat.

"Headmistress Seychelle, would it be possible to get a new copy of the spell please? It seems this one is smudged, and I'm having difficulty making out ingredient amounts."

Seychelle opened her mouth to speak, but the Queen beat her to it.

"Always wanting special consideration, aren't you, Lizbeth?" Queen Allanna Hammerstrike sighed. "I swear, Seychelle, my dear friend, if she weren't my very own daughter-in-law, I don't know what I'd do with her. I realize you probably only allowed her in this class in the first place out of consideration for me, but I won't permit her to take advantage of your kindness."

The Queen turned until she was looking directly at Headmistress Seychelle. "I set out those ingredients and spells with my own hands. There was nothing wrong with hers. She most likely spilled something on it, clumsy girl. There's a reason barbarians don't make good enchanters. I say make her use what she was given like everyone else or accept her failure."

Headmistress Seychelle nodded. "She's correct, Lizbeth, everyone was given the same materials to work with. I can't show favoritism. You'll have to use what's before you."

Lizbeth gulped and glanced back at the parchment.

*4: Add a generous pinch of Spirit Herbs to your mixture.*

*5: Quickly stir in one tablespoon of ground creature scale.*

*6: Into your hand, sprinkle flakes of Essence of Life and gingerly, so as not to bruise them, and one at a time, add—*

Again Lizbeth fought to see the real number under the smudge. It was either a three, an eight, a nine, or even a two. Tears threatened, and she swiped them away before they had the chance to fall.

She concentrated hard on the last part of the spell.

*7: Mix together thoroughly while chanting these words.*

*Though from scales of time or creature scales, bring forth life and let it not fail.*

*Essence and oils, herbs and sand, sprinkle of scale dust held in your hand.*

*Life for a moment or life everlasting, it's the choice you make while you're casting.*

Off to her right, Lizbeth heard a whoop and quickly looked in that direction. There, floating no more than a few inches above the dark-elf student's mortar and pestle was a tiny pink dragon. It flittered one way and then another until, finally with a poof, it was gone.

Headmistress Seychelle clapped her hands. "Excellent, excellent. That's precisely what I'm looking for, good job, Deedra. You pass."

Lizbeth looked back at the table before her, picked up her scale, and got busy grinding. She heard the door open and close and, for a moment, didn't bother looking up from her spell. Then, a shiver scampering down her spine and a sudden ache filling her chest told her all she needed to know.

Slowly, she lifted her face and turned to gaze at her husband. He had come to her exam. Why? He looked as if he hadn't slept any more than she had, and even though she doubted he would welcome it, she longed to go to him, wrap her arms about him, and kiss his worry lines away.

She didn't do that though. Instead, his angry words of the night before came rushing back to haunt her, and her feet refused to move. She forced the sob threatening to burst from her chest back down where no one would ever hear it and concentrated on the work before her.

He didn't believe her, he didn't trust her, he didn't want her, and he would never truly love her for who she was. He had probably only come here today to watch her fail. Well, she wouldn't give him or his mother the satisfaction.

The way things stood right now, the most she could hope for in life was to become the best enchantress she could be, and that meant successfully completing this spell. It had to be enough to make up for the coming years of her lonely, loveless marriage.

Taking a deep breath, Lizbeth said a quick prayer to Lord Draka and decided more was hopefully the better choice as she settled on what amounts of what she'd use.

Her hands were shaking as she allowed eight drops of Manna Oil to drip into the mortar, and she held her breath as she carefully counted out precisely twenty-eight grains of Blood of the Ancients and added them.

The human to her left shrieked, jumped backwards, lost her balance, and landed with a thud on the floor. Above the frightened girl's mortar and pestle floated a blob of green flesh with a head that looked somewhat dragonish with razor-sharp teeth, two tails, and six legs. It spun around three times as if seeking its creator, snapped its jaws loudly, then poofed.

Lizbeth trembled and let out the breath she'd been holding.

Headmistress Seychelle pointed to the still cowering girl. "Students, now that's what we call *You've failed Enchanter 101.* When I said precise measurements, I meant just that. If there's room, perhaps you can retake my class next semester. For now, please remove yourself from my sight, young lady. "

The girl scurried away, the sound of sobs fading in her wake.

Lizbeth fought the urge to follow her classmate through the door, wishing to be anywhere but here. Staring at her mortar, her pestle, and her spell, she sighed and did the only thing she could think to do. She continued.

Into the mixture of Manna Oil and Blood of the Ancients, she added a pinch of Spirit Herbs and quickly stirred in a heaping teaspoon of creature's scales. Next, and one at a time, she added six flakes of Essence of life. The mixture began to swirl and boil.

Lizbeth chanced a quick glance over her shoulder at Adan, and the thumbs-up and smile he awarded her not only surprised her, but caused her eyes to mist with tears. With a new lightness to her heart and a flick of her wrist, she grasped the pestle and began stirring as she quietly recited the words of the spell.

*"Though from scales of time or creature scales, bring forth life and let it not fail.*

*Essence and oils, herbs and sand, sprinkle of scale dust held in your hand.*

*Life for a moment or life everlasting, it's the choice you make while you're casting."*

## Chapter Sixteen

The hair on the back of Lizbeth's neck stood, and her fingers tingled as her entire body felt electrically charged. She tried to let go of the pestle but her fingers wouldn't—or couldn't—obey her command. Then, with a loud pop, followed by gasps throughout the room and finally stunned silence, it was there.

Her mouth gaped open as she slowly backed away from the table. It wasn't a dragon, or at least it didn't look like any dragon Lizbeth had ever seen. The only thing familiar about this creature was its color. A very deep, dark, midnight blue. The same blue as the scale she'd used. And it had those same scales now covering it from head to toe.

It was the head to toe part of the beast that really surprised her. It stood at least a head taller than the loftiest barbarian she'd ever seen. Thick, huge horns curled up and out from the top of its head, ending in needle-sharp tips.

The thing's face appeared almost humanoid, except its eyes were wide set with wild-looking, blood-red, bulging orbs. At the same time, its nose was not much more than two gaping, nearly flat, slits. Its nostrils flared as it sucked in air, and a growl constantly rumbled through its bared, fang-like teeth.

Its shoulders were broad, its arms muscular. Both hands boasted sharp, talon-like claws, and its long legs ended in cloven hooves. A whip-like, demonic-looking tail flicked to and fro from its backside, making a whooshing sound, as scale-covered wings, so long they dragged on the floor, protruded from between its shoulder blades.

It was the scariest creature Lizbeth had ever seen, and it didn't look for a moment as if it had any intention of poofing like the two previous student's creations had. As a matter of fact, a moment later, it spread its wings, gave a hair-raising screech, turned, and flew directly over Headmistress Seychelle's head and straight through the large windows behind her and the Queen.

Shards of glass rained, and Lizbeth covered her head with her hands and braced herself for impact. She was more than a little surprised when Adan's arms surrounded her, and pulled her safely out of the way. It was the most welcoming feeling she could imagine.

After long moments, the last of the sharp little window pieces tinkled to the floor, and then there was silence. Quiet as death, dark as midnight, as empty as a void, silence.

It didn't last long.

Headmistress Seychelle screamed. "How many flakes of Essence of Life did you use? Tell me quickly."

Lizbeth shrunk back even further into Adan's embrace, and stuttered. "Sa…sa…six."

The Headmistress's eyes looked ready to pop. "Six! The recipe called for three. This is bad. This is very bad." Her eyes glazed as she tried to calculate, her fingers moved frantically. After a moment, she stilled. "Thank God Draka you didn't use nine. The thing would've been virtually immortal if you had. As it is, it'll be almost impossible to kill."

Lizbeth's voice cracked. "Kill? What have I created?"

Ray jumped up and down pointing toward the broken window, yelling at the top of his lungs. "Nogard, nogard, nogard!"

Bile rose. It couldn't be, could it? Nogards were extinct and had been since shortly after humans arrived on this world with their magical weapon centuries ago. It wasn't possible. She couldn't have created something so vile, so hideous, so dangerous. Could she?

Taking two deep breaths, she lifted her face toward Headmistress Seychelle, ready to accept the fact she'd failed her enchanter final miserably. But it wasn't the Headmistress she saw. She couldn't take her eyes off Ray.

The little man ran in circles at his mistress's feet and continued shouting the word *nogard* without any end in sight. Lizbeth shook her head and shuddered. Of the limited vocabulary she'd come to expect being uttered from Ray's lips, *nogard* certainly hadn't been one of words. A weird, disjointed nostalgia came over her, and she wondered if she'd just lost her mind.

Lizbeth knew in her heart, she would forever prefer "Ray loves cock" over his crazed shouts of "Nogard, nogard, nogard" any day of the week.

****

Adan lifted Lizbeth into his arms, cradled her close to his heart, and turned to leave.

"Just where do you think you're going?" the queen shouted. "Put that...that woman down this instant. She must be made to answer for what she's done. It's only right."

Adan turned and glared at his mother. "I'm taking *Lizbeth*, my pregnant *wife,* back to our room and no one better get in my way."

"But don't you see?" the queen sputtered. This is your chance, Adan. Now you have a perfectly valid reason to rid yourself of her. To start fresh, with someone worthy. Turn her over to the magistrates, dear heart. Let them dispose of your…little problem."

Adan shook his head. "Your depth of abhorrence astounds me, Mother. But then I'm not sure why it should. You thrive on hatred, need it to sustain you." He looked her straight in the eye, not wanting there to be any doubt left in her mind as to the meaning of his words. "I know what you did, what you were a part of. I spoke with Master Seiger. I'll never forgive you, and if I had my way, I'd never set eyes on you again."

The queen gasped. "How can you say such a thing to me? How dare you choose," Queen Allanna pointed a finger toward Lizbeth, "the likes of…her over your own mother. Everything I've ever done, I've done for you."

If he could've managed a chuckle, he would've, though he found nothing remotely funny about the situation. "So I've been told" was all he could force between his lips before the desperate need to either kill his own mother or flee took over. Adan didn't say another word; he simply walked out with his wife in his arms, and no one tried to stop him this time.

The trip back down the corridor, and the path to their room and through the door into their bedchamber became no more than a blur. It didn't matter. He tucked her in their bed and cradled her in his arms.

"Make love to me, Adan. I need...I need you. I'm so numb inside. I need to know I'm still alive." Lizbeth pleaded.

His cock leapt in response, and his balls tightened. She didn't speak another word, and he didn't prompt her to. There would be plenty of time for conversation later. Years and years stretching endlessly for them to remember just what had been done to her and why.

Though his lovely young wife would probably never be able to forget the torture she'd endured because of him, let alone ever entrust him with her heart, he'd gladly take whatever she had to offer. It would have to be enough.

After all, she did admit she needed him. It was a start. Wasn't it?

She needed the comfort his body could give her, she needed his touch, she needed his protection, and their child needed his name. For now, that would suffice.

Slowly, Adan kissed her closed eyelids. "Your wish is my command, my lady."

She shivered in his arms, and the vibrations shot straight through his soul. A sigh escaped as her lips rose seeking his, and he was powerless to do anything but surrender his mouth to her kiss. Sweeter than honey, warmer than sunshine, fresher than the constant breeze blowing off the peaks of the Alarian mountain range she tasted, and he savored her.

Despair settled over him. God Draka, he loved his wife. How was he ever going to survive not having that love returned?

"Adan?" Lizbeth's voice trembled. "I'm so sorry about...everything. Can you ever forgive me?"

His arms tightened about her, and he nuzzled her neck. "There's nothing to forgive, love. You did nothing wrong, and I should've never doubted your word. It won't happen again, I promise. It's I who needs to beg your forgiveness."

She opened her mouth to speak, but Adan shushed her. "Later, after. Right now, please let me show you what I can't seem to find the words for."

Her skin was as molten silk, warm, alive, subtle, and responsive. Her nipples pebbled against his chest, and her nails scored his back as his hand journeyed toward its destination. Her clit was already swollen, and her pussy slick and ready as he pushed her thighs wide and entered her.

Though he'd been born a prince and from the moment of that birth had known he'd someday be king, for the first time in his life, Adan knew without a doubt, where he belonged. At this woman's side, joined forever.

\*\*\*\*

The loud banging of a gavel against smooth wood sounded more like the heralding of the end of her life, than it did the calling to order of a meeting. Lizbeth couldn't help but flinch, even though she'd been expecting that exact sound for two full days.

The room quieted, and Adan's warm hand encircling hers bolstered Lizbeth's courage as nothing else could have. She took a deep breath, lifted her eyes, and faced the Council.

Two days, that's how long it had taken Headmistress Seychelle to not only inform the governing body of Albrath and the Council of Elders of the nogard situation, but also to amass the council all in one place.

Lizbeth shuddered as she remembered the Headmistress's tirade later that very afternoon when she'd stomped into Adan's room and demanded to be heard.

"Oh, my God Draka, what've you done? I'll tell you what you've done. Fail…fail, that's what. I have already sent a missive to alert Uthiel Dragonheart. Being the leader of the Protectors of the Dragons, he'll know what to do. I've informed him that a dragon killer is once more on the loose. One who won't stop until every dragon in Albrath is dead. This is a catastrophe, a disaster of epic proportion. Didn't you realize what could happen when you decided to create a nogard? The end of dragons, that's what could happen, and with the extinction of dragons comes the loss of all magic. They are linked as everyone knows, completely and irrevocably linked. I must summon the council immediately. There will be repercussions and consequences. Of that, have no doubt."

The Headmistress's words had been followed by two long days of Lizbeth being confined to her quarters with Adan, which wouldn't have been such a bad thing except, though he'd held her and made love to her so tenderly her heart was bursting with words to share with him, he'd been unusually quiet and withdrawn. Reluctant to discuss anything more substantial than the weather.

Lizbeth felt so guilty they'd barely spoken more than a few words to each other. All she could think about was the why of it all. Had she somehow unconsciously created the nogard because of her fear of dragons? She didn't think so, but what if?

To make matters even worse, guards had been placed at her door and she hadn't been allowed to step so much as an inch outside to take in a breath of fresh air or feel raindrops upon her face. Even the balcony had been padlocked for fear of her escape.

Other than Adan's wonderful lovemaking sessions, the only things that had made the last two days bearable were the visits by Lark, Briar, and Laycee. But with the visits had come a whole new set of concerns.

It had been two tedious, frustrating days of hearing all kinds of rumors and not being able to defend herself to anyone except her closest friends. Adan assured her he believed in her and so did Lark and Briar, but it was the wild stories she couldn't get past. Everything from "Lizbeth created the nogard because of her deep-seated fear of dragons and she wanted them all dead" to "she knew her own magical ability was so pitiful she would rather have all magic leave the world than be exposed for the fraud of an enchanter she was."

There had even been talk that she had produced the nogard to make her husband and his family, especially the Queen, look as if they were part of some kind of conspiracy. There had also been rumors of the thing being fashioned for barbarian political gain and speculations of war.

Yes, Lizbeth was ready to face the council. It was past time to put the rumors to rest.

Adan squeezed her hand and Lizbeth's heart lurched. Though he stood at her side and had since the horrible mishap, the easy-going camaraderie they'd finally begun to share before he'd found out about the baby and Master Seiger's vile nature was gone. More often than not, he quickly averted his gaze whenever she caught him glancing her way. And though he no longer doubted what she'd said about Master Seiger and swore he was happy about becoming a father, the carefree conversations they'd enjoyed had been replaced with long sighs and mostly silence. It was as if the entire past semester at the Academy hadn't happened, and they were back to being strangers once again.

## Chapter Seventeen

"Are you prepared to explain yourself to this council and accept our judgment, young lady?"

Lizbeth gazed at the speaker.

Arizon Windstrider, great uncle to Sarco Sunwalker and the high-elf wizard responsible for single-handedly ending the Castle Kuropkat war long ago, was a sight to behold. He glared down at her, and she tried her best to smile, but her face refused to cooperate.

The leader of the council, with his white beard so long it nearly touched the ground, looked every moment of his almost nine hundred years. The passage of time showed plainly on his wrinkled, weathered face. Even the man's pointed ears drooped like the rest of his body. Some of those years hadn't been kind.

"Yes, sir," was all Lizbeth was capable of squeaking out.

The old wizard tapped his foot. "Well, get on with it then and get to explaining. These are serious charges you face, young lady."

Lizbeth cleared her throat, and the sound of it reverberated through the drafty hall. "It was an accident, sir. A horrible accident. It was never my intention to create a nogard. I didn't know any part of such a creature still existed before the other day. I truly thought the scale I found in the library's basement for my enchanter final exam was from a dragon, and my spell instruction parchment, well...it was smudged and..."

She made eye contact with each of the twelve members of the council before continuing. "I would never do anything to endanger anyone or anything on purpose. I swear I wouldn't."

As if in stereo, two voices, one belonging to an unfamiliar male and one to a very familiar female, rang out at the same time from opposite sides of the hall. "Liar!"

Once again, Wizard Arizon Windstrider struck his gavel on the block of wood. "Silence. There will come a time for discussion once the lass has her say."

Queen Allanna didn't heed the leader of the Council of Elder's warning. "I'll not be silent. She did this wicked deed on purpose, I tell you. She's trying to blemish my good family's name, turn my son against me, and tarnish his reputation. An annulment should be issued immediately. There should have never been a marriage to begin with. She's obviously below him. Lock her away in a tower, or better yet, chain her in a dungeon. She's evil and deserves to be punished. Not only does she deserve to be punished and set aside, but as queen of the Barbarians, I demand it."

Lizbeth closed her eyes tight to prevent the tears beneath her lids from falling. She opened them a moment later, however, as the gavel hit the block of wood so hard it split in two.

"I said silence!" Arizon roared as he looked directly at King Alfred. "If you can't control your wife, sir, I shall be forced to control her for you." He then turned his gaze to Adan. "Is what your mother says true? Do you wish an annulment from this girl?"

Lizbeth's heart pounded, and her hands sweated, though he'd touched her and had held her as if he loved her, she wasn't sure what Adan might say.

"No, sir," was the extent of his answer.

She had no sooner let out the breath she'd been holding when the unfamiliar male voice piped up once more. "Yout might be able to shout down a woman and her spineless husband with yout bluster, Arizon, but it won't work as easily on Krunto. As diplomatic liaison for the troll clans, I have a right to be heard. It's a filthy human, barbarian conspiracy, I'm telling yout. It's obvious to anyone who has eyes in their head, they're in cahoots." He stood and pointed toward Adan.

"Why, it's common knowledge the female's husband is good friends with that Uthiel, the human leader of the Paladins of Albrath, those dragon protectors. It's just one more attempt among many by the humans to get their filthy paws on the Blade of Gin. They know full well it's the only knife sharp enough to kill a nogard."

Krunto sneered. "Let him put his little hussy up to creating all the nasty beasts she wants. It's not going to work. They're not getting it. The Blade of Gin is a historical artifact, and a troll national treasure even if it was the humans who brought it to this world. They must not have valued it much. They tossed it away like garbage when they were done with it.

"It was discovered in the desert outside the Karza Swamps, and it's ours now. We found it fair and square. What do we trolls care about dragons or magic? We have no need of either. Now weapons? That's another story. We value a well-made weapon. The

Blade of Gin is ours and nobody's getting it, no matter what."

Lizbeth stared at Krunto, who was even taller and broader than her husband and shuddered. He had dark green skin, greasy-looking black hair, and thick yellowed tusks. She then glanced at her husband, and her heart filled with apprehension. Adan's face was red and contorted with anger, and the hand he was using to hold hers clenched so tight her fingers were numb.

He looked ready to respond and not with words, so Lizbeth held on tight and gripped the hem of his tunic with her other hand as she desperately tried to explain further in the hopes of avoiding a physical altercation between the troll and her husband.

"There's no conspiracy, I tell you," she yelled. "My husband had no idea. Neither did I until the creature was created. It was simply a horrible mistake. You must believe me."

Krunto bellowed. "Take the word of a barbarian? Especially a barbarian female? Not likely."

Queen Allanna shouted. "She's only half barbarian. I'm sure it's the wood-elf side that can't be trusted, though that's not my son's fault. He's as much of a victim in this as we all are. Not that a troll like you has anything of value to say in the matter."

Adan turned toward his mother. "Shut up, Mother! I stand by Lizbeth. There was no conspiracy, and she's no liar." He then turned and faced the troll. "You, sir, have insulted my wife. I would be glad to settle our differences in the arena. When this proceeding is over, we should let our swords declare who is just."

Krunto sneered again. "Oh, you't like that wouldn't yout? To slay a diplomat for merely stating his opinion?

How typical, how barbaric. I would expect nothing less from the likes of yout."

Once more, the sound of the gavel reverberated through the hall. "I said silence!"

Queen Allanna laughed. "Oh, I see how it is. You let the troll have his say but when——"

Wizard Arizon stretched out his hand, and a blinding light shot from the tip of his wand. The Queen grasped her throat, and her mouth opened and closed like a fish, but no sound came forth. She stomped her feet, poked her husband repeatedly in the arm, pointed angrily toward the wizard, and even gestured at Lizbeth, but still not even a syllable could be heard. King Alfred patted her hand.

Arizon calmly spoke. "I will have silence."

Even Krunto sat down.

Arizon nodded toward Lizbeth. "You said your spell parchment was smudged. Why didn't you simply ask for another?"

Lizbeth cringed as she wrung her hands together. "I did ask, but as it had been my mother-in-law, the Queen, who had set out the supplies for the exam, even the parchments, it was declared I must use what I had been given."

The wizard turned toward the Queen, who was still grasping her throat, and glared.

Lizbeth quickly explained. "Please don't misunderstand. I'm not trying to blame anyone else for my actions. I take full responsibility. If I'd known what was about to happen, I would've gladly taken the failure before creating that monster. I swear I would've."

Arizon nodded slowly. "And the scale? Are you

asking this council to believe you didn't know it to be something other than a dragon scale?"

She opened her mouth to speak, but from the back of the hall, Lizbeth heard a squeaky gnome voice.

"The lass wasn't the one ta find the scale. It was me. There were four of us down there in the library basement hunting for dragon scales that day, and ya can ask any one of them. I'm the one who found it. None of us thought for a minute it was anything but a dragon scale. So, if'n ya wanna punish someone for that mistake, it's gonna have ta be me, or find out who stored the damnable thing in the basement in the first place."

She could have kissed Laycee.

The weathered old wizard turned toward the rest of the council and, in hushed tones, spent the next few moments in discussions. Lizbeth wondered why she was so light-headed then realized she was once again holding her breath. With a whoosh, she let it out just as Arizon nodded toward the council and turned back to her.

The stern look he gave her did nothing to calm the herd of Alarian water buffalo stampeding through her belly, and it certainly didn't help to wet the desert her mouth had become.

Then he winked.

She didn't know why, but that single act of kindness made her want to cry more than anything else that had transpired over the last couple of days, and she almost did.

Arizon cleared his throat, and the drop of a single grain of sand could have been heard in the hall.

"We've reached a decision. It is the finding of this

council that the enchanter student, Lizbeth Hammerstrike, did not create a nogard on purpose during her final exam."

Happy shouts mixed with angry unbelieving ones. Lizbeth could manage nothing but to stare at the wizard as she reached with her free hand and held closed her mouth. Her jaw had become as rubbery as her knees.

Arizon raised his wand, and the room immediately quieted. "The council has spoken. We are in the positions we are because we're good at reading people and situations. We believe her, it's that simple. That doesn't mean there aren't still repercussions for her actions, accident or not. And there is still a nogard out there that must be dealt with. Above all, the dragons and the magic they bring to Albrath must be protected."

Arizon pointed at Lizbeth, and her heart pounded hard in her chest. "Expelled. That is the ruling of this council. You are to be expelled from the Academy of Magical Arts until such a time the nogard has been dealt with."

A boney finger shook toward Adan. "As her husband, the responsibility falls on your shoulders to hunt the beast down and kill it. We realize you don't have access to the Blade of Gin, so we suppose you'll simply have to improvise or do some fancy talking with the troll leaders. Whichever it is, don't return without the nogard's head, Adan Hammerstrike. May God Draka watch over you and keep you safe."

Gasps could be heard throughout the hall. Then a voice Lizbeth knew, but hadn't expected, spoke up. "Quiet, if you please. I have something important to impart."

The Ray who stepped forward no longer resembled

in any way the pet of Seychelle's he'd once been. This Ray was well dressed in a crisp black tunic and pants. Soft-looking, leather shoes were on his feet, and his nails appeared to be recently manicured. His sparse, dark brown hair was neatly slicked back, his face freshly scrubbed, and his tongue was no longer lolling off to the side. In his hands, he held a thick, leather-bound volume, and Lizbeth couldn't help but be surprised by the sight. This must have been what Ray looked like when he'd been Headmistress Seychelle's valued assistant. The little man even stood straighter and appeared taller than he had two days previous.

Ray walked right up in front of Adan and Lizbeth and addressed the council as if it were an everyday occurrence. "The Rules of Fair Engagement plainly state: When dealing with creatures that take magic to confront and defeat, all possible attempts must first be made to capture the beast for further study. It would be wrong to simply hunt down the defenseless animal and slaughter it without regard for what we might learn from it in captivity. This is an opportunity we can ill afford to lose. After all, there is no one living who has had the chance to study a nogard. Must we really throw away the possibility just because we fear what it may do?"

Lizbeth looked back and forth between Ray and Arizon, not liking the interest she saw shining in the old wizard's eyes.

"And, if there ends up being no choice but to kill the poor creature, is procuring the Blade of Gin even a reasonable possibility? All diplomatic avenues would have to be exhausted in the attempt. That would take time. Time the dragons probably don't have. Yes, capture instead of death is the only feasible, responsible plan. If it means sacrificing a barbarian or two along the way to get the job done, so be it."

Fear for Adan filled her heart, and Lizbeth shook her head. She opened her mouth to voice her opinion but didn't get the chance as Ray continued without skipping a beat.

"As far as the student, Lizbeth Hammerstrike, however, you have every right to expel her not for just while the nogard is being dealt with, but for the rest of her miserable life. I wish you would reconsider doing just that. Even if she didn't create the nogard on purpose, she's obviously reckless with her use of magic. There's no place at the Academy for such a lackadaisical attitude. We pride ourselves in being nothing if not professional at all times."

Lizbeth made a strangled, choking sound. Professional? Ray? Perhaps a professional cock-lover, but that was about it.

Adan squeezed her hand.

The old wizard shook his head. "Our judgment concerning the lass is final. As far as the nogard, though, you've made a valid point."

For a moment, he turned his gaze to Adan. "If there is any chance to capture instead of killing the creature, we should explore it. There is much we could potentially learn."

Once more, his eyes sought Ray. "Therefore, it is the decree of this council that you, Raynorel, accompany Prince Adan. See to it every and all opportunities to capture the beast alive have been exhausted before killing it, if you must. Report your findings back to us the moment you return."

The little man turned pale, gulped, and began to stutter. "I-I-I don't think I-I would be a good choice. I-I get motion sickness just stepping through portals. Perhaps I should coordinate things from here."

Arizon shook his head. "I have spoken." He glanced around the hall. "Now, who else among you is willing to pledge yourselves to Prince Adan's plight? I must warn you, though, it could very well be a suicide mission. To attempt to capture or kill a nogard is no easy task even if luck is on your side."

There was a sudden rustle at the back of the hall as Sarco Sunwalker stepped forward and faced his great uncle. "Adan Hammerstrike is friend, brother, and one of the most honorable men I know. I would consider it a privilege to pledge my wand to his service. Also, Uthiel Dragonheart has sent word ahead. His sword is at Adan's disposal. We will ride with the prince."

From the opposite side of the hall, another voice rang out. "What the pink feathers on the oversized hat of an ogre trollop doing a pole dance on a streetlamp are ya talking about, lad? Don't be thinking for a minute any of ya are going nogard hunting without Leeky Shortz!"

Arizon nodded. "It looks like you have plenty of help, Prince Hammerstrike. Good luck. Albrath is counting on you."

The gavel sounded once more. "Meeting adjourned."

## Chapter Eighteen

"It's not a request, Lizard. It's an order. You are to go home."

Lizbeth stood by the window of their room, staring out as the sun began to rise and wishing with all her heart she could stop time. There was too much not said between them and even more misunderstood. In less than a turn of the hourglass, he'd be gone and there might never be another chance to tell him or show him how she really felt. And now, to make matters worse, he just wanted to send her as far away from him as he could.

She straightened her spine and turned to face her husband. "Don't call me Lizard. You know I don't like it. And as far as going home, the only home I have is with you."

Adan shook his head. "I've already told you, you can't go with me, Lizbeth. You are with child, and even if you weren't, it's much too dangerous. You've been expelled from the Academy, so you can't stay here. As I see it, you have only two choices. Either return to Alaria with my parents, which even I don't want you to do, or go home to your brothers until this is over. It's up to you."

She bit her lip. "I can't go to my brothers. They're wonderful people, but they have their own families to care for. There's no place for me there. There hasn't

211

been for some time now."

Adan looked impatient.

She raised her chin an inch. "There's another option, you know. I could go wait for you at Castle Kuropkat with Uthiel, Briar, Lark, and Laycee. Briar did invite me."

He crossed his arms and looked stern. "What part of 'it's too dangerous, and you can't go' don't you seem to comprehend? You know as well as I do the caves surrounding Castle Kuropkat are home to the dragons. Just where do you think the nogard is headed? Have you forgotten already how afraid of dragons you are, let alone the fact you're with child, Lizbeth? Our child? If you care not for your own safety, at least consider his. Or deep down, do you feel about him as you do about me? Just one more thing you're being forced to endure?"

She looked at her husband as if seeing him for the very first time. Could it be true? Did he really think she didn't care? That she simply...endured his presence? "Why would you say such a thing?"

His dark blue eyes shown bright with moisture as his shoulders slumped slightly forward. "How could you not? I know what was done to you in my name, remember?"

Lizbeth wasn't sure if she wanted to cross the space separating them and kick him in the shins for being so stubbornly pigheaded or wrap him in her arms and hold him close. Either way, he wouldn't welcome her show of aggression or affection right this moment. Instead, she took a deep breath, blew it out, gathered her thoughts, and tried once more to convince her husband of her feelings about him and their unborn child.

"I'm not being forced to endure anything. There was a time perhaps that I blamed you, but not now, not anymore. I swear. And as for our son, our child, I love him, Adan, completely and unconditionally with all that I am. If you believe nothing else about me, believe that. I would gladly lay down my life for him."

She did make her away across the room then and gently cupped his face with her hands, forcing him to look her in the eye. "You promised me you wouldn't doubt my word again, remember?"

He nodded.

"Then know this. Our marriage may very well have started out as a duty, but I'm not here because of that reason anymore. I'm in love with you. I'm not sure when it happened or how it happened or even why it did, but it did. I know I haven't said it out loud before now, and I probably should have, and I know I tend to be stubborn and keep things to myself sometimes, but I'm not going to do that anymore. I love you, and I have for some time. I just want to be with you. It's where our child and I belong."

For a moment, his face almost softened, then he scoffed and pulled away. To Lizbeth, it was a slap in the face.

"Don't use my promise against me, Lizbeth, for there are some things that stretch even the bounds of those words. Do you really think saying what you think I want to hear will get you your way? You love me? Don't be ridiculous. Of course, you don't love me. How could you? I'm Queen Allanna's son, Master Seiger's prized pupil.

"I don't believe in such a frivolous thing as love

anymore. And anyway, love is the last thing I'd consider you have for me. I heard every horrid word of what happened to you straight from Master Seiger's filthy mouth. I understand why you were so reluctant to become my wife and why you wanted so desperately to run away to the Academy and why being something, anything, other than the wife of this barbarian prince was so important to you."

She opened her mouth to speak, but Adan raised a hand to silence her.

"I admit, when I thought it was just the killing of your rabbit and those ceaseless Adan Hammerstrike classes you were forced to take that made you dislike me so, I didn't understand. I thought, with time, we would get past it and at least exist in peace. But, if someone had done half to me what Master Seiger, with my mother's blessings, did to you, *because* of me, I wouldn't want to be my wife either. As a matter of fact, I'd want to be as far away from me and my family as I could get."

Tears filled her eyes, and she could tell Adan saw them as he slowly turned away and shook his head. "There's no reason to cry, Lizard. I understand, really I do, and I don't hold it against you. None of this is your fault. There's simply no need to say things you don't mean anymore. Most arranged marriages are like this and have nothing to do with silly ideas such as love. It is what it is." He sighed and his shoulders drooped.

"Look at my parents' marriage. Other than my mother being a complete psycho, it works quite well for them without adding in all those unnecessary, messy emotions. You have nothing to worry about, Lizbeth. And I want you to know, whether I survive the confrontation with the nogard or not, I'll still do my duty by you. I've already seen to it you and our child will be well cared for. I've made up a will. I've secured funds to be made ready at your disposal. Now, let's put this ridiculous love talk behind us, shall we? You need to get busy packing. We both have a long way to travel before this day is done."

She clamped her mouth shut, afraid if she opened it even a fraction of an inch, the sobs she'd been holding at bay would escape and she'd never get them to stop. Somewhere in the distance, thunder rumbled and Lizbeth knew she had to try at least once more to make this man understand. There was no way she could send him off into a danger she herself had created without him knowing on some level she cared deeply for him.

Slowly, she crossed the space between them and stood before her husband. Lifting the hem of her tunic, she pulled it up and over her head. Then she held it out at arm's length and let the only piece of clothing she wore flutter to the floor.

Adan's eyes widened in surprise, and that gave Lizbeth all the courage she needed. If she couldn't convince her husband of her true feelings with words, then she'd let her body do her talking.

He took three steps back. "What do you think you're doing, Lizbeth?"

She smiled and hoped it didn't look as forced as it felt. "Well, you're still my husband, aren't you?"

He nodded as he continued backing up until he was flat against the wall.

She followed. "And you do plan on being gone for what may be an extended period of time, don't you?"

This time he lifted his chin and looked her eye to

eye. "Most probably."

She slid her hands under his tunic and across his chest until she found what she was searching for, his nipples. She tweaked them both and enjoyed his gasp of pleasure. "Then as your wife, I'm demanding my conjugal rights before you go."

He sighed and looked away as if defeated.

Lizbeth genuinely smiled.

"That isn't necessary." Adan smiled. "You're already with child. You've done your duty. You aren't obligated to have sex with me anymore, Lizard. At least not until we want another child, if we ever do. Anyway, look at the time. The sun is almost up, and I wouldn't want to keep Sarco and Leeky waiting in the courtyard. We'll talk more when this is over."

He started to turn toward the door, and Lizbeth stopped him in his tracks with no more than a whisper.

"I wasn't thinking about obligations. I was hoping for a few moments of pleasure in my husband's arms."

\*\*\*\*

Adan closed his eyes for no more than a fraction of a second before reaching for her, and she slipped into his arms as if she really wanted to be there. Soft, warm, willing, and so very much alive. His heart ached in his chest, and he knew beyond any reason, until his dying day, he would want her and be powerless to deny her anything his body could give.

He bent his head and captured her soft sigh upon his lips as she molded herself against him. She tasted of the salt of fresh tears mixed with the intoxicating sweetness that made Lizbeth who she was. His tongue delved deeper into the recesses of her mouth, teasing, tempting, and drinking in her essence. Imprinting upon his memory every taste, every nuance, and every sound that was his wife.

His lips moved upward to the tip of her nose, then kissed each eyelid before finally coming to rest on the crisp point of one of her half-elf ears. Playfully, he nipped it.

She shivered against him. "I need you. I need you inside me, Adan, please."

He was a man undone, as he nearly dropped to his knees right then and there and begged her to really be in love with him. He had wanted to believe it so much when she said it moments ago. His heart still ached from it.

Instead, he silently lifted her into his arms, carried her to their bed, and threw back the coverlet. Gently, he laid her down. Perhaps Lizbeth didn't really love him as he wished and perhaps there would never come a time when she truly could or would, but, at least, in this moment, in this place, she desired him. Adan knew it would have to be enough to sustain him through the coming days.

Her arms lifted toward him as her eyes and fingers beckoned him to join her upon the soft bed. Without hesitation, he stripped off his traveling tunic, breeks, and boots, and did just that.

Her arms and legs wrapped tightly around him, cradling him, and pulling him in close. It was like coming home. This was where he belonged, and the only place he wanted to be. Without preamble, he entered her, and her warmth welcomed him. His powerful thrusts said what words couldn't, and hers answered the questions he'd been too afraid to ask. Perhaps she did care a little. He dared to hope.

Here in her arms, for this short time, there were no nogards or Master Seigers or kingdoms or kings and queens. Only a man, a woman, and an unquenchable need for each other.

He wanted to slow this down, to savor her pussy sheathed about him, to take the time to tease and tantalize her, but he simply couldn't. Never before Lizbeth, had the touch of any woman's hands or the quick little gasps of breaths and feminine moans made during lovemaking had the effect upon him as hers did.

When had fingernails grasping his buttocks, digging in, and holding on for dear life become so erotic? But, oh God Draka, hers were. And why were the little puffs of air rhythmically bombarding his neck causing tingles of excitement to shoot straight down his gut and into his cock? Her mewling moans of pleasure were making him dizzy with delight.

He watched her intently, loving the way her gaze locked with his. Never wavering, not blinking. An equal partner in every way in what they were doing. Equal and full of determination.

He thrust forward fast and hard, and Lizbeth's eyes widened. He did it again, and she grinned. She ran her nails up and down his back, and he gasped. She nipped at a nipple, and he groaned, though not from pain.

Sweat soaked their bodies as the fevered pitch of their lovemaking took both their breaths away. Over and over, they strove to get closer than their undulations could bring them, trying frantically to meld one into another. Each knowing once their climax was reached, and the moment was over, they'd have no choice but to part, perhaps forever.

But this wasn't that moment, not yet anyway.

In a single motion, Adan flipped them over until Lizbeth straddled him. She didn't miss a beat as she slowly rose the full length of his shaft then quickly slid back down, imbedding his shaft inside her. Sparks of light exploded behind his eyes while lightning-fast pleasure shot down his cock, through his spine, and all the way from the top of his head to the tips of his toes. She gave him that little smirk, that look all women gave when they knew they had their man at their mercy.

Adan laughed from the depths of his soul. It was the first genuine sound of joy he'd allowed himself to express for days.

"Like that, did you?" she purred.

All he could manage was a nod.

She tossed her long toffee-colored hair and grinned. "Hmm, would you say I learned at least a little something of value in those Adan Hammerstrike classes after all?" She winked. "Want more?"

His response was more of a growl than an actual word as he slid his hand between them until he found her moist, hard clit. For every upward movement she made, he gave her nub a downward stroke.

Lizbeth's eyes widened, and her nostrils flared. Her skin glistened with a golden peach sheen, and her lips fell open in a silent *oh*, as she began riding him in earnest. He tried to concentrate on pleasuring her first, but just when he thought he was gaining a grain of control, she varied either the speed of her stroke or the depth and he was lost again. Finally, he gave up or gave in, he wasn't sure which, and simply lay back to enjoy the ride.

Adan heard her cry of joy no more than a second before her legs clamped tight about him, and she shuddered. A moment later, his own world exploded with such sweet delight his eyes crossed, his mind went blank, and his thighs quivered.

Slowly, he came back to himself. His breathing calmed, and his heart no longer pounded as if it were a drum. He opened his eyes, and the sight of his well-loved wife with tears shining in her eyes brought moisture to his own. He pulled her into his embrace and held her tight, not wanting her to see his weakness.

"I don't want you to go." She sobbed.

He rocked her gently. "We both know I don't have a choice."

Snuggling her in close to his heart, Adan couldn't help but think it would be easier for both of them without the trauma of actually saying goodbye. So, he held her until her sobs subsided, her breathing evened, and she fell asleep.

He watched her for long minutes, just staring at her face in peaceful slumber and relishing the feel of her in his arms, unable to stop listening to the gentle cadence of the tiny puffs of air she exhaled.

He missed her already.

Sighing, he counted the steady drumming of the pulse at the base of her throat, knowing it matched exactly the rate the grains of sand were sifting through the hourglass. He needed to go. He should already have left. He didn't want to.

As carefully as possible, so as to not wake her, Adan slid his arm out from beneath Lizbeth, stood, and dressed. She didn't stir, and for a moment, he wished she would. It was wrong to leave without saying more. So much between them was still unsettled.

Adan shook his head. What was left to say? He

couldn't very well drop to his knees and declare his love and beg her for hers. After all he'd said earlier, it wouldn't be fair. He turned to leave, took two steps toward the door then turned back. It didn't matter if she could never love him, he needed to at least say something. It might be his last chance.

Kneeling at the bedside, he leaned over and with feather softness brushed her lips with his own. "Goodbye, Lizard. I'll be back as soon as I can, I promise."

Again, he stood then hesitated once more. With something akin to awe, Adan leaned over, placed a quick kiss on her tummy, and whispered, "Your father loves you, little one. Take care of your mother while I'm away. She means the world to me. You're the man of the keep till I get home."

Without another word, he straightened, turned, walked from the room, and closed the door behind him.

## Chapter Nineteen

"You've got to be kidding me." Adan sighed. "Don't you think being saddled with Ray is bad enough? He's going to throw a fit when he learns we're going after the Blade of Gin. We can't be adding kidnapping to our crimes."

Leeky Shortz rolled his eyes and extended his brown leather-clad hand straight out. "Ya might as well talk ta the digits."

Adan shook his head. "Under the circumstances, I can see where you'd think O.T.T. would be useful with his background in historical artifacts and all, but he hasn't done field work in a very long time. He gives lectures and sits behind a desk all day, for God Draka's sake. It's much too dangerous. Not to mention, I'd like to ride back out of Karza with the same body parts I had when I rode in. If you have need of a companion, Leeky, bring along Miss Bunny. She'd be a lot less trouble."

He tried to keep his expression stern as he stared at the little bald-headed man with the wire-rimmed glasses and pencil-thin mustache who was trussed up like a holiday bird across the rump of Leeky Shortz's steed. Adan had the feeling he was failing horribly.

"What the oozing canker sores on the bottom lip of a street-walking ogress deep-throating a dwarf for a platt and change are ya thinking, lad? Of course, we're taking O.T.T. with us." The gnome smiled widely. "Not only is he Albrath's leading expert on historical artifacts like the Blade of Gin, but he knows the newly elected troll magistrate intimately. Who better ta sweet-talk Karla than the man who once won her heart?"

Leeky's smile disappeared. "Anyway, Laycee wouldn't let me out the door with Miss Bunny this time around. Says she needs her ta help with the packing for the trip ta Castle Kuropkat. Can ya believe that? If ya ask me, I think she's developing a mean jealous streak."

O.T.T. slurred his words, and even though Leeky's horse was upwind, the strong smell of mead accosted Adan.

"It's not pronounced *gin* like the drink, ya daft, panty-stealing gnome. It's ga...gin, like begin or hen or fin but with a hard g. And my sister's never been jealous a day...hic...day in her life. And as for you, Adan Hammerstrike, don't ya be looking at me like ya smelled...hic...something bad. This wasn't my idea. I didn't tie myself ta this horse, ya know. I'm the assistant ta the assistant of Gnome/Ogre Affairs, and I'll be missed. Heads will roll...hic...I tell ya. I don't wanna go searchin' for the Blade of Gin with ya."

O.T.T. giggled, but instead of sounding funny, it resonated hysteria. "Anyway, Karla told me ta never come back ta Karza, and I take everything that woman says very seriously. I've only got one testicle left, ya know. Don't mean ta put that one in danger."

Leeky cackled. "As if ya need ta worry about your saggy old testicle. No woman's gonna give ya a second look anyway, so ya don't need it. And don't ya be thinking ya can correct my pronunciation. I'll call it blade of gin or ale or mead or whatever I want."

Adan tried unsuccessfully to rub the ache out from between his eyes. The throbbing pain had begun the moment he'd closed the door on Lizbeth, and had only gotten worse as he'd descended the stairs, walked out into the gray skies of morning, mounted his horse, and ridden into the bailey to meet his friends. "I'm pretty sure it's against the law to get your girlfriend's brother drunk and kidnap him, Leeky. Untie him and let him go."

The gnome shook his head. "Not gonna do it. You'll thank me later."

Ray rode up that moment, overhearing Adan's statement. He flipped through a shiny, new-looking leather notebook and made an entry. "I'm positive you'd be breaking at least one law, if not a few, by attempting to take an inebriated gnome along with us on a quest. And, if you are, it's my duty to report it. As far as that stupid knife, you should be spending your time thinking about how we're going to capture our prize, not kill it."

Leeky glared.

The sky darkened, matching Adan's mood. Fat, cold drops of rain began pelting the ground, some finding their way down the neck of his tunic, making him even more miserable than he'd already been.

He glanced up toward the window of his room, and the silhouette of Lizbeth with her face pressed against the glass could plainly be seen. He sighed. Having grown up with a sister who was a Spiritmaster, he had no doubt his son was now the one responsible for the day's foul weather. He wanted to go to Lizbeth right now and hold her and the baby both, but he couldn't. He had to get going. There was a nogard to deal with.

Adan was just about to climb down from his horse and untie Laycee's brother himself, when Sarco leaned over and whispered, "You know, it might not be such a bad idea if we did take O.T.T. with us. Though I do think we should probably sober him a bit before trying to convince him to come along. Kidnapping a diplomat, even a gnome diplomatic assistant, might get us in more trouble than we can afford."

O.T.T. chose that moment to show them just how inebriated he was. Loud, high pitched, and not in key by any stretch of the imagination, he broke out in song.

"Listen ta the story of the Blade of Gin...hic... the Blade of Gin, the Blade of Gin. Listen ta the story of the Blade of Gin, as so the humans say.

"It came from far away, the Blade of Gin, the Blade of Gin, the Blade of Gin. It came from far away, the Blade of Gin, so as the humans say.

"They killed the nogards with the Blade of Gin, the Blade of Gin, the Blade of Gin. They killed the nogards with the Blade of Gin...hic...so as the humans say.

"Cut right through their scales with the Blade of Gin, the Blade of Gin, the Blade of Gin. Cut right through their scales with the Blade of Gin, so as the humans say.

"The dragons bow down ta the Blade of Gin, the Blade of Gin, the Blade of Gin. The dragons bow down ta the Blade of Gin, so as the humans say...hic."

Adan nodded toward O.T.T. as he whispered back to Sarco, "We can't wait for him to sober up to get under way. I have no idea how much mead Leeky poured down him, but I'd wager it was enough to keep him inebriated for at least the remainder of this day and probably well into tomorrow."

Sarco rubbed his chin. "How much are you willing to bet I can get him sober and not only ready, but anxious to go with us?"

Adan laughed. "Oh, no, my friend. I know better than to bet with you. I always lose. But if you wish to try, have at it."

He wasn't the least bit surprised as Sarco hopped down from his horse, walked over to the nearby well, filled a bucket with water, and doused the trussed gnome.

O.T.T. coughed, sputtered, and squealed as cold water sluiced down his back and dripped to the ground below.

Adan didn't dismount as he sidled beside Leeky's horse, pulled his knife, cut the gnome's bonds, and helped O.T.T. into a sitting position. As soon as Laycee's brother had a leg securely against both sides of the horse, he turned and shook his fist at Sarco.

"The daft rain wasn't bad enough? Ya can try ta drown me if ya want, but I still ain't going ta Karza and ya can't make me."

Adan leaned back in his saddle and relaxed, secure in his elf friend's powers of persuasion. He didn't have long to wait before Sarco said, "You misunderstand. I'm on your side, O.T.T. I don't blame you for not wanting to come with us. I wouldn't want the responsibility of being declared a national hero either, if I could get out of it. Because that's exactly what you'd be if you somehow managed to talk the trolls into letting us use that knife for a few days. People like you and me prefer not to be in the limelight. We don't need frivolous praise and riches heaped on our heads to make us happy."

O.T.T.'s eyes lit, and Adan couldn't manage anything but a smile and a shake of his head as he listened to Sarco's manipulation speech.

"And you're probably right. It's much too dangerous for a scrawny little old gnome like yourself. Best to leave dangerous quests to the younger generation. Not to be disrespectful, but I doubt you still have the finesse to pull it off anyway, especially with Karla. Even if she did fancy you once, that was long ago, and it would take more of a gnome than you are to convince her. Leave the finessing to me. I have a way with women."

Sarco winked at O.T.T. "You still remember what I'm talking about, don't you? The power to have a female want to do your bidding? Yeah, best you stay here with your sister where it's safe. We'll tell you all about our adventure when we get back. Now, hop down off that horse so the rest of us can be on our way. We're wasting daylight."

Adan smiled at his brother-in-law's antics.

O.T.T. puffed out his chest. "Too dangerous? I'll have ya know I've stared down dangers so real they'd make your hair turn white and have ya jumping for cover. And scrawny?" The gnome pulled up his sleeve, exposing a thin little arm, and flexed it repeatedly. "Does this look scrawny ta ya? Bah, ya don't know scrawny from tightly defined. And if ya think for a minute I'm too old for a tussle, then come a little closer and I'll demonstrate how old I'm not, on the top of your pointy-eared elf head."

O.T.T. slid his sleeve down and thrust a spindly finger toward Sarco. "Ya think I have a lack of finesse? I'll have ya ta know, I was sealing diplomatic deals when ya were still at yer mama's tit. And not gnome enough? I'll show ya, I'll show all of ya."

O.T.T. shook a fist in Sarco's direction. "If ya think for a moment the lot of ya are going anywhere near my Karla or Karza without me, ya better think again. I'm the one who'll have Karla eatin' outta my hand again in no time, and that whatever-ya-wanna-call-it blade will be in Prince Adan's possession before ya know it."

Adan smiled his first genuine smile of the day as the gnome continued.

"Don't ya be worried about me, ya whipper-snapper of an elf. I still have one good testicle, and I'll guarantee it's better than both of yours put together. Now, quit gawking at me and let's get ta riding."

Ray flipped his notebook open once more. "This is highly irregular, and it's going in my report."

Adan turned his horse toward the gate. "Looks like that settles it then. We'd best be on our way. It's still the better part of a turn of the hourglass to the portal, then a long hot ride across the desert. We need to make it to the outskirts of Karza by nightfall to have any chance of meeting with magistrate Karla tomorrow."

O.T.T. didn't sound quite so brave when he opened his mouth a moment later. "Ta...ta...tomorrow? No need ta be in such a hurry, ya know. I happen ta know a nice scenic route we can take. All green and pretty, woods and flowers. Not near as hot and dusty as the desert. There's even a nice fishing hole we could stop at and catch our dinner. Yum, nothing like swamp trout ta hit the spot after a long day's ride. Trust me, Karla'll still be in Karza when we get there. She ain't going nowhere."

Adan didn't look back or slow his pace even a beat as the gates opened and he rode through them. "We'll take the fastest route possible. You can bet the nogard isn't wasting any time getting where he's headed. If we have any hope of catching him before he reaches Castle Kuropkat and the dragons, then neither can we. I just thank God Draka nogards never figured out how to use portals."

\*\*\*\*

Lizbeth bit her lip, said a prayer, and held her breath as she carefully sprinkled a pinch of coriander seeds into the mixture of motherwort and dill, and quickly ground them together. Then, she added the chunk of myrrh resin, and finally, four drops of essence of dragon. The mixture began to bubble in the mortar.

Carefully, she stirred the concoction and let the liquid dribble onto the square of leather lying on the table before her. As she recited the incantation, she couldn't resist the urge to look down and check and recheck her work from the book lying open before her.

Just as in her three previous attempts, there was nothing she was saying or doing different than she had for the last turn of the hourglass. This time, though, she spoke the words very slowly and made sure her articulation was precise.

*"Protect my body, protect my soul.*
*Let not harm take a toll.*
*Protect what's hidden, protect what's loved.*
*Let no danger come from above."*

Suddenly, with a loud poof, just like her three previous tries, the liquid simply vaporized, and all that was left was an empty container, a soggy piece of leather, and a disappointed enchantress.

As if every last speck of energy had drained from her along with the vapor of her spell, Lizbeth sat down heavily. Sobs racked her frame as she finally gave in to the tears she'd been holding at bay since the moment Adan had kissed her and their unborn child goodbye.

What was she going to do? How was she ever going to prove to her husband that her enchanter training could be of value if she couldn't even make a simple talisman of protection?

She stroked the worn pages of Goelz's *Book of Enchantments*. "It's not your fault. Sorry I let you down, old friend. Perhaps I wasn't meant to be an enchantress, after all. I suppose I'll have to settle for the daily simple protection spell and be happy with it, for now."

Gently, she closed the books leather bindings and held it close to her heart. "I'll unlock your secrets some day, you just wait and see. But until then, it'll be a cold day in VoT before I'll sit idly by and watch someone else I love ride off into danger without me."

She almost dropped her prized volume to the floor as the door to her room swooshed open and slammed against the wall with a loud bang.

"Aren't ya packed yet?"

Lizbeth stood and faced the female gnome and the two other women who had entered with her. "Don't wait for me. I'm not going to Castle Kuropkat, after all."

Briar looked surprised. "Why ever not? It's not because you're afraid of the dragons, is it? I swear no harm will come to you. Dragons really are quite friendly if you but give them a chance. At least, they are when Uthiel or I are around. I so want you to meet

Obsidian. He's so cute, and he's the first male dragon born in over a hundred years. But with the nogard out and about, Uthiel has him well hidden right now."

Lizbeth's face heated with embarrassment at the reminder of the danger to the magical creatures she'd caused.

The look on Briar's face became all seriousness. "You do realize, no matter what, you're always welcome at Castle Kuropkat, don't you?"

Lizbeth sat her book down on the bed and clasped her hands behind her. "I'm not staying behind because I'm afraid of dragons, though I am. It's simply that Adan wishes me to go to my brother's home until this is all over."

Lark narrowed her eyes. "And is that what you plan on doing, Lizbeth? Run home to your brothers? Somehow I can't bring myself to believe that."

She knew she wouldn't be able to come right out and lie to her friends, so she clamped her mouth tightly closed and tried to nod. She found she couldn't do that either. All Lizbeth could manage was to stand perfectly still and stare at the floor.

Her friends weren't having it.

Laycee began babbling. "Didn't I tell ya two we needed ta check on her earlier? Up ta something, I just knew it. Felt it even. Gnomes are sensitive ta things like that, didn't ya know. But no, ya said 'Don't worry, give her time ta pack in peace.' Now do ya see what 'give her time' has done? It's obvious she's come up with some half-baked, hair-brained scheme that's gonna get us all in trouble."

Lizbeth looked up quickly. "Oh, no, I would never involve any of you. You must all go to Castle Kuropkat just as you planned."

Lark wasn't having it. "We aren't going anywhere without you."

Tears burned Lizbeth's eyes and her voice cracked. "But you must. I can't be responsible for anyone else being harmed. Don't you see? This is my fault, all of it. My husband and yours are off risking their lives this very moment to correct a mistake I made.

"And Laycee," she implored, "your boyfriend and your own brother are with them. They may never come back from this. I can't hide away at my brother's home or even Castle Kuropkat and live with that."

Lizbeth squared her shoulders. "I've made up my mind. I'm going after them. I'll follow them all the way to Karza if need be, but I won't sit back and let someone else fight my battles for me ever again."

Briar grinned. "Guess that settles it then, ladies. It's off to Karza we go. I can't tell you how frustrated I was to be left behind when Uthiel, Sarco, Leeky, and Adan went off questing. And...and in your condition, you never know when you might find yourself in need of a healer."

Lark nodded. "Yes, it was horrible being left behind to wait and worry. We are smart women. I bet we could be quite useful on a quest."

Laycee cackled. "Can't wait ta see Leeky Shortz's face when he sees the lot of us riding up. Would almost be worth bringing along Miss Bunny. We better get going. They've got more than two turns of the hourglass start on us."

Lizbeth shook her head. "No, I can't ask any of you to come along. It's much too dangerous."

In unison, three voices rang out. "Who's asking?"

## Chapter Twenty

"What was that?"

Adan sighed as he rolled over, tucking his blanket in close about himself to ward off the night chill of the Karzan desert. "It's nothing but the wind, Ray. Just like the last ten times you thought you heard something. For God Draka's sake, I know it's still evening instead of the middle of the night, but we're all tired, and we've a long day ahead of us tomorrow. Please shut up."

He could hear the little man's disgruntled snort somewhere off to his right. He didn't care. He was too tired, too lonely, and too hungry to care about anything right now.

From the moment they'd stepped through the portal, the day had been one tedious turn of the hourglass after another. Even now, the stiffness of his backside and the soreness radiating from the insides of his thighs outward reminded him how much time had passed since he'd last sat a saddle for such a long trip.

And what had been the prize at the end of the lengthy day? A dinner that consisted of nothing more than dry bread and hard cheese. It was all that had been available since they'd failed to find suitable game. And being the mighty hunters they were, they hadn't thought to bring along anything else of substance.

Even though it really wasn't that late, it was dark, and there was nothing left to do but doze. Trying to find sleep with a mostly empty belly while lying on the ground with only one thin blanket between him and the cold hard pebbles had been challenging enough without having Ray announce every few minutes he was hearing things.

For not the first time since they'd left the Academy, Adan regretted having to bring the little man along.

He took in a deep breath and closed his eyes once more. Weariness finally overcame his hunger pangs and the worry of what tomorrow would bring. With one last wish that things could have been settled better between him and Lizbeth before he'd left, Adan drifted off to sleep.

"Don't tell me you didn't hear it that time? Something or someone's out there, I'm telling you, and it's getting closer."

Adan sat straight up, ready to throttle the little man. A nasty retort was on the tip of his tongue when he felt the sound more than he heard it. Horses, three, perhaps four, their steady gaits and soft clip-clopping coming closer with every passing moment.

In a single motion, he leapt, grabbed his sword from its scabbard, and looked toward his friends. Sarco, Leeky, and O.T.T. were already flanking him, weapons drawn, alert, and at attention.

Ray, however began rambling. "I knew I should've stayed at The Academy. I'm much too important to lose. We are all going to die, I tell you. I just know it."

Adan sighed and ignored the little human. It was common knowledge, no one without dubious intentions traveled the Karzan desert at night. There were too many quicksand traps, not to mention dangerous creatures, the most treacherous being of the two-legged variety. No one with two functioning brain cells traversed this desolate area after sunset, at least not anyone he'd hope to meet.

For a moment, Adan closed his eyes and concentrated, then pointed straight ahead. "There."

Though the sky above was clear and star-filled, and one of the three moons of Albrath was full and shining down upon them, he still had to squint into the darkness to make out the four figures.

It took a few moments to convince himself he really was seeing what he thought he saw. He wasn't the one who spoke though. That ability had fled him as soon as the face of the lead rider came into full view.

"What the pus-filled pimples on the raw underbelly of a street-walkin', toe-tappin' Ogre temptress in lime-green leotards do ya make of that, lads?"

Adan didn't look Leeky's way or even acknowledge the gnome's question. All he could manage to do was stare at the sight of his pretty little pregnant wife on a horse that was way too big for her, in a place she should have never been, and at nighttime no less. He wasn't sure what he wanted to do first, yell at her, throttle her, or kiss her silly.

He settled for yelling as the quartet rode into camp. "Have you lost your mind, Lizbeth? What the VoT are you doing here?"

Before his eyes, she became the queen he'd always known she'd one day be. She raised her chin a notch and looked down her nose. "You know I don't appreciate vulgar language, Adan, and I do wish you would refrain from using words like VoT, especially in mixed company. As far as the state of my mind goes, I think, for the first time in my life, I've finally found it instead of it being lost. I'm the one responsible for this mess, and I'm going to help fix it. I-I mean, *we* are going on this quest with you, and you aren't going to stop us."

Pandemonium broke out.

Sarco sputtered. "Larksong Sunwalker, I forbid you to do this. First thing in the morning, you're going straight back to the Academy. Do you hear me?"

Lark simply smiled at her husband and shook her head.

Leeky began pacing. "Everyone knows ya can't have a bunch of lasses along on a quest like this one. It's not seemly, bad luck even. Now, blow-up dolls, that's another story. They can be useful. But not a one of these is plastic."

He glanced hopefully at Laycee. "Ya didn't, by chance, bring my Miss Bunny along with ya, now did ya?"

A shrug of her shoulders was Laycee's only response.

Leeky cried, "We're doomed, I tell ya. Doomed for sure."

Laycee chuckled. "We're coming, and ya ain't got no say-so in it, Leeky Shortz. Yer stuck with the lot of us, so get used ta it. And as far as your Miss Bunny, maybe I brought her and maybe I didn't. Not telling ya 'til I feel like it."

Leeky's mouth opened and closed twice, but no sound came out. Then he simply sat down in a heap.

Ray jumped up and down. "Bet you'll believe me next time I say I heard something, won't you? Ears like a hawk, that's what I've got. Oh, and they can't be allowed to come along with us. They're females. It's a serious breach of the rules, I'm sure. I'll report it. Just you wait and see if I don't."

Adan ground his fingertips into his temples as he glanced at Sarco. "Look, they even have Briar with them. Uthiel's going to kill us when he finds out."

Sarco looked at his friend's wife and gulped.

Briar smiled benevolently. "Don't worry about Uthiel. I can handle him. Anyway, you never know when you may need a healer. I might come in handy, and what Uthiel doesn't know, won't hurt him."

It was Adan's turn to gulp. "Yeah, he's going to kill us for sure." He glanced at his own wife. "You can't do this, Lizbeth. For God Draka's sake, if you won't think about yourself, at least consider our child. You could be putting him in grave danger."

Lizbeth ignored his comments and hopped down from her steed unassisted. "It's been a long day, Adan, and we're all tired and a little cranky. There's really nothing to be done 'til morning anyway, so we might as well try to be civil to each other and make the best of the situation. I hope you don't mind if we make use of your fire."

His head felt fuzzy as if this were some strange dream. "Fire?"

Laycee beamed and pointed to something tied to the back of her horse. "We got a boar, a young one. Gonna cook him and eat him."

"Boar?" was all Adan could manage.

Lark chuckled. "You should've seen us. You would've been so proud. Laycee spotted it, I hit it dead on with a fireball and knocked it out, Lizbeth enchanted a knife to kill it quickly, and Briar gutted it and cleaned it all proper. He's not very big, mind you, but he'll make a nice meal."

Adan's mouth watered, and his stomach rumbled. "A wild boar?" His mind raced. Meat or not, hungry or not, he really should put up more of an argument.

The four women grinned from ear to ear as Laycee cut the bindings and the gutted boar slipped to the ground. Lizbeth, Lark, and Briar lifted their prize high for all to see.

Laycee linked her arms across her chest and stared at the men. "Well, ya going ta stand there all night gawking at us, or are ya going ta help us get this thing cookin'."

Adan, Sarco, Leeky, O.T.T., and even Ray, quickly stepped forward.

****

Lizbeth licked the last remnants of meaty juice from her fingertips, leaned against a boulder at the edge of camp, and sighed with contentment. Happy finally to have Adan all to herself for a few moments, she was hoping to be able to convince her husband of her value on this trip, so he wouldn't be so quick to try and send her away.

She turned to him and smiled. "Now I know exactly what my brothers meant when they used to say meat tastes so much sweeter if you've caught it yourself. I never dreamed I'd be a good huntress."

Adan cleared his throat. "Speaking of your brothers, come first light that's where you're going, and I refuse to argue this matter."

She shook her head slowly. "No, I'm not. I'm going on this quest with you for the Blade of Gin."

"Lizbeth, my little lizard, listen to reason. I can't

do what I need to do if I have to constantly worry about the well-being of you and our child."

Heat burned her cheeks. "Stop calling me Lizard. You know I hate it. You don't have to worry about me, Adan. I can take care of myself."

He shook his head back and forth and for a moment, Lizbeth's fingers itched to run rampant through his golden curls. Then he spoke and ruined the effect. "That's the whole point. You really can't seem to take care of yourself. I know you think you can, but left to your own devices, you make bad decisions and get yourself in trouble."

He held up a finger. "For example, one, you forgot your PDUP spell and ended up with child before we even had a chance to discuss starting a family." He shrugged his shoulders. "Not that I mind, for I don't. I'm even looking forward to becoming a father, truly I am. It's just one example of your not thinking things through."

Hot tears stung the back of Lizbeth's eyes.

Adan sighed and held up a second finger. "Then, you lost your temper and accosted my mother. She most assuredly deserved it, but as a future queen, you no longer have the luxury of doing whatever you wish whenever you get angry. You must think out each and every action and reaction you contemplate. The future of the kingdom may one day depend upon your being able to control your temper."

She fought hard, but a single tear escaped and slid down her cheek. She wiped it quickly away.

Adan didn't seem to notice as he lifted yet a third finger and continued. "Then, you failed miserably at your enchanter final exam and created a monster. Your fault totally or not, and I don't believe for a moment it was, it was still you who spoke the nogard into being. I do wish you would forget this nonsense about becoming an enchantress. You simply aren't magical."

Though the lump in her throat threatened to choke her, Lizbeth whispered past it. "I will become an enchantress, I must. It's the only way. I have to protect us."

A growl emanated from Adan's throat one moment before he jumped to his feet. "Again, you seriously don't believe I can take care of my family? Why must you always be so disagreeable, Lizbeth? Why can't you find it in yourself to be just a little trusting? And why can't you at least pretend to be sweet and pliable, or even quiet and obedient to your husband's wishes as your instructors were commissioned to teach you to be?"

Lizbeth glared as she stood. She faced her husband toe to toe with not more than a breath separating them. "Is that what you really want in a wife, Adan? Someone who'll blindly obey your every whim and lie at your feet like a pet? You'll have to forgive my instructors, my lord. Though they were quite diligent in their task, not in a thousand years could they have turned me into such as you wish for. Not even Master Seiger could accomplish that, though he certainly tried."

For a moment, Adan looked as if she'd slapped him, then as quickly as the hurt had formed in his eyes, it was gone, and a cold, empty mask was once more in its place.

"Go to sleep, Lizbeth, for in the morning you are to return to your brother's keep, and that's my final declaration." Without another word, he picked up his blanket, turned, and stomped out of camp.

"I'm going on this quest with you, Adan, whether you like it or not," she shouted after him.

****

He didn't know how long he'd been sitting, watching Lizbeth sleep. All he knew was, she was the most beautiful creature he'd ever seen and he was hopelessly in love with his wife.

With a single finger, he tentatively stroked the rose-petal softness of her cheek. Not only was she beautiful, but she was stubborn to the core. Even in sleep, Lizbeth's brow furrowed, her chin stuck straight out, and her fists clenched as if ready to do battle. She tossed first one way then the other, fighting to stay asleep on the cold, hard, uncomfortable ground.

What was he going to do with her? He couldn't possibly let her come along with him, could he? It would be irresponsible of him. It would be madness. Men didn't take their women on dangerous quests with them anymore. These were modern times. Women stayed home where they belonged, watching and waiting for their men to return.

She was half barbarian though, so perhaps the same rules didn't need apply. How many nights had he sat and listened to the stories his father told of his great grandmother? A woman who'd fought and died at her husband's side.

Adan shuddered, and his stomach turned, the thought of Lizbeth in harm's way enough to make the succulent boar meat dance in his belly. There had to be a compromise, something they both could live with. The sheen of a single tear caught Adan's eye, and he gently kissed it away. In her sleep, Lizbeth tossed once more.

Adan chuckled. Perhaps he couldn't make her obey him, and perhaps he wasn't so sure he really wanted her to. Lizbeth's fire was one of the things he loved best about her. Not that he would ever tell her that. There would be no living with her at all if he did.

So, what should he do with his wife?

His groin tightened as his fingertips brushed across her tunic and settled upon a pert nipple. He rolled the hard nub between his fingers before lightly squeezing her breast. Lizbeth sighed in her sleep, and Adan's cock begged to be set free of his breeks.

He loosened the ties of her tunic and freed her flesh instead. As the cool, desert night air touched her skin, he marveled at the perfection of her rose-pink pebbly-hard nipples. The worry lines in Lizbeth's brow unfurled, and he bent, captured the nipple in his mouth, and sucked. He heard her gasp of surprise, but he didn't look up and he didn't stop.

She tasted of warm ambrosia, of sweet night air, and of more, much…much more. Even though his hunger for food had been well sated, his hunger for this woman never would be. He needed her in his life. He needed her with each breath he took. Without Lizbeth at his side, his heart would simply cease to beat.

Adan lifted his head and looked at her then, and she was staring back at him. She smiled, and he finally understood. There were still many things he didn't know about this woman, his wife, but one thing he did know was there was love between them. A fledgling love perhaps, but it was there. It was alive, it was raw, it was real, and it was precious.

"Are you just going to stare at me all night, or do

you mean to put that…thing I feel pressing against me through your breeks to use?"

Adan chuckled as he rubbed his cock against her leg once more. "What did you have in mind, Lizard?"

She scowled. "I'm not a lizard. Quit calling me that."

He laughed. "Oh, my dear wife, you are very much like a squirming little lizard at times. Like when you're beneath me and my cock is buried deep inside you. You wiggle that sexy ass of yours in the cutest way."

Lizbeth opened her mouth to comment, but whatever she was about to say was lost as Adan seized her lips with his own. The heat of her breath, combined with the teasing of her tongue, fueled his passion.

They sparred, the barbarian side of them both taking over. His tongue attacked hers while her mouth captured his. It was primal. It was instinctive. It was barbaric.

His hunger for her refused to be sated. He plundered the tender skin of her neck before sucking first one nipple then the other. Lizbeth gasped, leaned up, and nipped his neck, hard.

Adan growled, but there was no anger in his voice, only passion. "My little barbarian lizard is full of surprises tonight. You did learn a thing or two from those Adan Hammerstrike classes after all, didn't you? Let's see you put them to use."

She flipped him off her as if he weighed no more than a feather and straddled him before he could take another breath. "I was a very good student, my lord. Prepare to be plundered." Then she grinned.

Lizbeth made a production of removing what was left of her tunic. Her breasts jutted out proudly, her nipples kissed by the moonlight. Adan watched in wonder as she stood, slid off her traveling pants, and with a gleam in her eye issued an order. "Get naked, Barbarian."

He complied.

"Now touch yourself."

His cock spasmed with need. "I'd rather you touched me," he demanded.

She shook her head and wagged her finger at the same time. "No, no, no, Barbarian. Not yet anyway."

Lizbeth slid her hand down her belly and between her legs, gripping her mound. With her other hand, she motioned to his cock. "If you wish to put that in here, then you're going to have to do what you're told…first."

He liked this game. He liked this new Lizbeth. He liked this woman who refused to shrink or cower. And though he'd never admit it, even on penalty of being tossed into the fiery pits of VoT, he very much liked the wife who'd dared to ride across a desert and defy her husband.

Adan grabbed his cock with both hands and pumped. There was something about masturbating himself in front of her that was beyond erotic. It was powerful and freeing.

Her eyes gleamed with the same passion he knew she saw reflected back in his own as she watched him. It was mesmerizing. He held his breath as she loosened her grip on her mound and slid one finger deep inside then out, over and over. He almost came.

"Have mercy, Lizbeth."

She grinned. "Is this what you want, Barbarian?" She slid her finger from her pussy, leaned over, and ran it across the head of his rock-hard cock.

Spasms shook him. "Oh, yes."

She didn't slide down and mount him like Adan thought she would. Instead, she turned until her cute little ass faced him, went down on her knees, and straddled him backwards. Reaching back, she grabbed his cock, and guided it into her welcoming warmth. Without preamble, she rode him hard.

He couldn't breathe, and he was going to die. Pleasure shot from the pit of his belly and straight out his ass.

She was magnificent. All Adan could do was hold onto Lizbeth's hips and enjoy the ride as, from this vantage point, he watched his own cock slide in and out of her sweet pussy.

And what a ride it was. With her every glide up his cock, his toes curled and the roots of his hair tingled, and with each plunge downward, spasms of pleasure raced down his spine.

Faster and faster, she rode until Adan was no longer sure where his body ended and hers began. Time slowed, the universe drifted away, and all that was left was sensation. Mind-blowing, breath-taking, ball-exploding sensation.

Lizbeth's muscles clenched hard around him, and Adan gave up the fight to hold back his orgasm. With a shout of release, he let it all go. Hot fluid shot forth, spurting deep within her still quivering depths, and with one last spasm, Adan relaxed.

She eased off his spent shaft, turned, and cuddled into Adan's embrace. "So, did I pass my exam as an Adan Hammerstrike student?"

He chuckled. "Oh, honey, you didn't just pass, you

are the master."

The sound of her gentle snort was her only response.

Cradling her in his arms, he held her close to his heart. She immediately fell back to sleep.

Adan used his body to protect hers from the hard ground. She didn't wake but snuggled contently and covered him like the warmest of blankets. Tomorrow would bring what tomorrow would bring. For this night, though, he would do the only thing he had energy left to do.

He slept with his wife.

## Chapter Twenty-One

The camp was utter chaos.

Lizbeth stood with her hands on her hips and fire in her eyes, glaring at Sarco. "Would you please at least give us the falling of a few grains of sand through the hourglass to explain our plan before you shoot it down?"

Adan had the sudden desire to cheer his wife on and champion her cause, but fear for the safety of not only her but also their child kept him quiet for the moment.

"Karla is a woman. We are women. Let us at least try talking with her first. What can it hurt? If you men go riding into Karza, demanding she allow you the use of the Blade of Gin, the outcome will be disastrous. After all, it is trolls we're talking about here. They aren't known for their hospitality. Look what she did to poor O.T.T. when she got angry."

Adan almost chuckled as he watched a look of horror cross the faces of the other men.

Lizbeth didn't seem to notice, or at least the men's reactions didn't slow her down at all. She just kept championing her cause. "Laycee has come up with an idea, and, well, we believe we have something we can use to bargain with Karla. What can it hurt to let us try? If we fail, then it's your turn."

Sarco shook his head. "Lark's not going anywhere

near Karza."

Thunder rumbled across the desert.

He stood his ground as he glared at his wife. "Go ahead, make it rain. Make it pour. I'll still not allow it."

Lark smiled. A dark gray cloud appeared overhead, and a torrential downpour fell on Sarco. Just Sarco.

"I'll have you know I'm your wife, not your property, Sarco Sunwalker, and I don't need your permission. I love you with all I am, but I'm going to Karza with you or without you, and that's that. We all are. We have just as much invested in the outcome of this venture as you men do. Either see reason, or prepare yourself for a very long, wet, miserable day, husband."

Sarco shook his head and droplets of water flew from the tips of his hair. "Lark, be reasonable."

He pointed toward Briar, and the hue of his skin turned a sick shade of green. "And…and…and her! We can't take her with us. Uthiel will kill us. He'll have our heads for sure."

Briar shrugged her shoulders and smiled. "I'm already here. There's nothing to be done about that. Which do you think would make my husband angrier? That I went on a simple overnight trip to Karza within the protection of big strong men like yourselves, or that I was sent back across a dangerous desert, all alone, by men he considers to be his very best friends in the whole world?"

Adan laughed. "She's got us there. If we stand around arguing with them all day, Sarco, no one will be going to Karza."

Sarco sputtered. "Okay, okay, okay, I give up. Make the rain stop, Lark. I'll agree to let you come along. Not because you've soaked me to the skin, mind you, but because it's the only way to keep all of you out of harm's way."

The rain stopped, and the sky cleared.

Leeky Shortz began pacing back and forth. "Ya say it was Laycee who came up with this plan? God Draka, help us."

The female gnome snorted and was about to open her mouth when her brother spoke. "If it's my sister's plan, then I for one say let's try it. What can it hurt? Anyway, she's always been the really smart one in the family. I trust her judgment completely."

Adan wasn't sure if it was a moment of guilt, surprise, or panic he saw streak across Laycee's face. Right then, it didn't matter. He needed to get them moving.

The sun was already high in the sky, and he knew for a fact the nogard wouldn't be wasting time getting to what it would consider its feeding ground—the dragon caves high above Castle Kuropkat. And furthermore, he needed to give in to Lizbeth, without letting her know that was exactly what he was doing. A moment later, Ray gave him the perfect opportunity to do just that.

"I thought I made myself perfectly clear last evening when I said the women must not be allowed to accompany us. They have no place here. This is men's work. I will not only inform the council, but also your mother. I gave Queen Allanna my personal assurance that quest protocol would not be breached in any way." He pointed toward Lizbeth. "Especially by her."

When had seeing his wife's eyes fill with tears become so much more important than even his next breath?

Adan stood and raised a hand for silence. "I'm leading this quest, and it is I who will say who goes and who does not. As far as the council and my mother, to VoT with the lot of them. Tell them whatever you wish."

He winked at his wife and smiled. "The women can come along if they like, and they can even speak to Karla first if they wish." He took a moment to look directly at each of them. "But you better be able to keep up, because we won't be waiting around or slowing down for anyone."

The look Lizbeth gave him wasn't quite a smile, but it wasn't a glare either. Adan considered it progress.

****

Though the dry air surrounding her was still hot enough to parch her throat, chills skittered nonstop the length of Lizbeth's spine and had done so from the moment they left the desert and entered the Karzan Swamps. Strange little blue insects flittered to and fro, forcing her to swat at them while trying to keep an eye out for whatever was making the horrible water-slapping, teeth-grinding, loud-breathing sounds off to her right.

And Adan, he certainly wasn't being helpful. As a matter of fact, he was making the situation worse. And if the sounds coming from his direction were any indication, he was enjoying that fact immensely.

With his horse being a full hand taller than anyone else's, his pace was almost impossible to keep up with. He was at the lead of the pack, and not once since they'd left camp had he so much as glanced backward at her. For all he knew, she could have been eaten by whatever was making those horrendous noises or swallowed by the swamp itself. Not that he would've heard it with what he was doing.

Eyes straight forward, relaxed in his saddle, Adan looked every inch the prince. A prince she would very much like to throttle at the moment. He was whistling loudly, not just whistling, but over and over whistling the same incessant tune, and it was driving her mad. It was as if he were out for a ride in the park instead of in the middle of a dangerous swamp on an important quest. After last night, she'd expected to be treated differently.

Suddenly, he stopped and held up a hand. Even the sounds of the swamp around them ceased.

Then the foliage opened and out of nowhere, at least a dozen angry-looking trolls surrounded them. "State yout business and be quick about it."

Adan hopped down from his horse and extended a hand toward the troll who had spoken. "We've traveled far and have need to speak with your leader."

The troll ignored the hand and glared. "Speak with our leader, yout say? With Karla?" He chuckled, but the sound held no humor. "Yout picked a fine day for it. Hope yout aren't too overly fond of yout heads. She's been in a foul mood all morning."

Adan's shoulders heaved, and Lizbeth almost felt sorry for him as his deep sigh penetrated all the way to her very core.

"Well, of course, she is," he said. "Why wouldn't she be? After all, she's female, isn't she?"

The troll cackled out loud. "That she is for certain, Barbarian. That she is."

In unison, the trolls turned, parted the greenery

before them, and led the group into the village of Karza.

Lizbeth looked first to Lark, then to Briar, and finally toward Laycee. She straightened her spine, took three deep breaths, sent a quick prayer to Draka, and followed. The time had come to negotiate.

\*\*\*\*

The heat, not to mention the smell of unwashed troll inside the confines of the meeting hall, was stifling. Lizbeth dabbed at her forehead, took in deep gulps of stale air, and fought back her nausea. The last thing she could afford right now was to be sick all over the leader of the trolls.

Karla was bigger than she had imagined. Being half barbarian, not many females could stand toe-to-toe with Lizbeth and look her straight in the eye, but Karla easily could and did so without flinching.

Lizbeth averted her gaze downward out of respect and tried not to steal a peek at the dark green female with the stringy black hair and razor-sharp tusks. This only served to bring her gaze level with the troll leader's tight-fitting leather breeks and the distinctive outline of the camel toe she'd heard so much about. She wasn't sure which urge was stronger, the one to laugh or the one to gag.

"My men tell me yout think yout have business with me. What could a barbarian possibly want with the leader of the troll clan? Speak and be quick about it before yout all become my lunch. It's been a long time since I've tasted fresh, white meat."

Karla bent and tweaked Laycee's cheek. "Especially gnome."

Laycee balled up her fist but stood her ground.

Lizbeth cleared her throat. "A nogard is loose and

on the way to kill the dragons. If it's not stopped, magic will cease to exist on Albrath. We have need of the Blade of Gin to defeat the nogard. We'll return the knife to you as soon as our quest is done. You have my word."

Karla scoffed. "A nogard? What do yout take me for, an idiot? Nogards have been extinct for centuries. I should have yout head removed from yout worthless body for telling such a tale."

Lark, Briar, and Laycee all started to speak, but Lizbeth held up a hand to silence them. She raised her eyes and looked directly at Karla. "I speak the truth. It was I who accidentally created the creature, and it is I who must see it destroyed. We realize your people hold The Blade of Gin in high regard, and we don't expect you to simply hand it over without assurances it will be returned. Perhaps we have something with which to bargain."

Karla laughed. "Bargain with barbarians, elves, and gnomes? I think not. What on Albrath would the four of yout have that I could possibly want?"

Lizbeth, Lark, Briar, and Laycee looked at each other and smiled.

****

The sun glinted so brightly off the length of metal, Adan was momentarily blinded. He shook his head once and then shook it again. He couldn't believe his eyes. They had done it. Somehow, Lizbeth and the other three women had actually talked Karla into relinquishing the Blade of Gin. Would wonders never cease?

When she placed the knife reverently in his hand, it was as if it pulsed with a power of its own. Somewhere in the back of his mind, Adan, realized the energy most probably came from the heat of Lizbeth's touch, but it didn't matter. It was still magical.

Grasping the wooden handle while running the pad of his thumb along its eight inches of serrated blade, he marveled at the sharpness of the instrument. Tiny droplets of his blood welled along its length. Even after centuries, the knife still had a razor's edge.

He studied the knife closely. At its base, right above the handle, was some ancient writing. The word *Gin* could plainly be seen. Adan used a corner of his tunic to rub off the blood and was immediately amazed. It didn't say just Gin at all, it said *Ginsu*. Right under that, it read "Made in Ohio." What an amazing knife, and what amazing creatures the humans were for bringing it to this world.

Adan strove to remember his history. Was Ohio a human world all of its own or simply a major country from the world of London spoke of in the Chronicles of Sha Spere? It didn't matter, all that mattered was they had in their possession the magical Ginsu Blade, and they now had the power to stop the nogard.

He glanced at Lizbeth. "How?"

He watched as her face turned a bright shade of crimson, and she began wringing her hands.

"Lizbeth, what did you promise Karla for the knife?"

She opened her mouth to speak, but no words came out, only a garbled squeak.

Suddenly the door in front of them flew open and out walked Karla in all her troll splendor. "Where's my Thad?"

Adan's blood rushed to his feet as realization of

what the girls had used as a bargaining chip filled his mind. He stared at Lizbeth, hoping to be wrong. "You didn't. You couldn't have? Laycee would've never? Would she?"

Lizbeth shrugged.

Karla wasn't wasting any time as she advanced on the group. "Thaddeus Titwilder, yout little rascal, yout. Where be thee? Come give Karla a big kiss. I've missed yout."

Even though O.T.T. was small, Adan heard him hit the ground like a boulder. He turned just in time to see the poor little gnome lying face down in the dirt. He couldn't believe it.

Adan shook his head and glared at Laycee. "Your own brother? You gave your very own brother to a...a troll? And not just any troll, but the troll who unmanned him?"

Laycee hung her head, shuffled from one foot to another then back again before looking up once more. "He'll be fine, and it's only 'til we return the knife. It'll be for the best, you'll see. O.T.T. isn't stupid. He'll be careful with what he says this time around. And just look at her. It's obvious ta anyone who's got two eyes in their head, Karla's still plenty sweet on him."

O.T.T. gained consciousness just long enough to gaze into the face of the big green female who held him tightly in her arms. His eyes widened, his breathing came in short strangled little gasps, and he promptly passed out once again.

Ray took notes, lots and lots of notes.

## Chapter Twenty-Two

The castle's subterranean vault was not only dark and damp but chilly. Lizbeth attempted to draw her shawl closer about herself in hopes of staving off the shivers running the length of her spine. It didn't work. Not only were both her hands too full to accomplish the feat, but instinctively, she realized the cold wasn't so much from the temperature of the air, as it was from fear.

Time had run out.

In a matter of a few hours, when the sun rose high above the stone walls of Castle Kuropkat, Adan would leave this place they'd arrived at earlier in the day and go in search of the nogard. Tomorrow the full weight of the mistake she'd made during her final exam would come to bear.

Unless she could manage to accomplish what she'd failed miserably at so many times before, she knew in her heart of hearts she stood a very good chance of losing the only man she would ever love. The talisman of protection was the lone answer. It was now or never.

She placed the candle she held onto the rough wooden table before her and gently set down her most prized possession. As they always did when in close proximity to the old volume, her fingers tingled in anticipation of opening it. She allowed them free rein for a few moments and stroked the familiar, worn leather binding of Goelz's *Study of Enchantments*.

She quickly flipped through its pages, and the book, as if realizing what she needed, fell open to the one set of spells Lizbeth hadn't yet been able to master. The enchantments of protection.

Taking a deep breath, she closed her eyes and concentrated on steadying her shaking hands. This time there could be no mistakes, no failure. She could do this. She simply must.

The babe chose that moment to remind her of his presence as thunder rumbled somewhere off in the distance. Lizbeth emptied the pockets of her tunic and set down the remaining items she'd been carrying.

With both hands, she cradled the small paunch her tummy had become. "Shush, Zander. Momma has work to do. You don't want to wake your father, do you? I'm already in enough trouble with him. Go back to sleep." And even though she wasn't sure if it was for the baby's benefit or her own, she added, "Everything will be fine, you'll see."

The skies outside quieted, and Lizbeth smiled. When exactly had she begun to know the child growing within her body as Zander? No longer was he thought of as the mischievous little Spiritmaster, but he had become an honest-to-goodness person and so much more than the conglomeration of cells of just a few weeks ago. He was growing rapidly these days, and when she was quiet and still, he moved within her and tucked himself securely under her heart.

Even though Adan's mother certainly would never be counted among her favorite people, the Royal House of Hammerstrike tradition was still tradition and very important to the realm. Barbarian custom dictated it was the mother's responsibility and right to name the children. The King, the Queen, and all of their children, except for Lark, shared the same initials, A.Z.C.H., as had the majority of the King's direct ancestors as far back as the royal family could be traced.

So would this child.

Lizbeth fervently hoped Adan would be pleased with the name she had chosen for his heir. Upon his birth, Alex Zander Collin Hammerstrike, Zander to his mother, would take his rightful place as the next prince of Alaria.

Remembering suddenly why she had sneaked down into the bowels of the castle in the middle of the night, Lizbeth sighed. When tomorrow was done, would Adan still be alive to see his son born? She shook off the fears and strengthened her resolve. If she had anything to say about it, not only would he live to see the birth of his son, but he would also be there to place the barbarian crown on Zander's head someday.

Lizbeth ran a fingertip along the rough rim of her mortar, closed her eyes, and attempted to clear her mind. She had no doubt that one of the most valuable bits of advice Headmistress Seychelle had ever given her in class was "If you don't believe you can accomplish what you set out to do, then you won't. Even a mediocre enchantress can rise to greatness with the right attitude, but no enchantress ever got to the level of being a master without first believing in the magic of herself."

After flattening out the small soft, supple square of leather meant to hold the contents of the talisman, she got to work.

Grinding the coriander seeds in the mortar, Lizbeth

carefully read and reread the protection spell as she slowly added the motherwort powder, the dill leaf, the chunk of myrrh resin, and, finally, the four drops of essence of dragon. The concoction began to bubble.

Carefully, she stirred the ingredients with her pestle and drizzled it upon the square of leather while reciting her chant.

*"Protect his body, protect his soul.*

*Let not harm take a toll.*

*Protect my love, protect Prince Adan*

*From first morning light 'til the sun's rays have faded."*

With a loud poof, the liquid simply vaporized, and all that was left was an empty mortar and a bare piece of leather.

Lizbeth slumped to the floor in a heap and sobbed.

"What are you doing?"

The familiar voice right behind her startled Lizbeth and immediately stifled her tears. It couldn't, however, suppress her groan. Slowly, she plastered a smile on her face, rose, and turned to face her husband.

"Adan, whatever are you doing? It's the middle of the night. You should be resting. You have a big day ahead of you tomorrow. I couldn't sleep, so I thought I'd practice a few simple little spells. You know, just something to take my mind off…things. Go back to bed. I'll be up shortly."

He crossed his arms, tilted his head, lifted his chin ever so perceptively, and glared at her.

Lizbeth groaned again. How many occasions had she watched Adan do this same pose? Every single time she'd tried to get away with not explaining her actions to him, that's how many times.

He added tapping his foot impatiently to his already angry demeanor. "I was awakened by thunder, Lizard. However, the air smells much more of snow than it does of rain. I wasn't sure if it really was an honest-to-goodness storm brewing or if perhaps my sister or even my unborn son were up to late-night mischief. You can imagine my surprise when I found you missing from our bed and followed strange, chanting-like noises down here. I now realize it is my wife who is once again up to only God Draka knows what."

He grasped her shoulders, though it was not a grip to showcase his superior strength, but rather one of tenderness. "I don't need magic, and I especially don't need a silly talisman, Lizbeth. That is what you're doing down here, isn't it? Instead of getting the rest you and the babe so desperately need. I'm a big strong barbarian, and I can take care of myself, love. How many times must I tell you this before you'll believe me?"

Tears filled her eyes even though she fought them back. Gritting her teeth, Lizbeth dared them to fall. "Perhaps you don't require my assistance or even something so basic and probably so completely silly as a protection talisman." She reached up and stroked his cheek. "Perhaps I'm the one who needs you to have one. Is it so very wrong of me to desire you to need me, to need something, anything, from me?"

Surprise gleamed in his eyes. Adan's hands slipped from her shoulders. He held both hands, palm up and out toward his wife. "Is that what you really think of me, that I don't need you?" He ran his fingers through his hair. "I need you, Lizbeth, more than you could ever know. How can you doubt that? What will it take to prove to you I not only need you but want you as my wife?"

"Believe in me," she cried.

He ran his fingers through his hair once more then looked her straight in the eye. "I do believe in you. What will it take to convince you that I do? Will acting as your servant this night and wearing your talisman on the morrow convince you? If it will, then tell me what it is I can do to help you so we can both seek our bed. I may not believe I have need of magic, Lizbeth, but I do know I have need of you."

Those were the last words she'd expected to hear from her barbarian husband, and Lizbeth had no idea how to respond. She stood paralyzed, staring openmouthed, unable to fully comprehend what had just transpired.

The slight uplifting of the edges of his lips snapped her out of her trance.

"You would really help me?"

He raised his eyebrow and nodded.

Her voice broke ever so slightly. "You wouldn't jest with me about something so important, would you?"

He slowly shook his head, sighed, and crossed his heart.

The tears she'd been holding back tumbled forth, and Lizbeth didn't realize Adan had moved until his strong arms enveloped her.

Her skin began to tingle from the top of her head to the very tips of her toes as he whispered against her hair. "Morning will be here soon, Lizard. Perhaps we should cease the weeping and get to work."

She almost laughed. Leave it to Adan to get right to the point. She pulled away, just enough so she could still feel the heat his body generated yet clear her mind and look him in the eye. "You're right, husband, let's get started. Oh, and how many times have I asked you to not call me Lizard?"

****

"Are you sure you've been adding everything you're supposed to and reciting the spell correctly? We've been at this a long time, Lizbeth. Perhaps you should give me a chance to do something other than just hand you...stuff."

Lizbeth glared at her helper, but he didn't seem to notice.

"Like, I could be the one to hold the book and read the spell to you for a change. Maybe I'll see something you've been missing. Want to try it that way?"

She wanted to hit him. Not just a small companionable thump on the arm, but an all-out I-am-not-the-idiot-you-obviously-think-me-to-be punch right in the nose.

Lizbeth sighed. How could she have thought for a moment help from Adan would be anything but the disaster it had been for the last turn of the hourglass? After all, the man was a barbarian. She swallowed back a sudden giggle, realizing Adan wasn't the only barbarian in the room.

Perhaps he had a point.

Lovingly caressing the leather of Goelz's *Study of Enchantments* one last time, she silently handed it over to her husband and pointed out the spell.

He smiled at her and her heart lifted as his voice rang out loud and clear. "Continuously grind five medium-sized coriander seeds as you slowly add a pinch of motherwort powder. Next, crumble in one dried leaf of dill, and a crushed chunk of myrrh resin."

He didn't even have time to say slowly add four drops of essence of dragon before the concoction, once again, went up in a puff of smoke.

Lizbeth groaned as she gazed at Adan in defeat. "It's no use. You were right all along. There's nothing magical about me. I'm sorry, I've failed you."

Adan looked as if she'd slapped him. "No, don't say that. I didn't mean it, Lizbeth. I swear I didn't. You are the essence of magic. I don't know what had gotten into me when I said those hurtful words to you. I think I was just jealous and afraid you wouldn't need me anymore if you had magic to rely on. I was wrong, so very wrong. Try again, please! Don't ever give up because of me."

Lizbeth had an overwhelming urge to rush into Adan's arms. Her eyes roamed the length of him, taking in not only the sincerity in his eyes and the fullness of his lips, but also how the fine leather of his tunic molded itself perfectly to his broad-chested frame. For a moment, her breathing quickened as heat rushed up her neck and down into the pit of her belly.

Then, an entirely new thought occurred to her. "Strip, Barbarian, hurry."

## Chapter Twenty-Three

Adan coughed. "Now? Here? Really? Umm...okay. It's kind of dusty in this basement, and there's really nowhere to lie but on the cold stone floor, but you know me, Lizbeth. I'm ready whenever, wherever you wish. I'm just surprised you'd want to stop what we're doing and have sex right now is all."

She did punch him then, but playfully.

"Not that, silly. I have another idea, and I need your leather garments to test it."

"Another idea?"

She couldn't contain her excitement. "Yes!"

Adan lifted his tunic over his head and tossed it to his wife. He then made a production of slowly pushing his breeks over his hips and down his legs, before kicking them off and toward her. "Umm...while I'm already in a state of undress, you wouldn't, by chance, want to take advantage of me, would you?"

Lizbeth smiled as his cock proudly rose to attention and bobbed under her scrutiny. "If this works, I'll gleefully ride you the rest of the night, Barbarian. Right now, though, I need to concentrate on my spell, so make that thing behave for a while longer."

His eyes were upon her as she turned first the tunic then the breeks inside out. Finding just the right section of leather she was looking for, she held out a hand. "Knife."

Adan chuckled. "And just where do you think I would be hiding a knife right now, Lizard? I'm naked remember."

She had the grace to pinken. "Oh, I forgot."

Reaching into her tunic pocket, she pulled out the small knife she used for eating. "Guess this will have to do." With more hacking and sawing than cutting, Lizbeth managed to extract a small square of leather from the hem of Adan's tunic where it wouldn't be quite so noticeable. She laid it on the table and glanced at her husband.

"This talisman of protection is for you, so I'm hoping by using a piece of leather that is personally yours to contain it, the spell will work this time."

Adan nodded and began reading the requirements of the enchantment. "Grind the coriander seeds."

Into the mortar Lizbeth dropped the five coriander seeds and ground them with her pestle until they were the consistency of dust.

"Add the pinch of motherwort powder."

She did so and ground the ingredients together.

"Now, it's time for the crumbled leaf of dill and the crushed myrrh resin."

Lizbeth held her breath as she added them both to the mixture. Her fingers started to tingle and the substance within the mortar began to shimmer. She looked at her prince and smiled.

Adan locked gazes with her. "Slowly add four drops of essence of dragon."

She drew the dragon's essence up, but the dropper shook so violently in her hand, Lizbeth was afraid she'd either miss the mortar completely or accidentally add too much. The sudden steadying touch of Adan's hand was a welcome relief.

They counted the drops together as they fell. "One, two, three, four."

The mixture started to bubble, and Lizbeth began the process of slowly drizzling it upon the square of Adan's leather. While praying silently to herself, she recited the chant out loud.

*"Protect his body, protect his soul.*

*Let not harm take a toll.*

*Protect my love, protect Prince Adan*

*From first morning light 'til the sun's rays have faded."*

She held her breath and waited.

The square of leather shot from the table. A streak of blinding, white light emanated from it. Suddenly, the leather piece folded itself into a packet, trapping the light within. Just as quickly as it rose, it landed back down, coming to rest in the same spot it first had begun.

Lizbeth gingerly scooped it and held it toward Adan as carefully as if it were made of the finest crystals.

He grinned. "It worked then? I knew you could do it. Didn't I tell you, you are the very essence of magic?"

Lizbeth shook her head but couldn't seem to stop grinning. "I'm not sure why it finally worked this time. Was it simply using something personal of yours, or was it a combination of that and you believing in me? I don't know and I don't care. It worked."

Picking up his breeks, Adan ripped the hem off a leg. Taking the shimmering piece of leather Lizbeth offered, he attached the strip to the talisman and looped it over his neck. It settled snuggly between his pecs and pulsed with energy.

"Now that I'm protected from all danger, have your wicked way with me, wife. I have a powerful need of thee."

Lizbeth laughed all the way to her soul. "I'd love to do just that right this very moment, husband, but morning will be here before we know it, and there are still four talismans to make."

Adan looked confused. "Four more?"

Lizbeth nodded. "Yes, for Sarco, Uthiel, Leeky, and Ray. Now that I know how to make the spell work, we must protect them also. Hurry and fetch me a small piece of leather from each of their garments. If we do this quickly, there may still be time for us to have our way with each other."

He grabbed her about the waist and brought her up tight against his hard, hot body. His cock pulsed with a life of its own along the junction of her thighs "Oh, no, Lizard. We may not have a later. There's no way of knowing what tomorrow will bring. The talismans will wait a little while longer."

The shimmering, leather pouch nestled between them vibrated to the same mesmerizing rhythm Adan's cock did. Lizbeth couldn't resist rubbing herself against his length. Her tunic overheated her already too-warm skin and restricted her movement. She leaned up on tiptoes, a breath from Adan's ear, and whispered. "We can't do anything 'til you get me undressed, Barbarian."

Before the word *Barbarian* was even completely out of her mouth, Adan had the tunic up and over her head and tossed to the side. Skin to skin, heart to heart, they stood a moment, relishing the passion reflected in each other's eyes.

It was Adan who finally broke the spell. His voice

was low, gravelly, and winded, as if he'd run a race. "God Draka, Lizbeth, what you do to me. I need you so badly." His cock drove home his point as it expanded to an even greater length and width against her belly. "I want to take you now, fast and hard, up against the wall, on the table across the room, even on this cold stone floor. I don't care." He sighed and leaned his forehead to hers. "But I won't. You are a princess, *my* princess, and with my child. You deserve a soft bed, my lady."

He lifted her into his arms and began up the steps.

Lizbeth squealed. "Put me down. We're naked. Someone's going to see us."

Adan laughed. "Let the world watch, Lizard. I don't care. It's much too late to stop now."

**** 

Silk sheets and downy softness enveloped Lizbeth and cooled her heated skin as Adan laid her gently upon their bed. Her proud barbarian stood above her, staring down with a look of pure determination on his handsome face. His eyes burned blue-hot heat, his nostrils flared, his lips opened in invitation, and his rock-hard cock riveted her attention like a cobra about to strike.

Lizbeth wanted to cry. Adan was right. This could be their very last chance to make love, and it was all her fault. Instead of crying though, she smiled up at the man she loved. Last time or not, she would make it an experience they'd both never forget.

Smugly she reached out a finger and stroked the velvety-soft head of his cock. "My, what a wild-looking serpent you have there, my lord. Is it dangerous? Does it bite?" She leaned forward, bracing herself on one elbow, and flicked out her tongue, licking just the very tip.

He sucked in a breath. "Don't tease me, Lizbeth. My control is at an end."

She gave him her most innocent smile. "Promise?" She winked as she slowly slid her lips over the head and down the shaft, sucking as she went.

Adan growled. "You little minx. I warned you."

Before she'd taken another breath, Lizbeth found herself flat on her back with Adan firmly settled between her thighs. He took her mouth in a kiss filled with promise yet laced with regret. Their lips melded, their tongues warred, and their breath became as one.

"Now, Adan, please," she whispered against his skin.

His answer was a quick plunge into her pussy. His cock filled her completely while his balls slapped her ass. He pounded in and out of her slick passage in a frenzy. As if this really would be his last chance to ever show her his heart.

Lizbeth throbbed and clenched around his cock as he pounded mercilessly into her pussy. She gloried in his possession, breathing in his essence of pure barbarian and lustful sensuality. Shocks of pleasure shot through her. They radiated from her eyebrows all the way to the tips of her toes. She tingled and quivered as sweat wet her skin and glistened off Adan's shoulders and chest. It eased the friction and added to the mutual slide of the grinding of their bodies.

Suddenly, he slowed his thrusts to a steady rhythm, and Lizbeth matched him stroke for stroke. She closed her eyes and laid wide open her heart. Trying to convey with her body the words her husband, her lover, her prince, her life had refused to believe, that she loved him.

The walls of her pussy contracted around him, seeking to keep his cock buried deep, never to allow it to escape. Her heart pounded wildly, desperately needing Adan to speed his stroke to match its cadence, yet at the same time, her mind and body gloried in the wondrous torture his slow steady thrusts delivered.

Excitement skittered along every nerve ending as pressure built in her core. She opened her eyes and locked gazes with Adan. She wanted him to watch when she found release. She wanted him to know he'd pleasured her beyond any doubts, and she wanted him to know he had complete possession of her heart. Tomorrow would bring what tomorrow would bring, but for this night, Adan would not doubt her love.

"I love you," she whispered.

Adan's nostrils flared.

"I love you, husband." Tears threatened.

Adan stared at her.

"I love you, you blockheaded barbarian," she cried.

The look on his face never changed, but a new determination burned in his eyes. He thrust into her wildly, stroke after stroke taking her breath away. Pleasure centered deep within her core and shot up and outward. She shattered into a million tiny fragments with Adan being the only solid thing holding her together.

A heartbeat later, Adan found his release as he plunged deep within Lizbeth one last time. "I love you too, wife. God Draka help us both. I love you with all that I am."

\*\*\*\*

"I don't need to make talismans for myself or the other women. Our everyday personal protection spell should suffice since we'll be staying well out of harm's way unless we're needed."

Lizbeth stood before her mortar and pestle with her arms folded, tapping her foot.

Adan looked at her as if she'd lost her mind. "You bet you'll be well out of harm's way. You aren't leaving this castle."

Lizbeth laughed. "Of course, I am, silly. You didn't think I came all this way to be left behind now, did you?"

Adan frowned. "There are dragons out there, Lizard. Lots and lots of dragons. I thought you were afraid of them almost as much as you are of the nogard?"

Lizbeth shrugged. "Childish fears, nothing more. I'll be fine come morning."

"I'm not going to argue this point with you, Lizbeth. You aren't going, and that's that. I'll get the piece of leather from Uthiel, Sarco, Leeky, and Ray, so you can make their talismans, but that's it."

Quickly, he turned, but Lizbeth's next words stopped him momentarily in his tracks. "I'm going and you can't stop me."

He turned around and faced her once more, flashing a grin. "Want to bet?"

## Chapter Twenty-Four

Adan smacked his hands together in glee. "That was an awe-inspiring performance, my friend. The poem was perfection, and you were brilliant in your storytelling. I can't convey to you how much I appreciate what you've done. Making Lizbeth think it was her idea to stay behind was genius."

Sarco grinned. "You think that was something? I'm an amateur compared to our two friends here. After we kill this beast and get back to the castle, I'd almost pay to watch Uthiel try and convince Briar he didn't actually drug her yet again to keep her from tagging along. She's going to be so mad I'd be surprised if the castle is still standing when this day is said and done."

Uthiel shook his head. "The castle will still be there...I hope. I'd rather see it in rubble again, though, and suffer Briar's wrath any day than allow her to put herself in danger."

Adan nodded, then another thought struck him and he laughed out loud. "Oh, and what Leeky did with Laycee. That was pure talent. How long do you think it'll take Lark and Lizbeth to locate her?"

"What the stiff ironed creases in the puce pant legs of a dwarf dandy dancing a jig on a pickle barrel are ya talking about, lad? Locate her? Why, I hid Laycee so good, I'd be surprised if even I can find her when we get back."

Ray cleared his throat. "If I had a wife, she'd obey my every word without question. You three are pathetic, having to resort to trickery to control your women. I'm much too refined for this task. You should be concentrating on how you plan to capture the nogard. Not on your silly women issues. I can't wait until I get back to The Academy and give my Mistress, the Council, and the Queen my report. Tsk, tsk, I've never seen such incompetence."

Uthiel glanced at Adan. "I liked the other Ray much better."

Adan laughed. "Trust me, my friend, we all did."

Ray snorted. "Other Ray? What other Ray?"

Leeky cackled. "What Ray do ya think they're talking about, lad? The one who loves cock, of course."

Ray sputtered. "Why, I'd never! This harassment is going into my report."

Adan, Sarco, Uthiel, and Leeky simply smiled at each other and kicked their horses into a gallop. Ray followed.

****

Standing in the middle of Castle Kuropkat's courtyard and staring into the gray, cloudy sky while fat flakes of snow fluttered all about wasn't where Lizbeth had planned on being this morning.

She sighed in frustration.

She should be on the hunt for the nogard with Adan. After all, it had been she who had breathed life into the creature and brought it into being. And it was she whose responsibility it now was to see to its demise.

Lizbeth shuddered.

How could she have been so cowardly? Had she

really come all this way to be left standing in the cold all alone? With child or not, she should have known better than to allow her silly childhood fear of dragons to sway her common sense. Even Ray wasn't as much of a coward as she was.

How could she have been so easily convinced to stay behind? To sit and wait for someone else to bring her news? To hide where it was safe? And worst of all, to lose the bet?

She knew exactly how it had happened. She simply didn't like the fact she'd let it happen today of all days. Why had she allowed long-ago memories of her brother's sick versions of bedtime stories, mixed with that stupid poem Master Seiger used to frighten her with, get the best of her?

But then, why had she wasted time breaking her fast this morning at all? She should have been busy packing the items she'd deemed necessary to confront the nogard. But, no, that's not what she'd done. Hunger had outweighed common sense, and Lizbeth had found herself sitting at the same table with not only her handsome barbarian of a husband, but his sister and brother-in-law. She'd eaten her fill while listening avidly to Sarco Sunwalker tell dragon tales.

Sarco! Even if he was her wizard instructor, Lark's husband, and one of Adan's best friends, what she wouldn't give to have his throat between her two hands this very moment. She'd squeeze it until he was no longer capable of speech, let alone scaring the wits out of people.

Lizbeth seethed. If truth be told, Adan himself had probably been the one to put Sarco up to declaring it was *only* those of human heritage who were in any way safe amongst dragons. And she had no doubt it had been her barbarian prince who had convinced Sarco to recite the very same dreadful poem Master Seiger had taunted her with as a child.

Not that Sarco had precisely recited it. He'd sung it really, over and over and over, undoubtedly in the hope she and Lark would be frightened and stay behind.

*"Watch when ye wander, little children, and where.*
*Be careful, don't disturb a dragon in its lair.*
*Be it high on a mountain or deep in a wood,*
*Walk softly, tread lightly, and always be good.*
*For dragons read hearts be they obedient or not.*
*In the darkest of night, the bad will be sought.*
*For though dragons by morning can be quite gay,*
*And afternoon dragons may be found in play,*
*When the sun doth set and dusk draws near,*
*If ye've misbehaved, ye have reason to fear.*
*For by darkness of night, wings take flight*
*And seek out the naughty to devour by next light."*

Men!

It had worked, too. Well, at least it had worked with Lizbeth. Lark had only agreed to stay behind because she hadn't wanted to go without the other women, especially Laycee.

And what of Laycee? She certainly hadn't been around when needed.

Lizbeth's thoughts centered on the female gnome. Where exactly was Laycee? The morning was half gone, and there hadn't been even a glimpse of her as of yet.

Lizbeth sighed, Laycee was probably sleeping in, the poor dear, and who could blame her. The far north, high mountain air certainly had the same effect on her.

If this weren't such a dire situation, she'd love to take a nap herself right about now. But it was dire, so who in their right mind would be able to sleep through it?

That thought brought Briar to mind. She was another story all together. No one could ever accuse Briarlarn Dragonheart of being the least bit afraid of dragons. But then why should she be? Not only was she a very powerful healer and half human, but she had a one hundred percent human husband in Uthiel Dragonheart, who was not only a well-known paladin in his own right, but also the sworn protector of all dragons. Not to mention Briar had a personal pet dragon, Obsidian, whom she'd helped rescue a couple of years back.

Oh, no, Briar hadn't stayed behind out of fear. She had simply fallen fast asleep right in the middle of breaking her fast and didn't awaken even when the men left. It had been the strangest thing.

Lizbeth shivered, and though common sense told her dragons were good and nogards bad, try as she might, she couldn't shake the stupid poem Sarco had rattled off so gleefully earlier. Again, the song invaded her mind.

She gathered her shawl tightly about her and groped for something, anything else to focus on. When she did finally find something to take her mind off of dragons, she almost wished she hadn't.

The spell, oh God Draka, would the talismans still be successful in this weather? She'd worked so hard on them. Had all her effort been in vain? Would the small, magical leather pouches still protect the five men they were meant for if the sun was obscured? The last line of the chant played once more in her mind, and she spoke it to the gray clouds overhead. "From first morning light 'til the sun's rays have faded."

The same thought that had plagued her from the moment she watched Adan, Uthiel, Sarco, Leeky, and Ray ride through the gates of Castle Kuropkat and disappear from sight, consumed her now. What would happen if there were no rays of sun to shine down upon them?

Lizbeth once more raised her face toward the heavens, but this time in prayer. "Watch over them for me, Lord Draka, at least until I get there and can kill them myself."

She turned and hurried inside.

\*\*\*\*

The skies had grown so dark it was difficult to see for more than a few feet in any direction, and the blizzard-like snowfall wasn't helping visibility either. To make matters worse, the incline had become so steep that forward progression was painfully slow. But forward they trudged.

The path began to narrow the higher up the mountain they rode, and the horses were in constant danger of bumping each other off the side. Even riding single file became treacherous.

Uthiel raised a hand. "I know this path well, and we must tether our mounts here. We have no choice but to walk the rest of the way to the dragon caves. Carnelian awaits us there, along with the other mature dragons and my very best paladins. That's where we must make our stand."

Adan looped his horse's bridle to a nearby tree and bent to examine the snow-covered ground at his feet. The distinct indentations going in every direction had him breaking out in a sweat. "Tracks, cloven hoof tracks."

Somewhere from behind, Leeky cackled with glee. "Has ta be the nogard for sure then, lads. We must be getting close."

Sarco wasn't paying attention. Turning to his right, he gazed out into the woods, squinting at something. Slowly, he pointed. "I think I saw movement over there." Suddenly, something big and running upright streaked between nearby trees.

"There, did you see it that time?"

Ray screamed. "Nogard! Nogard! Nogard!"

Chills scurried down Adan's back. The creature stopped, turned, and stared right at them. It was even bigger than Adan remembered. Huge horns curled up and out from the top of its head, ending in needle-sharp tips. The thing's humanoid face grimaced at them, and its blood-red eyes glared with their bulging orbs. Its flat nostrils flared as if it had been running fast and hard for a long time, and a low-pitched growl rumbled through its bared, fang-like teeth.

Adan quickly unsheathed the Ginsu Blade and began advancing upon the beast. The closer he got, the bigger it looked. Its shoulders were broad and its arms muscular. Both its hands boasted sharp, talon-like claws, and its long legs ended in the same cloven hooves as the tracks he had just seen. Suddenly, it lifted its face toward the heavens, flicked out its tongue, and sniffed the air.

Looking directly at Adan, it almost appeared to smile as it flipped its whip-like tail toward him, making a whooshing sound. Then, in the blink of an eye, the beast unfurled its scale-covered wings and took flight.

Back in the direction of the village and castle it flew.

"It knows, oh, my God Draka, it knows." Uthiel yelled.

"It knows what?" Adan demanded. The fear in Uthiel's eyes told the whole story, but he still needed to ask, to hear it for himself. "Tell me quickly. What does it know?"

"The cave halfway down the waterfall." Uthiel glanced toward Sarco and Leeky. "You two remember the cave, don't you? The same one Briar and Obsidian were once stuck in. It's the safest hiding place and hardest location in all of Castle Kuropkat to find and get to. At least, I thought it was."

His voice rose in decibels. "I didn't mean to put them in danger, you must believe me. It's my duty to protect Obsidian. He's the future of the dragon race. The first male dragling born in well over a hundred years. But...but, oh, my God Draka, in doing so, I've left Briar not only drugged but unprotected in the castle. And the other women...they won't be able to defend themselves against a nogard. None of them will."

"Tell me if I truly understand. Are you saying you hid the dragling in the waterfall cave and didn't tell me? Isn't that the same place Leeky hid Laycee? The cave not far from the castle and certainly not very far from our wives?"

Uthiel gulped and nodded. "If that's where Leeky hid her, then I'm afraid so, my friend. Seemed like a good idea at the time. And I didn't think it important enough to mention. I was certain the nogard would go for the rich feeding grounds found at the high-mountain dragon caves first. As far as Laycee being in the same cave, trust me. Obsidian would die protecting her if need be."

"What the slime-covered belly of a hung-over dwarf skinny-dipping in a mud pond with a group of troll trollops were ya thinking, lad? Ya know as well as I do that half-grown dragon's as likely ta eat my Laycee as he is ta protect her." He quickly slipped off his charcoal-gray looking-at-tracks gloves and replaced them with his soft leather riding ones.

Adan turned toward his gnome friend to offer reassurance, but all he saw was his backside. Leeky Shortz was already on his horse galloping full speed down the mountainside.

A heartbeat later, so were Adan, Uthiel, Sarco, and Ray.

## Chapter Twenty-Five

"Hurry! We really must hurry." Briar's voice penetrated Lizbeth's brain, causing her to forget once more what she just remembered she'd been looking for.

The castle was in a state of panic. Servants running to and fro, townspeople flooding the gates in a panic, and even the castle's stray cat sat shaking in the corner with his yellow eyes wide with fear and his black fur standing on end.

Lizbeth glared at Briar but continued stuffing various articles into her bag. "I am hurrying. You said to bring everything I have that has anything to do with magic, didn't you?"

Briar nodded.

"Then, go find Lark. I'll be ready by the time you get back."

"I don't need to be found. I'm here," a voice rang out.

Lizbeth quickly glanced at her sister-in-law as she jammed the last and most important item into her bag—her book of enchantments. "I'm ready, too."

"What about Laycee?" Lark asked. "I still can't find her."

Briar's voice sounded almost calm, but the twinge of fear in her eyes spoke volumes. "Don't worry about Laycee. She's already where we're going. She's with Obsidian right this moment, and she's...fine. He told me so."

Lizbeth shuddered. "Laycee's alone with a dragon? Your dragon? Isn't gnome one of a dragon's favorite snacks?"

Briar grimaced. "Well, I did mention the need to hurry, didn't I?"

The terrain was rough and the going slow. More than once, Lizbeth lost her footing and slipped, the heavy snowfall making it almost impossible to see where to next put her feet. Suddenly, a hand shot out and stopped all forward progress.

For no more than a handful of heartbeats, the sky almost cleared and Lizbeth gasped at the sight before her. The three women stood at the very edge of a tumbling, watery precipice. She couldn't help herself, she backed up a full two-and-a-half steps.

"Tell me we don't have to go to the bottom of that, do we? Please say we don't."

Briar scoffed. "No, don't be silly. Well, we at least don't have to go all the way to the bottom. See the ledge sticking out about halfway? We only have to go that far. There's a cave behind it, and that's where Obsidian and Laycee are. Don't worry, you'll see. It's easy. Obsidian will fly us down one at a time."

Lizbeth gulped and backed up a couple more steps. "I seriously don't think I can touch a dragon let alone ride upon one. Perhaps it's best if I do my part from here?"

Briar placed her hands on her hips. "Nonsense! I know you're no coward, Lizbeth Hammerstrike. We need your help down there. Obsidian and Laycee need your help. As a matter of fact, you need to go first and get set up."

She was in the process of shaking her head while backing farther away when the sky was obscured by a sudden darkness. It took only a moment to realize the reason for the loss of light was getting closer and had wings, big wings. With a yelp, Lizbeth jumped, lost her footing, and landed hard on her backside as two taloned feet came to rest directly before her.

Briar patted the dragling's midnight black scales. "Lizbeth meet my friend, Obsidian, and Obsidian, this is Lizbeth. You must fly her to the cave, then come back for Lark and I."

There wasn't time to jump and run or even to cry out before the dragon's talons wrapped themselves about her middle and lifted her up and away. Lizbeth closed her eyes tight. She couldn't move, she couldn't think, and she didn't dare even breathe as with a whoosh, those huge wings unfurled once more and over the side of the waterfall they flew.

She wasn't going to open her eyes, she really wasn't, but curiosity got the better of her fear and Lizbeth cracked open one eyelid and gasped. It was amazing. In a spiraling motion, downward the dragon flew. One moment a solid wall of water was before her gaze, and the next an expanse of mountains and valleys.

The wind buffeted her face while the updraft of air cushioned her body. For a moment, she stretched her arms wide, straightened her legs behind herself, and reveled in flight.

All too soon, the ledge came into view and through a curtain of water they flew. Before Lizbeth had a chance to realize Obsidian had released her, he was once more out the entrance and gone. Suddenly, she felt alone in the expanse of the dark cave. Then she saw

Laycee and couldn't help but sigh in relief.

The sight of the female gnome with her ill-fitting blonde wig hanging cockeyed on her oversized head was a welcome vision. She was shaking her fist in the air, and it took Lizbeth a moment to understand what her friend was yelling.

"Yeah, I'd run off again too if I was you, ya oversized coward. Ya just wait till my Leeky gets ahold of ya. He'll show ya whats what. Try ta eat me, will ya. And don't ya think for a minute I took any of those licks as affection, no matter how impressive your tongue is or where ya might have thought ta place it. Ya can't tell me ya weren't either tasting or basting me."

Lizbeth didn't want to think about the implications of either of those possibilities.

Within moments, what had looked to be a good sized cave became ridiculously small as Obsidian returned first with Lark then Briar. The four women were crammed in so close to each other there wasn't room to take a deep breath let alone move around freely. The added heat generated by the dragon's breaths sent trickles of sweat scampering down Lizbeth's back. She tried to ignore it. She tried to ignore him. It wasn't an easy task as each and every move she made brought her into contact with either one of her companions or the dragon itself.

"Let's get ready."

Lizbeth glanced sideways at Briar. "What did you have in mind?"

It was too dark in the cave to clearly see her expression, but the determination in Briar's voice was certain. "We must do whatever is in our power to protect Obsidian until the men and Carnelian arrive."

Lizbeth had one more question. "How?"

"Well, you're the enchantress. Enchant the cave with a protection spell. I'm the channeler, I'll channel your magic, boost it so to speak. Lark can do that spirtmaster-wizard stuff she does and fend off the nogard. If we work together, we can do this."

"What ya want me ta do?"

Lizbeth could almost hear the smile in Briar's voice. "You have the most important job of all, Laycee. Keep Obsidian calm."

The female gnome groaned. "Keep him calm! Just how am I supposed ta keep a two-ton dragon calm? Other than becoming a midday morsel that is." She crossed her arms and scuffed her booted toe along the ground.

Lark had an answer for her. "Why not do what you used to do with my sisters and me? Sing him a song or tell him a story. Worked well enough with us."

Conversation died away, and though she fought them, doubts filled Lizbeth's mind. *What if I can't do it?* She'd never tried to put a protection spell on an entire cave before. She didn't think she was magical enough to accomplish it.

Lark spoke directly to Lizbeth's mind though no actual sound was heard. *"We've all had our reservations when it came to our abilities. The trick is not to let your doubts get the better of you, Lizbeth. What is magic anyway but the determination to bend what isn't bendable to your will? You're a very strong-willed woman. You can do this. We can all do this together."*

Lizbeth nodded as she pulled her book of enchantments from her bag. A moment later, however, she was completely distracted by another book. One Laycee was now reading to Obsidian.

"She gasped as he flicked out his tongue and licked his eyebrows. Lillian Cuntalicious had never seen such a man as the debonair Gnoma Sutra. She simply had to have him.

"Purposefully, he strode toward her and, the moment he was within hand's reach, ripped her bodice wide and exposed her globes of milky-white breasts. He fondled them, tweaking the pert, rosy red nipples.

"She gasped and held her breath, waiting, wanting him to take her there and then, yet, at the same time, afraid if she did, she'd be spoiled for any other man. How many times had her mother told her, 'Once you go gnome, you'll never again roam?'

"And what a gnome he was. His turgid member—"

"Laycee!" Briar cried. "What on Albrath are you reading to my dragon?"

Laycee scoffed. "What do ya think I read ta Lark and her sisters when they were little, fairy tales? Nope, it was romance novels. And if ya gonna read a romance novel, ya might as well read a steamy one that makes your thighs stick together and your panties stand up by themselves when ya finally take 'em off."

She held the paperback up for all to see. *"Romancing the Gnome.* It's one of my favorites. It's written by Selvig Gnomenclature herself. I don't leave home without at least one good fuck-me-silly book. Never know when it'll come in handy."

Briar shook her head no.

Laycee sighed. "Fine then. I'll sing him a lullaby."

Her voice rose to almost a screech. "Forty-three cocks and balls on the wall, forty-three cocks and balls.

Take one down and pass it around, forty-two cocks and balls on the wall."

Lizbeth hid her grin, took a deep breath, placed three amethyst stones at the entrance of the cave, walked through the curtain of water, and began chanting the protection spell she'd chosen."

\*\*\*\*

Adan blinked twice then blinked once again, not wanting to believe his eyes. His wife, his pregnant wife, stood boldly on the ledge, halfway down the waterfall with a book in her hands and a look of intense concentration on her face. What did she think she was doing? She wasn't supposed to be here. She was supposed to be back in the castle, safe. She was supposed to be where he'd left her.

He balled his hands into fists, took deep breaths, and tried not to lose what tiny grip on his temper he still had. He made a promise to himself, though. If Lizbeth didn't fall and kill herself before he got to her, he was going to make sure she never again got the chance to put herself in danger even if it meant locking her inside their castle and throwing away the key.

A moment later, Leeky broke Adan's train of thought. The gnome tugged on his pant leg with one of his leather-gloved hands while pointing skyward with the other.

"What the red-painted lips of a toothless dwarf streetwalker giving a gummer ta a drunken halfling in the middle of town square and charging onlookers the price of admission ta watch do ya make of that, lads? Damn, looks like the nogard's gonna beat us ta the cave after all."

Adan looked up as did Uthiel, Sarco, and Ray. His

breath caught in his chest, and his blood ran cold. The nogard was heading straight for the ledge. "I have to get down there now!"

He grabbed a length of rope and began heaving it over the side. Uthiel stayed his arm. "There isn't time to climb the distance. Wait just a moment. Carnelian is almost here."

Adan shook his head and pulled away as the nogard landed on the very edge of the ledge and began walking directly toward Lizbeth. "No time."

Sarco took hold of Adan's other arm. "You'll get there faster on Carnelian's back, my friend. And take a good look at what's going on below. Our wives don't appear to be in any immediate danger. We have time. Carnelian can fly you down a lot faster than you can climb, then she can come back for the rest of us."

Adan did look. He really looked this time. Lizbeth wasn't simply standing there, she was orchestrating some type of spell, and she wasn't alone. The sheet of water covering the cave had parted and behind Lizbeth stood Lark and Briar. A triangle of blue lights danced back and forth between the three women and through their hands.

The nogard was close enough to almost touch them, but it didn't seem to be able to close the distance. Even though snow continued to fall in fat flakes all around, thunder crashed in the distance and lightning streaked the clouded sky.

For a moment, he was mesmerized, and more than just a touch in awe and proud of his wife...of all of them really. He'd always known there was magic in the world. He'd seen it up close from his sister more times than he could count. But this magic was beyond anything he'd ever envisioned. Lizbeth stood proudly, competently, directing her own brand of magic, and Lark and Briar were following her lead. It was mystical poetry in motion.

The sky above darkened even more as Carnelian flew directly overhead, circled, then landed. As if the dragon already understood what needed to be done, she wrapped her talons around Adan's middle and lifted him.

"I'll send her right back."

Uthiel, Sarco, and Leeky nodded, but Ray wasn't having it. "I will observe from here, thank you. I'm not overly fond of water or heights, and I'm much too important to be taking unnecessary risks. After all, someone reliable must be left to report back to the Council and the Queen."

Adan ignored the little human, tapped the dragon on her talon, and pointed downwards. He pulled the Blade of Gin from its sheath, readied it, and offered up a prayer to God Draka.

## Chapter Twenty-Six

*"Tempest of passion, tempest of light, protect what's within with all of your might. Tempest of truth, tempest of wonder, keep safe this dragon with a voice of thunder."*

It was working, she wasn't sure for how long, but for now, it was working. Power coursed through her veins as the nogard backed up another step, almost tumbling over the side of the ledge before regaining its balance.

Lizbeth concentrated even harder, redoubling her effort.

Elation warred with fear. She hadn't made a mistake this time. She'd picked the right spell for the right circumstance, after all. By combining what she knew of Lark's spiritmaster control-of-the-weather, along with Briar's ability to channel, and this particular protection spell from the book of enchantments, they were successfully staving off the beast a mere few feet away.

Venom dripped from its sharp fangs, and fury shot daggers from its blood-red, bulging eyes.

Lizbeth was so tired, though. Her arms ached from holding the book of enchantments tightly so the wind couldn't whip it from her grasp, and her fingers had long ago gone numb from the cold. Her throat burned from shouting into the wind, and her legs threatened to no longer hold her weight.

Though fatigue sapped her of what little energy she had, Lizbeth took yet another deep breath and began chanting the protection spell once more. How much longer could they keep this up? Where was Adan? Where were Sarco, Uthiel, and Leeky, for that matter? If there was ever a time they desperately needed them, it was now.

She'd even be glad to see Ray. Lizbeth giggled, though she wasn't sure if it was from hysteria or the thought she'd just had. What would she give to be safe, sound, and warm at The Academy right now, even if Ray were back to his old self, running around yelling "Ray loves cock. Ray loves cock. Ray loves cock." at the top of his lungs?

She shuddered, not sure which would be worse, the nogard standing before her right this moment or the crazed little human?

\*\*\*\*

Adan couldn't breathe. He wasn't going to get to her in time. Before Carnelian had completely released her hold upon him and before his feet had a chance to settle upon the ledge, he ran directly toward the nogard. He drew the Blade of Gin from its sheath and readied it to strike, his only thought to protect his wife and unborn child.

The nogard paid him no mind. From the top of its horned head to the tip of its scaled tail, it was of a single purpose, and that purpose was to get to and past Lizbeth. That couldn't be allowed to happen.

Adan timed the swishing of the nogard's tail. He ducked and rolled between and through the outstretched legs of the beast, popping up directly between it and

Lizbeth. The creature's blood-red eyes shifted their focus from the women and directly onto him. Adan was once again able to breathe.

They faced off, Adan, with his spine ramrod-straight, standing tall, with determination rippling through every fiber of his being while the nogard stood inches away, hissing at him. Its wild gaze penetrated with a deadly stare while its slit-like nostrils flared. Its thick horns shook back and forth like an angry bull.

"Get inside the cave, Lizbeth, now."

She didn't argue with him. She simply ignored him while continuing to chant. Adan wasn't sure who he wanted to kill first. He couldn't turn to glare at her to emphasize his point, afraid to take his eyes from the monster before him. "I said, get back inside that cave, now!" he yelled.

A growl rumbled through the bared, fang-like teeth of the nogard while its whip-like, demonic tail flicked to and fro making a whooshing sound.

*"Tempest of passion, tempest of light, protect what's within with all of your might. Tempest of truth, tempest of wonder, keep safe this dragon with a voice of thunder."*

The ledge below his feet shook so violently with the crash and rumble of sound, Adan almost lost his footing. It told him one thing. Lizbeth wasn't going to stop, no matter what he demanded, until this was finished, so he might as well get it done. Though the thought of her putting herself in the line of danger chilled him to the bone, it also filled him with pride.

From the corner of his eye, Adan watched as first Uthiel, Sarco, then Leeky, were deposited on the ledge directly behind the nogard. Up again Carnelian flew.

Only Ray was left to be collected.

Uthiel hefted his broadsword, Sarco readied a fireball, and Leeky removed his leather gloves and replaced them with his golden wielding-daggers ones. It was now or never.

Adan lunged, aiming for the space between the nogard's scales on the left side of its chest. The beast was quick, though, and side-stepped the assault.

The nogard lashed out with its sharp talons and slashed across the top of the arm Adan used to handle the Blade of Gin. Blood oozed from the cut and ran freely, dripping to his wrist.

From behind, he heard Lizbeth gasp, but her voice didn't falter. Adan switched hands. Again, the nogard lunged, but this time he was ready. Adan nodded toward his companions. Uthiel brought down his broadsword, and the impact of the blade against impenetrable scale slowed the forward progression of the monster.

Sarco let fly his fireball, and the nogard screamed in anger. Leeky ran toward the beast and, with lightning speed, plunged both daggers between its taloned toes. The nogard glanced down at the gnome and kicked him. Leeky went flying across the ledge, barely managing to hang onto the side.

Adan plunged the Blade of Gin deep into the nogard's chest, slicing through the scale as if it were no denser than butter and burying itself deep.

The beast screeched, twisted, and backed away. The momentum took Adan along.

The last sight Adan Hammerstrike had before plunging over the side of the ledge and down into the watery abyss was the look of sheer horror in his wife's eyes.

\*\*\*\*

Lizbeth's heart stopped, and time slowed.

The flapping of wings overhead filled Lizbeth's ears with a roar, but at the same time, broke her heart. It told her two things. One, Carnelian was finally bringing Ray down to the ledge, and two, the dragon wouldn't have time to deliver Ray and still save Adan.

She watched in helpless desperation as the man who held her heart tumbled backwards. Lizbeth flung out both arms as if to catch him, her precious book of enchantments falling, unheeded, to the ground. It was of no use, though.

She couldn't glance away for even the dropping of a single grain of sand as Adan and the nogard toppled. He clung to the knife still embedded in the nogard's chest and gazed back at her, a look of regret in his eyes.

Lizbeth screamed, but the wind swallowed the sound.

A single ray of sunshine broke through the clouds at the same time there was a sudden commotion behind her. Lizbeth turned, stunned by the sight. Obsidian stood, his scaled wings unfurled, once black as midnight, they now glowed golden where the sun's rays lit upon them.

With a whoosh, the dragon flew over the side of the cliff, and Lizbeth tried to follow. The only thing stopping her were the arms of Uthiel and Sarco, holding her back, while Leeky clung to one of her legs.

The gnome let go and wagged his finger at her. "What the puked-up pork rinds from the belly of an inebriated dwarf dandy doing the hokey-pokey with a trio of troll transvestites were ya thinking, lass? Ya can't help him. Give Obsidian a chance, ya'll see. If it's possible, he'll bring Adan back safe and sound. Jumping off the side of a ledge after him is just plain insane."

Lizbeth did stop. There was no fight left in her. Silently, she slumped to the ground and sobbed.

The sunshine disappeared, angry lightning streaked the sky, thunder crashed, the wind howled, and snow so heavy it blanketed the landscape fell.

****

He wasn't dead.

Adan wasn't quite sure why he wasn't dead, but he wasn't. What he was, though, was wet and cold, very wet and cold. Though the water was no deeper than his chest, the impact into the lake below the waterfall had drenched him to the skin. The snow falling on him wasn't helping matters, either.

The nogard, however, was another story. Adan stared at the creature. Its bulging eyes were closed. No more did its nostrils flair or its mouth hiss. It simply floated upon the surface of the lake, the Blade of Gin protruding from its chest. He poked it once, then poked it again. Dead, yes, it was most assuredly dead.

But why wasn't he dead? A fall from that height should've killed any normal mortal. Though Adan knew he was bigger and stronger than most, he had no illusions of immortality.

Then he felt it. Then he knew. It pulsed against his chest and gave off a soul-warming heat. It glowed even through the leather of his clothing.

Adan grasped the talisman of protection Lizbeth had fashioned for him. He pulled it out from beneath his tunic and stared at it. The talisman had worked. The spell she'd spoken had really worked. He was alive, and he had his wonderfully magical enchantress of a wife to thank for it.

The sight of Obsidian landing gracefully upon the lake brought a sigh of relief to Adan's lips. The thought of lugging the heavy dead nogard out of the lake and up the snowy hill wasn't something Adan had looked forward to. The dragon scooped up the lifeless beast with one talon and Adan in the other.

The barbarian smiled all the way to the ledge. The nogard was dead, he and Lizbeth could get on with their lives, and now he'd have the chance to make sure his Lizard, never forgot just how magical she was.

****

There almost wasn't room on the ledge for Obsidian to land. Lark, Briar, and Laycee had come out from the cave, and along with Carnelian, Uthiel, Sarco, Leeky, and Ray, they all lined the small space.

Adan couldn't help but grin as he yelled down to them. "Clear the runway, dragon about to land."

They scattered, all of them that is except for Lizbeth. She stood rooted to her spot at the edge of the ledge as if frozen.

The moment Obsidian released him, Adan wrapped his wife in his arms. She melted against him, and he kissed away her tears.

"I-I-I thought you were dead."

With a finger, Adan tucked an errant strand of toffee-colored hair behind her slightly pointed ear and stroked her cheek. "If it hadn't been for you, my little enchantress, I would have been."

Lizbeth shook her head. "What?"

Adan lifted the talisman of protection from beneath

his tunic and held it out. It still glowed with energy. "It worked, Lizbeth. Your magic worked. I'll never again doubt you or your abilities. You can protect us whenever you like."

Tears filled her eyes and spilled down her cheeks once more. Adan waited, anxious for her response, when the sound of someone else sobbing distracted not only him, but everyone else as well.

It was the strangest sight. There sat Ray, kneeling before the dead nogard, crying as if his heart were broken.

The little human glared up at Adan. "Murderer!" His face filled with rage. "You didn't even try to capture it. Look what you've done. All is lost. I was going to be so rich. Your mother, the Queen, promised me all the platt I could carry if we brought the nogard back alive. She said as long as the beast lived, people would never forgive and forget what your...your wife did."

Ray stood, blew his nose, and wiped it on his shirtsleeve. "You just wait. I'll get all of you. I've been keeping notes, you know. I'm going to tell the Council every dirty little detail I can think of and some I've even made up. You'll be outcasts when I get finished with you, all of you."

Leeky crossed the short space between them and patted Ray gently on the back. "What the bald belly on a feather-plucking parrot watching an ogre orgy from the confines of his cage are ya talking about, lad? Ya know as well as the rest of us do there was no choice but ta kill the thing. It was either the nogard or us. It's over, let it go."

Ray backed away. "You...you...you struck me!

You're trying to kill me. You think you can silence me, don't you? But you can't." He continued to backup. Just as Ray stepped perilously close to the edge of the ledge, Adan, Uthiel, and Sarco rushed forward to catch him.

It was too late.

By the time they reached him, Ray had lost his balance and plummeted over the edge. With arms and legs flailing, he yelled, "Murderers, murderers, murderers."

Adan rubbed his jaw. "I suppose someone should go get him."

Lizbeth wasn't so calm. "Oh, my God. We've killed Ray!" Adan stroked her back. "He's not dead. We couldn't get that lucky. He's wearing the talisman you made him, remember?"

Uthiel spoke. "I'll send Carnelian. She can fish him out of the lake."

Leeky objected. "Naw, don't waste the dragons. We need them ta carry the lasses back up top, not ta mention the dead nogard. I'll go get him. It's my fault he fell off in the first place. Never should've touched the little peckerhead." He glanced over the edge as he took off his golden dagger-wielding gloves and replaced them with a pair of muddy-looking brown ones. "Shimmying-down-things-and-climbing-back-up-'em gloves."

The gnome smiled then sighed. "Anyway, I better get going. It ain't getting any lighter. If ya all get a move on now, ya can be through the portal and back ta the Academy before morning. Ray and I will meet ya there."

Laycee placed her hands on her hips and stuck out

her jaw. "And just how was ya thinking of getting down there ta Ray, Leeky Shortz? Did ya think ya could climb all the way down without falling and busting ya head? Or was ya just gonna throw yaself over the edge like ya was afraid Lizbeth was gonna do a few grains of sand ago?"

Leeky chuckled and shrugged his shoulders. "Seemed like a reasonable plan."

Laycee sighed as she pulled something plastic from the pocket of her pants. "I was saving this for just the right time. I guess that's now."

Leeky's face lit up like a sunrise when he spotted the only thing not plastic on the object. It was a little white, furry bunny tail. "My Miss Bunny! Aww, Laycee, lass. Ya do know how ta make my short and curlies stand up and wiggle, don't ya?"

Laycee pinkened. "Flatterer."

Adan almost choked. "What on Albrath are you going to do with the doll this time, Leeky?"

The gnome grinned from ear to ear as he slipped off the shimmying-climbing gloves and replaced them with his soft, fuzzy pink touching-a-lady pair. He squeezed Miss Bunny's nipples and popped out the air tubes hidden within them. "Well, as soon as you lads blow her up for me, I plan ta surf her down the side of this waterfall. Uthiel, ya take the right tit and Sarco can have a go at the left one."

He grinned at Adan as he turned Miss Bunny around and lifted her furry little tail out of the way, exposing yet another air tube right between her ass cheeks. "Saved the best one for ya, Adan. Once ya've tasted plastic, there's nothing more fantastic. Okay, boys, get ta blowing."

## Chapter Twenty-Seven

Though it was still more the middle of the night than morning, Lizbeth was anxious to get the presentation of the nogard over with. A momentary twinge of guilt plagued her for tolling The Academy's emergency bells, but not enough to prevent her from doing it. She tugged once more on the heavy cord, ringing them for the third time. The vibrations shook the tower.

She sighed. The Council would undoubtedly be angry with her for waking them, but she couldn't help it. There was no way she could wait even one more turn of the hourglass to learn her fate.

As quickly as they could travel, with Adan, Uthiel, and Sarco carrying the dead nogard, the group made its way to the formal meeting hall.

No sooner had the heavy double doors of the hall closed behind them than an angry voice rang out. "This had better be important. I'm over nine hundred years old, and you can bet I get a little cranky when awakened before my usual hour."

Lizbeth stepped forward, looked around, and gulped. She knew ringing the emergency bell would bring The Academy officials, but she hadn't expected this. The hall was near to bursting at its seams. It looked as if every single resident was in attendance.

Even the Queen, with King Alfred at her side, sat

next to Headmistress Seychelle, a look of complete disdain upon her face.

Lizbeth gulped once more and stiffened her spine. "I am sorry for waking you, Wizard Arizon, but I thought you'd want to know straight away that the nogard is no longer a threat."

Adan, Uthiel, and Sarco walked forward and laid the body of the dead nogard, with the Blade of Gin still protruding from its chest, at Arizon's feet.

The old wizard nodded. "So I see."

He didn't get to say anything else before an ear-splitting scream deafened the room.

Queen Allanna Zanlynn Calista Hammerstrike stood, her face a picture of rage. She pointed one perfectly manicured finger toward Lizbeth. "You did this. You're responsible. The nogard was supposed to be brought back alive for study. Where is Raynorel? What have you done with him? I demand to hear his report!" She tapped her toe. "Well, where is he?"

Whispers and speculation came from every corner of the hall.

Adan glared at his mother. "I killed the nogard. No one else. It was him or me. There was no other choice."

The Queen scoffed. "I see you've been taken in by your...your...wife. Him or you, poppycock. I don't believe that for a moment. I should've guessed this would happen. Men, you're all alike. Only thinking with your...nether parts. I expected more of my son, though. Where is Raynorel, or did you kill him, too?"

Lizbeth gulped, her cheeks burned with a combination of anger and guilt. She was about to try and explain when the doors of the hall crashed open.

In swaggered Leeky Shortz with his blow-up doll

under one arm and leading a sopping wet Ray with the other. The little human dripped with every step he took. His eyes were glassy, and his stringy brown hair lay plastered in clumps on his head. Even his boots squished as he walked.

Leeky bowed before Arizon. "Sorry we're late for the party. What the prickly heat rash on the backside of a sunburnt, nakey halfling, skinny-dipping in the local honeypot did we miss?"

Queen Allanna huffed. "It's about time you got here. Gnome, you be quiet. Raynorel, give the council your report."

The Queen smirked at Lizbeth. "I'm sure we would all like to hear what *really* happened."

Leeky flipped off the queen, but still urged Ray forward until the little human stood directly before Wizard Arizon.

Lizbeth held her breath. She knew from his stiff stance, Adan was holding his, too. Neither had any idea what Ray would say nor how damaging it would be.

A hush fell over the hall, every eye glued to Ray.

The soggy human looked up at Arizon, pulled his ruined notebook from his pocket, opened it, and grinned. "Ray loves cock," he yelled.

Queen Allanna screeched. "What have you done to him?"

Leeky shrugged his shoulders. "He fell in the water, I pulled him out, and all he's been saying all the way here is how much he loves cock. The dip in the pool must've traumatized him back to his old self is all I can figure."

High Wizard Arizon leaned toward Adan and Lizbeth, and whispered, "Is she always like this, the

Queen?"

Adan nodded, but Lizbeth simply sighed.

"How do you stand it? Never mind. Remind me after these proceedings, I think I have just the thing. It'll make your lives more...bearable. Trust me." To the assembly in the hall, his voice boomed. "I will have silence!"

Ray jumped up and down. "Ray loves cock. Ray loves cock. Ray loves cock."

"Silence!" Arizon demanded.

Headmistress Seychelle rushed forward. "Of course, you love cock, sweetums. Come along with Mistress, and I'll get you one."

Ray turned toward the headmistress, looked up at her with such sadness in his eyes, and whimpered, "Ray loves cock."

"I know you do, pet." Seychelle placed a protective arm about Ray's shoulder and led him away.

Wizard Arizon pointed to the blade protruding from the nogard's chest. "I see you were able to procure the Blade of Gin, after all. Knowing the leader of the trolls as I do, that couldn't have been an easy task. What kind of bargain did you have to strike with, Camel Toe...I mean, Karla, to get your hands on it?"

Queen Allanna shouted. "I have no doubt my daughter-in-law obtained it by illegal means. She needs to be punished."

Lizbeth's cheeks burned. She opened her mouth to answer, but no sound came forth.

Adan didn't seem to have that problem. He cleared his throat, bent down, and extracted the knife, then wiped it clean upon his breeks and glared at his mother before turning toward Arizon. "It was completely legal and surprisingly easy. We offered Karla something she couldn't resist as a deposit, so to speak, until such time as we returned the blade."

A look of wonder crossed Arizon's wrinkled old face. "What on Albrath did you offer?"

Adan mumbled. "O.T.T."

Arizon leaned in a little closer. "Come again?"

The entire group began talking at once. Lizbeth finally found her voice. "We didn't force him. Well, not really, anyway.

Uthiel shouted, "It was a brilliant strategy if you think about it."

Briar cried, "It was the only way."

"It had to be done," Lark insisted while Sarco nodded furiously.

Laycee dropped to her knees before the old wizard and cried, "He would've wanted it that way. I just know he would've."

Leeky patted her on the back.

Arizon raised a hand for silence and pointed toward Adan. "Explain."

Once more, Adan cleared his throat. "By all rights, O.T.T. should go down in history as the greatest diplomatic strategist Albrath has ever known. Even after losing a testicle to Karla years ago, he offered himself up as collateral for the use of the blade. Not a braver gnome have I ever seen. Even as we speak, he's in Karza…with Karla, awaiting our return. In the morning, we'll take the blade back and collect our friend. As intact as we left him, I hope."

Arizon nodded and wiped what suspiciously looked like a tear from his eye. "I see a medal of honor in that gnome's future. What selflessness and dedication." He waved his arms outward encompassing the hall. "Let it be known. The nogard has been dispatched, and Lizbeth Hammerstrike is reinstated as an enchantress student here at the Academy of Magic."

The Queen fainted.

****

No bed had ever felt so welcoming.

Lizbeth snuggled beneath the furs and up against the warm, naked body of her husband, tingling with joy and anticipation.

Adan chuckled. "Be careful where you put that lush bottom of yours, Lizard. Even though I'm tired all the way to the marrow of my bones, some things are near impossible to resist."

She turned to him and ran her hand the length of his torso, marveling in the rock-hard plains of his chest and abdomen before finally coming to rest on his expanding cock.

She grasped his balls, squeezing gently as she grinned. "Perhaps I don't wish to be resisted. I think we deserve a reward for our fine work of these past few days, my lord. Would you like another Adan Hammerstrike class demonstration by chance?"

Adan gulped, and Lizbeth felt his cock spasm beneath her fingers.

"Lizard, I'm game if you are, my love, but you've had a very long day, and you're with child, remember? You need your rest. I'll devour you when we wake."

She giggled. "Don't call me Lizard, and as for our child…" She turned and glanced toward the window. Outside, the morning sun was just beginning to peak in the eastern sky, a gentle breeze blew through the drapes, and birds sang. "Zander seems quite content at the moment. I think he's sleeping."

She ran a single finger across the head of Adan's cock, swirling it around and around before bringing it to her lips and slowly licking. "If we're quiet, we won't wake the baby."

Lizbeth slid her hand back down his body and grasped him once more. She opened and closed about his completely rigid cock, stroking as she went. He groaned, and it was like music to her ears.

"Shush," she whispered against the scratchy stubble of tomorrow's beard while kissing her way to his mouth. "Just lie back and relax. This one's on me."

She captured his lips with hers and forgot who was seducing whom as his arms enveloped her and his tongue plundered her mouth. Lightning fast jolts of pleasure raced along her spine and straight to her pussy. Her toes curled of their own volition, and the tiny hairs on the back of her neck stood at attention, waiting, wanting, needing.

She didn't have to wait long as, with a growl, Adan flipped her onto her stomach and began a slow descent of kisses from the top of her shoulder blades to the small of her back. She wiggled beneath him, the warmth of his lips combined with the stubble on his cheeks driving her insane. Every nerve ending in Lizbeth's body zinged to life.

He parted her thighs and slid one finger deep into her pussy while still feathering kisses along her hips. "Want to bet there are still things you don't know about me when it comes to making love, Lizard? I think I still have a surprise or two up my sleeve. Or in this case, down my pants." Then he nipped her right ass cheek, hard.

Lizbeth shivered, as chill bumps popped and her flesh burned with fevered desire. "I think I've leaned my lesson about betting with you, my lord. I'll take you at your word, this time."

He nipped her again, and she moaned. Never had she experienced such a feeling of wantonness, yet at the same time, knew herself to be completely safe.

It made sense now. She didn't have to be afraid of marriage with this man. He would never hurt her. They were a couple, a husband and a wife, separate yet one. Equals, not only here in this bed, in the love they made, but also in day-to-day life.

Each would always give as good as they got, and more than good was what she was getting now as Adan pulled her up until all that touched the bed were her knees, feet, and hands. His cock nestled snugly between her legs as if it were her own, and his arms wrapped about her, her back to his front.

He ran his hands freely over her, tweaking first one taut nipple then the other before moving down her belly and back up again. His lips tickled her tender skin, kissing and sucking a path from the tips of her pointed ears, down her neck, and along her shoulder blades.

Lizbeth couldn't breathe, and she couldn't think. Jolts of delight shot throughout her body, paralyzing her with pleasure. Everywhere he touched, spasms of ecstasy followed in his wake. It was on the tip of her tongue to tell him it didn't get any better than this when it did.

Adan leaned into her, and in one swift plunge, entered her. He fisted both his hands in her hair and rode. The walls of Lizbeth's pussy clenched about him, and her juices flowed.

Throbbing with need, she met him stroke for stroke. The faster and deeper he plunged, the quicker she reciprocated by slamming her ass against him.

This was no cultured gentleman and his sweet lady dallying. And this was no gently bred dandy with his civilized doxie. This was two barbarians fucking, this was raw, this was untamed, and this was real.

Lizbeth quivered with the absolute bliss of it.

A throbbing so intense it almost hurt built deep within. She fought it, trying to stave off what she knew was coming, wanting this moment to last longer, to last forever.

Adan was having none of it, however. He slipped a hand around Lizbeth's waist, down between her folds, and matched the strokes of his cock with caresses against her clit.

Lizbeth lost the fight to keep from orgasming as spasms—his filling her with hot liquid and hers rocking her to the very core—had her shuddering with surrender. She collapsed in Adan's arms, spent, satisfied, complete.

It was long moments later, after her heart had ceased pounding and her breathing slowed, that she found the energy to glance up. He was grinning at her like the arrogant prince he was, and she couldn't help but smile right back at him. Oh, my God Draka, he was sexy.

She sighed, no longer afraid, but finally content with the thought of being Adan Hammerstrike's wife, their son's mother, and the next barbarian queen. But there was still unfinished business to attend to. What did the immediate future hold?

"So, what's the plan for tomorrow and all the other

tomorrows after that? That is, after we go rescue O.T.T." Lizbeth hoped the anxiousness didn't show in her voice. She didn't want Adan to know how important his answer was to her.

He hugged her close, then tipped her face up until they were eye to eye. "What do you want our tomorrows to hold?"

Lizbeth took a deep breath. "Well, I'd like to finish this next semester here at The Academy if that's possible. Then I suppose we must return to your parent's castle for the birth of our child, mustn't we?"

Adan kissed her forehead and sighed. "One more semester doesn't sound unreasonable. Zander isn't due for a few moons yet. As for his birth, by decree, the heir to the throne must be born on Alarian soil. However, that doesn't mean we have to live with my parents. I asked my father to have a separate castle built just for the two of us, remember? Something small, one we can live in until it's time for us to rule. That way, we can go back and forth and spend what time we need to at The Academy finishing our studies and still have a place of our own to come home to. Does that sound acceptable?"

Lizbeth smiled. "That sounds perfect. I love you, Barbarian."

Adan laughed. "I love you, too, Lizard."

Her heart swelled near to bursting. To her way of thinking, those were the most beautiful words Lizbeth had ever heard.

## Epilogue

"You may now kiss the bride."

Adan glanced at his own bride of a short year ago and smiled in wonder. Lizbeth sat at the back of the hall, stroking the downy, soft head of their son and cooing nonsense to him in order to keep Zander quiet and the lightning from striking the castle. She was beautiful. They both were. They were his life. He could watch them forever and never grow tired of the sight.

The clearing of a throat somewhere off to the side brought his attention back to his current duty. Tearing his eyes from his family, Adan gestured for the happy couple to turn and face the crowd.

In a voice that boomed, he exclaimed, "As ruler of the kingdom of Alaria, it is my proud honor and duty to be the first to present to you Leeky and Laycee Shortz, man and wife. May God Draka bless this union."

Even Tug McGroin, dressed in a tux and acting as best man, and Miss Bunny, in pink chiffon, as the maid of honor, looked happy for the couple.

The hall broke out in cheers, and it didn't take more than a minute for the wedding reception to commence in full swing. Music blared, and spirits flowed freely.

Then Lark asked the question Lizbeth had been dreading all day. "Okay, you've kept us in suspense long enough. Out with it. I'm dying to hear. How on

Albrath did you convince my parents to let you paint the walls of this dusty old castle every color of the rainbow, and why did Father step down from his throne? And where is Mother? Has Father locked her away somewhere, finally?"

Lizbeth handed the sleeping infant over to his great-grandmother, Ava, and glanced toward Adan. He held up both hands. "Oh, no, my little Lizard. I've been talking all day. It's your turn."

Looking at the room full of anxious faces, including the bride and groom, O.T.T. and Karla, Uthiel, and Briar, Sarco, and Lark, Lizbeth felt her cheeks burn. Where to start? She took two deep breaths and blew them out.

"You remember that the king was having a separate castle built just for Adan and I, don't you?"

Everyone nodded.

"Well, it wasn't quite finished when time came for us to return to Alaria for Zander's birth. The Queen, of course, was her typical self, and I was...let's just say, a little...hormonal at the time. Something simply had to be done so that one of us didn't kill the other. There really was no choice."

For a moment, Lark looked concerned, then she laughed. "You two didn't by chance really lock them away somewhere, did you? It would certainly serve Mother right, if you did...but..."

Lizbeth shook her head, but Adan chuckled. "Oh, Lizard did better than lock them away. Tell them, darling."

The words tumbled from her lips in a rush. "I enchanted them out of their very own home. And I don't even regret it. I'm the most horrible of daughter-in-laws. There, I've said it."

Lark did look concerned now. "Just how did you enchant my parents out? They do still exist, don't they? I mean, my mother may not care for me, but I do still care for her."

It took a moment for Lark's words to sink in, but when they did, Lizbeth was horrified. "Oh, no, it's nothing like that. They're fine, really they are. They just live in that little castle on the far side of the city your father was having built for us. I guess you could say, we traded residences."

Lark grinned. "So, what's the catch? I know my mother, and she wouldn't have given up her castle, let alone her throne, without a very good reason."

"It's the paint," Adan shouted excitingly.

Not another sound was made as every eye in the room turned and locked on Lizbeth, waiting.

She wrung her hands together and cleared her throat. Looking straight at Sarco Sunwalker, she explained, "It was your uncle who gave me the idea. Arizon presented us with a packet of special powder as a gift. When mixed with something else, anything else, it enchants that product with happy thoughts…forever. Thereby making it impossible to say or do cruel or mean things while in its presence."

She forced herself to relax her stance. "I hadn't meant to use it as I did. I'd planed on sprinkling it in the evening's stew on special occasions. You know, just to have a peaceful meal once in awhile. Perhaps during the Yulemass when the whole family's home. But…"

Lizbeth took a deep breath as heat wicked up her neck. She hurried to get the words out before she lost her nerve. "Queen Allanna said something particularly nasty about my size not soon after we arrived, and I lost it. I put the magical powder in the paint, all of the powder in all of the paint. Then, I purposely used the paint in every single room of the castle, even the dungeon. Within two days, she couldn't take it any more. The king turned over his crown to Adan, and they moved out. She hasn't visited even once since then. Not even to see her grandson. Thankfully, Grandmother Ava decided to stay with us. She's been a godsend."

Adan grinned from ear to ear. "We can't even say mean things to each other. If we want to fight about something, we have to take it outside. And since it's so blasted cold here, that makes for very short and to the point arguments, with long, sizzling hot make-up sessions."

Leeky cackled as he wiped tears of laughter from his eyes. "What the worn-out boulder holder on a troll trollop in a too-tight tutu trying ta do a gaggle of limp ogres all at the same time do ya make of that, lads?"

There was a sudden sound of choking from across the room.

O.T.T. frowned at his brother-in-law. "Mind what ya be saying bout trolls, Leeky Shortz, lest ya find yaself at the business end of my..." His last words were never heard as the enchantment in the paint took over.

Instead, he climbed on a chair and wrapped his arm protectively about Camel Toe Karla's pink tutu-clothed waist and glared.

"Now, O.T.T.," Laycee said. "Ya know as well as I do, Leeky didn't mean no disrespect. We're proud ta have Karla as our sister-in-law. We just want ta have fun."

The almost bald gnome with the wire-rimmed

glasses took another swig of his ale. "Didn't I ask ya not ta call me O.T.T. anymore, sis? The name's Thaddeus, and I don't have just one testicle anymore, I've got a pair again."

He reached up and pulled what looked to be a brown, dried-up, wrinkly object hanging on a strip of leather from inside his tunic. "Got it right here. Karla gave it back ta me as a present at our wedding night. She'd been wearing it herself since the day she bit it off. Kept it right by her heart, she did, ta remember me by. Isn't that just the most romantic thing ya ever did hear?"

Adan, Uthiel, and Sarco gagged, but Thaddeus Titwilder didn't seem to notice. He leaned in close and kissed Karla on the tummy. "And I'm living proof all ya need is one functioning testicle ta get the job done. Karla and I want ya all ta be the first ta know that six moons from now we're gonna have a little trome of our own."

"Trome?" Lizbeth asked.

Karla smiled shyly. "That's our pet name for the little bundle of joy. Half troll, half gnome, a trome."

A bell sounding and another voice, this one coming from the dinning room, saved Lizbeth from having to respond.

"Dinner's served."

\*\*\*\*

"Chili, seriously? What were you thinking?" Sarco grimaced.

Adan shook his head. "You don't like chili? It's what Leeky and Laycee both insisted they wanted served for their wedding dinner. And this is extra special chili. It's made from Alarian water buffalo. Try it, you'll like it."

Sarco sighed. "Gnomes and chili aren't a good mix."

Adan's eyes widened. "Oh, VoT, I forgot."

Sarco laughed. "Yep, it's like a drug to them. How could you have forgotten? Remember what happened at their last party?"

Adan gulped. "You're right."

Leeky and Laycee finished off their third bowl, burped, farted, and jumped up from their seats. They both hopped onto the table and began dancing. Before long, Thaddeus and Karla joined them.

The dance soon got out of control, and Adan shook his head, silent, watching.

Leeky snatched Laycee's blond wig from her head and put it on his own. He stripped off his tunic, tweaked his own nipples, then proceeded to hop down and give Tug a lap dance.

Laycee, not to be out-done, flipped up her skirt, exposing her pasty white bottom. She grabbed a cucumber from the veggie tray and had it on its way to her bare essentials when Lark seized it from her grasp.

Lizbeth clung to Adan's arm. "You've got to do something. Make them stop."

Adan stood and tapped his spoon against his glass to get the gnome's attention. It didn't work.

Leeky dropped his draws and let out a fart so long and loud a green cloud formed in the air above him. "Let's see ya beat that one, honey tits!"

Laycee beamed. "Ya've always been a sweet talker, Leeky Shortz. But I'm gonna win this one." She lifted her skirt even higher, bent until her head touched her toes, and let it rip.

Leeky came up behind his wife, and they began a bizarre dance. She gyrated in front of him, and he acted as if he were smacking her on the ass.

Then Karla and Thaddeus began disrobing.

Adan's eyes burned and not just from the smell. He tried to yell for them to stop, but no sound came forth. The paint, it was the damn paint. He grabbed Lizbeth's hand, motioned to Sarco, Lark, Uthiel, and Briar to follow, and ran for the door. Only one word echoed in the courtyard as Adan drew his first breath of fresh, cold Alarian night air.

"Leeky!"

## About the Author

Maxine Mansfield writes erotic-fantasy romances for The Wild Rose Press from the comfort of her home in the far northern state of Alaska, where the summer days are long and the winter nights even longer.

She has one very special man, his three equally special children, and their six delightful grandchildren to keep her busy when not typing away on her next book. Not to mention her very bossy African grey parrot named Gabriel.

Oh, and gnomes! Many, many gnomes.

Visit Maxine at
Web site: www.maxinemansfield.com
Blog: http://www.maxinemansfield.com/blog.html
Email: Maxine-mansfield@hotmail.com
Twitter: https://twitter.com/LeekyShortz

To chat with Maxine Mansfield and other Wild Rose Press authors of erotic romance, join us at www.groups.yahoo.com/group/thewilderroses.

Also Available

# Tempted By The Storm

## by

## Maxine Mansfield

Larksong Hammerstrike has always been just the younger sister of Princess Aryanna, never quite as pretty or as smart, always lacking, a mere empath whose power gets her into trouble more often than not. But at Carnalval, the festival of all things sexual, she unleashes her sensual side for a night in the arms of a masked stranger. When morning dawns, Lark can't resist a peek beneath the mask of her lover and is once again crushed by fate. The man of her lusty adventure is none other than the future Lord of the High Elves and destined to marry her sister.

As heir to the kingdom of Landis and current instructor of wizardry at the Academy of Magical Arts, Sarco Sunwalker is honor bound to rise above the temptation of the beautiful empathic student who invades his mind, body, and soul. But when sparks fly, lightning strikes, and thunder rolls, Sarco finds himself more than tempted by the storm of Lark's passion and vows to find a solution that will prevent a war between races, fulfill an infamous quest, and win Lark's hand.

*"It's ice and fire*
*that forms a maiden's desire.*
*It's searing heat*
*where metal and gemstone first meet.*
*It's with love in mind*
*that a treasure becomes divine.*
*It's a champion you must defeat*
*for a heart you wish to seek.*
*It's your choice to make*
*for the wife you will take."*

## Chapter One

Lark sighed.

If ever a man was born to be laid upon silken sheets and devoured like an ice cream sundae, the handsome, dark-haired high-elf across the room was that man. He leaned nonchalantly against a pillar and my, oh my, how she'd like to practice a little good old-fashioned debauchery with him.

What was she thinking? Even though this was the pleasure city of Carnalval and lusting after strange men was not only acceptable, but expected and condoned, that didn't mean she could simply stroll over and take what her heart desired.

Still, she gazed at him with longing and let her mind wander where it would. Perhaps, if given the chance, she'd even top that man-sundae with hot fudge and whipped cream, sprinkle it with nuts and cherries, and slowly lick off the entire concoction. The thought made her smile and her tongue tingle with anticipation.

Even with his face partially concealed by a mask,

he was gorgeous. Absolutely, mind-bogglingly, breathtakingly gorgeous. In all her twenty-one years, Lark had never seen anything or anyone to compare with the sight. She sighed once more as her mind filled to overflowing with the possibilities.

What would it be like to have those long, robe-covered legs nestled between her own? How would it feel to lace her hands through that thick, black mane of hair? To tease, stroke, and draw him down beside her? When would be the perfect moment to kiss those lips, delve into their recesses, and taste heaven? Where in Albrath was there a place private enough to have him buried deep within her and adequately secluded so they'd be free to shout their pleasure to the rooftops?

For once in her boring, predictable life, Larksong Hammerstrike would very much like to be desired and taken by a man such as this one.

She adjusted her feathered mask, drew a deep breath, and took a step toward him when she recognized another woman making a beeline straight for the man of her dreams.

Lark stepped back into the shadows. There had never been a time in her life she could compete with her sister, Aryanna, and she certainly wasn't going to start trying now.

Why had she come to this silly ball in the first place? Why had she come to Carnalval for that matter? Lark took another deep breath and squared her shoulders. She would not feel sorry for herself tonight. She had long ago recognized her place in this world and, if she were completely honest with herself, was comfortable in it.

She understood and accepted her duty and, though

there were those who didn't appreciate her abilities, Lark knew she was good at what she did. Darkly handsome men were meant for women of stature and beauty, like her sister, not those relegated to companion status, such as herself.

Despite her resolve, tears threatened and Lark fought a losing battle to stave them off. Perhaps she should make it an early evening and go back to the castle. A good wallow in self-pity and a warm cup of cocoa would be perfect. The day had been long and exhausting. She wouldn't have even been at this asinine ball in the first place if Ary hadn't insisted upon it.

Lark turned from the vision of the handsome, masked man across the room smiling down at her sister and headed toward the door. Perhaps it was for the best if she left the debauching to those more suited to it.

****

He tried to concentrate on what the female before him had to say, but couldn't. Sarco Sunwalker was having too much trouble trying not to chase after the beautiful barbarian female walking toward the door. He'd noticed her the moment he'd stepped into the room and had been about to go speak with her, when he'd been waylaid. For a heartbeat, he'd been sure the feather-masked beauty had meant to come to him and then, she simply hadn't.

Sarco shook his head. Carnalval on its best day was a strange place, and this season had certainly proved to be no exception to that rule. Why had he even come? Intimately cavorting with strangers had never been on the top of his to-do list.

The damn gnome, that's why. He shuddered. There would be time to dwell on Leeky Shortz and his motives later. Right now, he needed to catch the fleeing beauty.

Knowing he was being rude but unable to stop himself, Sarco bowed quickly before the woman in front of him and headed toward the door. He caught a quick glimpse of the barbarian beauty slipping into the darkness.

With only one thought in mind, he followed. If he must be at Carnalval, he meant to make the best of this one night, his last evening of no responsibility. Tomorrow, he'd head back to the Academy of Magical Arts and to his duty, but for this one last night, his life was still his own.

He found her standing silently in the shadows of the late summer evening, her face tilted to the pale light of the three moons of Albrath and her eyes closed. In her mask and glittery white gown, she reminded him of a fabled goddess he'd once read of. He was almost afraid to speak, fearful she would be but a figment of his imagination and disappear before his eyes. Sarco gathered his courage.

"Warm, don't you think?"

The woman startled at the sound of his voice. The air whooshed from Sarco's lungs. She was even more beautiful up close than she'd been from a distance. Hair the color of warm amber cascaded down pale shoulders. Eyes of molten silver gazed back at him through the white feathers of her mask. Lips full and pink—the kind begging to be kissed—curved upward in a slight smile. There was only one word that could describe the creature standing before him. Wonderful.

"Yes, it is a little warm, I suppose." Her voice was warm honey.

Much like an untrained schoolboy, for the first time in his twenty-six years, high-elf wizard Sarco Sunwalker stumbled for something to say. "Umm, may I have this dance?"

He longed to touch her. The low-cut gown she wore clung to—but still did too good of a job hiding—her full breasts and lush, womanly curves. He yearned to caress her naked skin and discover the different textures of every inch. Her sigh broke into his erotic thoughts.

"There's no music," she whispered.

"There's music all around, my dear Wonderful, if you but close your eyes and listen."

He watched, enthralled, as long, dark lashes caressed white feathers. Her eyes closed and a smile graced her gentle features.

"Can you hear the music now?" he whispered. "Do you not notice the melodies sung by the birds of the night, the tempo of the wind, the added harmony of tiny insect wings in flight, mixed with the percussion of our very own heartbeats?"

He leaned in close and inhaled the fragrance of wildflowers mixed with lust. His cock hardened. "Can you not feel the music, Wonderful? Allow it to seduce you, give into the moment. Taste it, embrace it, dare to embrace me."

She opened her eyes and nodded.

Sarco held out a hand. "Shall we then?"

Sweeping her into his arms and close against his chest, he twirled her to the rhythm of nature's night song.

****

If she could have, Lark would have pinched herself

to make sure she wasn't dreaming. He had called her *Wonderful*, and in a voice so rich and deep, it rumbled all the way to her toes. No man had ever left her so breathless.

Her skin tingled and tiny shivers skittered along her spine. Being held in the arms of the most mystifying man in all of Albrath and dancing, actually waltzing beneath the stars, were what dreams were made of. Not reality.

Not wanting to break the spell, she chanced a glance at his face anyway. Although his simple, black half-mask concealed his identity, nothing could hide those eyes. They reminded her of the hungry eyes of a large cat—rich brown, streaked with gold, mesmerizing. Where had she seen eyes like his before? An inkling of a memory stirred, but Lark pushed it away.

Now was not the time for dwelling. Now was the time to misbehave. This was Carnalval. This was allowed.

Crisply pointed ears told her of his high-elf heritage. And his lips…Lark trembled with the desire to lift up on tiptoes the mere inch it would take to savor their fullness, to chance a nip, to slide her tongue deep inside and relish a taste. The sly smile he gifted her with told Lark this man knew exactly what she'd been thinking, and heat warmed her cheeks.

His arms tightened about her, and for the first time in her life, Lark knew what it meant to be under a spell. Looking away wasn't a possibility as, ever so slowly, his head dipped. He was going to kiss her, and even though she told herself to relax and breathe, her treacherous heart pounded erratically.

He tasted of exotic spice and stardust, of sweet passion and the promise of sizzling desire. His tongue teased and tempted. His hands roamed, his body molded to hers. She was lost and knew it. Whatever this man wanted, he could have. He needn't ask, simply take.

What was wrong with her? It wasn't as if she were some virginal schoolgirl. Her barbarian father's castle was well staffed with a team of professionals to teach all the specifics of carnal knowledge. Lark had not only passed, but excelled in her sex education classes and graduated with honors.

Why, then, did this man make her knees feel they could not hold her weight? Why did her heart pound near to bursting with just a kiss?

"Shall we find somewhere more private to continue our…dance, Wonderful?"

The whisper against Lark's skin sent shivers racing straight down her spine, tightening her nipples along the way before scattering throughout her belly. "Do you mind if we go to your room? Laycee, my gnome— umm—governess, would never forgive me if I brought a man back to mine."

He chuckled against the skin of her neck and Lark quivered.

"I understand that statement, Wonderful. I too have a pesky gnome in my life."

Lark couldn't stop the soft moan that escaped as she struggled to maintain her composure while his lips continued their exquisite exploration. "Does your gnome have rules for every situation he demands you follow, like Laycee Titwilder does to me?"

The sound of the man's laughter and his softly

spoken words of "Oh yes, his name should be 'Rules' instead of Leeky" warmed Lark's heart and settled the butterflies fluttering in her tummy.

He unwrapped himself from around her and tucked her arm in his. Together they strolled the lantern-lit lane.

The man turned slightly toward her and grinned. "Leeky Shortz really does have a rule for everything. For this trip to Carnalval alone, he had three in particular."

He held up three fingers. "One," he lowered his ring finger, "stay at the biggest castle you can find. That way if you get too intoxicated you can still find your way back to your room or find someone to at least point you in the right direction." His middle finger joined the others. "Two, divide your money into three equal parts; one part in your tunic, one in your breeks, and one in your boots. That way, if you end up losing everything except your boots, you might be naked, but you still aren't broke. And last but not least," he shook the remaining finger, "never venture down a dark alley alone, because that's just dumb."

Lark laughed. "Your Leeky should meet my Laycee. They sound much alike."

The man grinned, and Lark's heart hammered in her chest. He leaned in close and nuzzled her neck. "Let's not waste time talking gnomes, Wonderful. All I want to discuss is how long it's going to take before I have you naked and squirming beneath me."

She looked him straight in the eye. "Me, too."

****

Sarco knew himself to be undeserving of the gift waiting before him and yet, at the same time, he couldn't force himself to walk away. In a matter of no more than a season—and certainly by the appearance of the once-a-century, triple-full-phasing of Albrath's three moons—he was duty-bound to take a wife. And not just any wife, but a barbarian-human princess of a wife.

So why was he here now, doing something so completely foreign to his character? One-night stands and lusty encounters for the sake of sexual release alone had never been his style.

And yet, here he stood in the middle of his rented room, facing a lovely stranger and set upon a path of total intimacy with her. There was something about this woman, something he couldn't resist.

Something beyond her obvious beauty drew Sarco to her. Something he didn't understand and wasn't sure he wanted to. Something almost spiritual had called to his soul the moment he glimpsed her standing across the expanse of the ballroom, and yet he dare not even ask her name. The freedom of Carnalval came with few restrictions, but anonymity was the most important one.

The trembling of his hand as he undid the closures holding his tunic together and slipped it awkwardly over his head told him more about himself than he wanted to know. When had he last made love to a woman for the purpose of pure, simple pleasure? He couldn't remember. Had he really allowed his life to become so burdened with day-to-day responsibilities that he'd forgotten how to live?

Perhaps Leeky Shortz had been right when he told him, "Boy, life is much too short ta not enjoy every single breath. Live life like ya're arse is on fire. That's my motto."

Sarco chuckled.

"Did you say something?" the woman whispered.

He shook his head. "Nothing, I just can't believe my luck. You really are real and here with me."

She smiled, but her smile didn't extend to her eyes.

Before another heartbeat passed or another breath taken, he stood at her side. With tenderness, he gazed into her gentle, masked face and took both of her hands in his. He was humbled as her fingers trembled even more than his own did. "We don't have to do this if you'd rather not."

She smiled wider, and her eyes gleamed with mischief. "I suppose we might as well. After all, we're already here, and you're at least halfway undressed."

Sliding his hands up her arms and around her shoulders to her back, Sarco felt for and found the clasps holding her gown together. With the flick of a wrist, they gave way, and with a swish, the silky fabric fell to her hips exposing lush, rose-tipped breasts. Just the right size to hold in both hands, to fondle, to caress, to taste.

"Hmm, it seems you're halfway undressed yourself."

With a fingertip, Sarco grazed one pert nipple and was rewarded with the soft sound of a gasp. Replacing the finger with his lips, he sucked, then grinned to himself as the woman before him forgot to breathe and shivered. Easing the gown slowly over her hips and down her legs until it floated quietly to the floor, Sarco stepped back an inch to gaze. "Exquisite."

Although she still wore a mask, Sarco didn't miss the look of doubt as she opened her silver, passion-filled eyes.

Slowly, he caressed her cheek, running a finger down her neck, between her breasts, across her belly and resting it lightly at the top of her smooth mound before reversing and retracing his way back up.

"It isn't necessary to say pretty words and tell me things like I'm exquisite," she whispered. "I've always known I'm not. Being ordinary is fine with me, really it is. Let's simply enjoy what we have to offer each other for this one night. This is Carnalval. It's the only chance we'll ever have."

Confusion muddled his thoughts. Was it possible this woman really didn't know how very beautiful she was? Sarco placed his hands on her shoulders and turned her until she faced a tall mirror standing behind her. He took her hands into his, and one at a time, positioned them firmly on the sides of the mirror's dark-wood frame. He held them there. Sliding a foot between her feet, he pushed with his knee and slightly parted her legs.

His voice was more a growl than a whisper when he dipped his head and nuzzled the skin below her ear. "Watch yourself, Wonderful, and see the woman I see."